ALL IN

ALL IN

To Ilana-
Hope you enjoy the
read. This is one of my
favorites- Wrote it about 10
years ago-

[signature] 3/17/19

A Novel by Harry Brooks

This story is a work of fiction. All of the characters, events, and
places are products of the author's imagination and in no way are
intended to misrepresent any real-life incidents, with the
following exceptions: the training to become a member of
Sayeret Matkal, references to the Entebbe hostage crisis, the
assassination of the Palestine Liberation Organization military chief,
and the Warsaw Ghetto Uprising were all true. However, the author
integrated fictional characters. The use of other public places, personalities,
celebrities, or publicized events are used only to dramatize and to
establish a time frame. The story is not intended to be
a true-life experience of any one person or event.

This book was printed in the United States of America.

To order additional copies of this book, contact:
Xlibris Corporation
1-888-795-4274
www.Xlibris.com
Orders@Xlibris.com
55387

This book is dedicated to my wife, Joan,
my best friend and true love.

IN LIFE LIKE IN POKER,

YOU MUST PLAY THE HAND YOU ARE DEALT.

DEFINITION OF

ASSASSINATION

Wikipedia: The Free Encyclopedia

ASSASSINATION. The targeted killing of a high-profile person. An added distinction between assassination and other forms of killing is that the *assassin* (one who performs an assassination) usually has an ideological or political motivation. Other motivations may be money, revenge, or a military operation.

Oxford English Dictionary

THE ACT OF ASSASSINATING. The taking of the life of anyone by treacherous violence, especially by a hired emissary or one who has taken upon him to execute the deed.

CHAPTER ONE

June 20, 1995, New York City

The two men sitting in the gray Lexus parked on East Seventy-ninth Street were getting inpatient. "Where the hell is this guy? If a cop comes by, we're gonna have to move."

"Relax, Tozzi, he'll be here."

The cell phone rang, and Tozzi answered. The conversation was short and one-sided. "His jet landed about an hour ago. It took a while for his limo to get clearance from the Newark Airport to drive on to the field. He's on his way. He should be there in the next ten to fifteen minutes."

Tozzi responded with, "Great, we're all set on this end." The man with Tozzi was the Sharpshooter. His real name, Carl Wilson. He got the name Sharpshooter when he was a Green Beret. That was the reason Tozzi hired him to help with this job. What Tozzi didn't like was Wilson insisted he hire his good friend Sal Morreti as the fourth member of the crew. He knew the two of them were very tight. And he had heard rumors they were bisexual. To make matters worse, they had the reputation of pimping kids to all kind of perverts. Tozzi was by no means an angel, but he didn't go for that type of shit. However, Wilson was good at his job as a shooter, and that was the important thing. He turned to Tozzi as if to ask him what was happening. "He's on his way. I'm gonna call Angie so he can watch for the limo." Angie was the third man of the four-man crew whose job was to assassinate Walter Lippincott, one of the richest and most powerful men in the country. Angie was parked at the corner of Seventy-ninth and Lexington. It was his job to place a blockade barrier marked Do Not Enter—Street Under Repair across Seventy-ninth Street as soon as Walter Lippincott's limo passed the corner. This would prevent any traffic from entering Seventy-ninth Street while the Sharpshooter performed his night's work.

As soon as the shiny black Lincoln Town Car pulled to a stop across the street from where Tozzi and Carl were parked, the Sharpshooter tried to position himself so that he could get a clean shot at his target. He had moved from the front of the Lexus to the backseat after Tozzi received the call informing them Walter Lippincott was on his way home. The Sharpshooter took his high-powered rifle from its case and adjusted the lens. However, as he looked through the lens, he realized that Lippincott was going to exit the car on the curbside; and the limo would block his vision. He was pissed at himself for not taking this into account. This was not how a Green Beret was taught to prepare. However, they are taught to have a backup plan. And so he put his backup plan into immediate action. "Tozzi, take out your gun and follow me," he said as he took out his own weapon and opened the rear door of the car.

"What's going on?" Tozzi asked as he followed his partner's instructions.

"I can't get a clean shot. We got to do them close-up," the Sharpshooter said as he started across the street, holding his gun by his side

Tozzi, right behind him and almost across Seventy-ninth Street also with gun in hand, whispered, "How about anybody else there? You know, the driver, the—"

The Sharpshooter interrupted him as he glanced over his shoulder and whispered back, "Shoot 'em all!"

Walter Lippincott was returning to New York from Las Vegas with his personal assistant, Alan Gold. They had attended a fund-raising dinner for Republican Senator Guy Baxter, the man who appeared to be the front-runner in the 1996 presidential election, which was about eighteen months away.

Walter was one of the major contributors to the Republican Party and was believed to have a lot of influence in the party's decisions. No sooner had his car pulled to a stop in front of the luxury condominium building in which he lived than the doorman was out to greet him and open the back door of the limo. At the same time, the driver got out and opened the trunk to take out the suitcases. Alan Gold was saying goodbye and remained in the car as Lippincott got out. It was at that instant the driver saw the two men approaching from the shadows, holding their hands outstretched each with a gun. Before he could say a word, Tozzi fired two shots directly at his head. The driver fell into the trunk of the limo, causing the trunk door to slowly close on his back. The Sharpshooter was already in back of Walter Lippincott and fired three shots to the back of his head. As one of the richest men in the country fell to his knees in the gutter, his head half blown off, the Sharpshooter then fired into the backseat of the limo, killing Alan Gold. The doorman who would have retired in two years was shot and killed by Tozzi while the Sharpshooter was completing his job. The entire killing took less than thirty seconds.

Both killers quickly returned to the stolen Lexus they left parked across the street. Tozzi handed his cell phone to his partner and got behind the wheel of the car and slowly pulled away from the curb, crossed Park Avenue, and turned north on Seventh Avenue. The Sharpshooter called Angie. When Angie answered, the Sharpshooter said, "Meet you at the corner of 129th and Eighth Avenue in ten minutes."

"See you there," was the response.

Then he called Sal Morreti who was already on his way into New York from the Newark Airport. All he said was, "129th and Eighth, see you soon, lover boy."

"See you," was the response. Tozzi looked at Wilson in disgust. Wilson just smiled. Tozzi, Wilson, and Angie all arrived at about the same time. It took Sal about forty minutes longer to get there. He had rented a car using a stolen license and credit card. He parked the car on 129th Street. After making sure there were no fingerprints or other evidence in either car that might lead to them, they left the keys in both cars, and all got into Angie's car. The hope was some punks would find the cars, steal them, and get caught by the police. Let them talk their way out of it.

As the four men drove down Fifth Avenue toward the Lincoln Tunnel, Tozzi dialed a number in his cell phone. The voice that answered was almost muffled. "Is that you?" Tozzi asked.

"Yes, it's me. Is it over?"

"Yeah, it's over. There was a little complication, but it's okay."

The muffled voice became a little clearer but was still unsteady. "What do you mean complications? What happened?"

"Well, we had to do everyone."

"Everyone . . . what do you mean everyone?"

"Well, we couldn't get a clear shot of the target. So we ended up having to take care of the driver, some other guy in the car, and, oh yeah, the doorman. But it's all done. No extra charge. By the way, did you hear from Vegas?" Tozzi asked.

"No," the voice on the other end answered, hesitated for a moment, then said, "Good job," and hung up the phone.

CHAPTER TWO

Same night in Las Vegas

PJ was playing in a high-stakes Texas Hold'em poker game at the Golden Nugget Casino in Las Vegas when he received the phone call from his good friend Johnny King. King was a reporter for the *Las Vegas Sun*. "PJ, I have some bad news for you." PJ listened as he watched the dealer turn the first three cards over. This was called the *flop*.

"What kind of bad news?" PJ asked matter-of-factly. "It's Walter. He and his assistant were shot and killed in front of his apartment building. According to someone who was looking out of her apartment window, two men ran up to his car when the driver pulled up in front of Walter's building and started shooting. He was on his way home from the airport. It just came over the newswire. Did you see him when he was here?" One of the players bet $25,000. Two players before PJ mucked their cards (dropped out of the hand). PJ looked at his two cards, a 2 of spades and a 3 of clubs. He had the worst hand possible. He hesitated a moment and then said, "I call," Johnny King's words still ringing in his ears. The heavyset man at the end of the table with an unlit cigar in his mouth, the man whose real name was Sam Boron but because of his style of play was called the Pusher, smiled and raised the bet by another $25,000. PJ looked at his cards again and said, "I call." The three cards that came out in the flop were a king of diamonds, an 8 of spades, and a 6 of diamonds. Absolutely no help to PJ. Not even a draw.

It was the Pusher's turn to bet. He said, "I check." PJ knocked on the table signifying that he too checked. The dealer turned over the next card, a 7 of hearts, which was called the "turn." The Pusher looked at PJ and then at his own cards. He had a king and a 6, which meant he had two pair—kings and 6s. He bet $20,000. Without hesitation, PJ called the bet. The dealer then turned over the final community card, which was called the *river*. It was an ace of clubs. It was of no help to either player.

"PJ, are you there? Did you hear what I just said? Walter was shot. He's dead."

"I heard you, Johnny," PJ said, finding it difficult to talk. "You said Walter has been shot. And in answer to your question, no, I didn't see him when he was here. The luncheon was $5,000 a plate. That's a pretty expensive lunch." PJ knew he was not reacting the way he should. His brother had just been murdered, and he continued playing cards. What kind of a man was he? How could he be so unconcerned? But strange as it was, PJ felt no emotion. It was like he just heard the weather forecast. "Rain and heavy winds by sundown!" His mind started to blur. He looked around the table, and all eyes were on him. The other players at the table had all stopped whatever it was they were doing and looked at PJ.

He then moved the mouthpiece of the phone away from his mouth, looked down at his chips, took another look at his two worthless cards, looked at the Pusher, smiled, and said, "I'm all in." The other players continued to stare as PJ played his cards.

The Pusher who was usually very calm sat up in his chair and showed his displeasure with PJ's bet. He had no interest in overhearing that PJ's brother had been shot. There was a lot of money at stake here. "Are you crazy, PJ? You don't have shit. You're trying to bluff me. You checked after the flop, just called on the turn, and now you go all in." The Pusher played with his cards, then asked PJ, "How much you got?"

PJ quickly counted his chips and answered, "A hundred and ten thousand, give or take a thousand." The Pusher was calm now. He smiled, thinking to himself if he could call the all-in bet. It would cost him another $110,000. "That ace gave you two pair, didn't it?" PJ just looked at the Pusher, showing absolutely no emotion. "Son of a bitch, PJ, you're trying to bluff me. I know I got you beat. I got kings up. Maybe you got three 8s, PJ? Yeah, you been sittin' on a set waiting to hook me. Is that what you got, PJ, three 8s?" Still no emotion from PJ.

One of the other players at the table finally lost his patience. "Goddamn it, Sam, either call the bet or fold. Let's get on with it." The Pusher simply looked at the other player and smiled. He then looked at PJ.

"Tell you what, PJ, I figured it out. You had a small pair and pulled a pair of aces on the river. You got aces up, don't you?" Still nothing from PJ.

Johnny King shouted into the phone. "PJ, what the hell is going on?"

"Be with you in a minute, Johnny. I'm in the middle of a poker game."

"Jesus Christ," Johnny said in disgust.

"All right, PJ," the Pusher said, "I'm gonna let you take the pot. But I need to see your aces up, or else I won't be able to sleep. I'll give you a thousand bucks to show me your hand."

PJ looked at his opponent and smiled. "Throw in your cards, and I'll let you know."

"Man, you are a real ballbuster," Pusher said as he threw his cards in the middle and, at the same time, reached for a thousand-dollar chip from his pile of chips in front of him.

As PJ pulled in the chips from the middle of the table, he turned over his cards and quietly said, "Keep your thousand dollars, Sam. Bluffing you was worth more than the money." All of the players stared at the worthless cards PJ turned over. He had made an unbelievable bluff. PJ then thanked his friend Johnny King for calling and politely said he would speak to him later. He got up from the table, motioned for the floor person to cash in his chips, and started to walk away. Then casually, he turned and said, "I won't be around for a while. I have to go back East on some family business. See you when I get back."

As soon as he left the casino area, PJ ducked into a men's room and walked to the sink where he splashed cold water on his face and then looked at himself in the mirror. He didn't like the man he saw looking back at him. How could he not show more emotion when hearing such terrible news? Was playing a game of poker more important than his brother being shot and killed? He couldn't answer that because he knew that wasn't the real question. He had been taught not to feel, to be tough, to be fearless. And why didn't he go to the fund-raiser? He knew why. He didn't like Guy Baxter. He thought he was a douche bag, and he told that to Walter. He knew that the squeaky-clean senator from "the good old South" made frequent clandestine visits to Vegas—always arriving by private plane, traveling from the airport in an unmarked limo, and each time, to a different hotel-casino, staying in the nicest villa or most expensive VIP suite. He ate, drank, gambled, screwed around, and left owing markers but never once paid a dime.

Walter didn't agree; he told him JFK did the same thing, and look how he's revered. "Except," PJ said, "JFK never tied up the girls and beat the shit out of them while he was screwing them."

"You don't know for sure Baxter did that," Walter said.

"I do, brother. I saw some of them after his little soiree. Some of them ended up in the hospital, were given $1,000, and told if they ever said anything about what happened, they would never work in Vegas again."

The door to the men's room opened, and a man PJ knew walked in. "Hey, PJ, how you doin'?"

PJ just stared at him and smiled. "Not so good, Tony, not so good."

CHAPTER THREE

When PJ left the Golden Nugget Casino, he went straight home. He lived in a town house not too far from the Strip, but far enough away so that you didn't see the neon lights. He returned to the States from London eight years ago where he lived for the last twenty years, spending most of that time traveling between Europe and the Middle East, occasionally returning to New York. His former business cards read Gould Security International—PJ Gould, President. What the business card did not say was "professional killer, hit man, and assassin." That was PJ's main business before he retired in 1986. He drove his Porsche into the garage and closed the garage door before getting out of his car. Just a habit to always be cautious. He smiled when he saw Cindy's car already parked in the garage. She worked in the chorus line at Caesars, and he was a little bit surprised she was home before him. The last show at Caesars didn't finish until midnight, and it was only eleven thirty. The car was still warm; she must have just come home. He guessed she took the night off. Caesars lets the girls do that every so often.

He walked around the back of her car to the door leading to the house. He glanced at her personalized license plate: CIA. Cindy Ingrid Abbott. Cute. He punched in the code on the security pad on the wall, and a small white light started to blink, meaning the system was unalarmed. After entering the house, he reset the alarm. It was a split-level town house with the bedroom suite on the second level. As he made his way up the short stairway leading to the bedroom, he could hear Ol' Blue Eyes on the stereo. Nice sound. He just about reached the landing that led into the bedroom, and he could see Cindy half uncovered, lying naked on the bed on her side. She looked beautiful. Her rear end was exposed, which

PJ thought was her biggest asset, that is, if he had to pick one thing. She appeared to be sleeping. PJ was surprised she didn't hear him come in. Her clothes were lying half on the bed, some on a chair, and her underwear on the floor. Very contrived.

And suddenly, PJ froze. He almost stopped breathing. Something was wrong. He had been trained all his life to be able to recognize something out of the norm. Cindy was a neat freak. She would never leave her clothes thrown around, even to set up something sexy. That was not her shtick. And Frank Sinatra was not her sound. The Beatles, maybe even Billy Joel, but not Sinatra. And why would she be asleep so soon and so sound? Her car was still warm. And then he smelled it. Tobacco. The smell of cigarettes on someone's clothes. He knew it well from the casino. He hated it. And neither he or Cindy smoked. His eyes darted around the room as he very slowly took the small .38-caliber handgun from his jacket pocket. With one hand, he was able to release the safety catch; however, he knew that if he needed a weapon this night, it would not be the .38. He slowly turned to go back down the stairs to the first level. "I'll be right up, baby. I think I need a glass of milk. And wait until I tell you how I bluffed Sam Boran. It was beautiful." He hoped that whoever was in the room would continue to wait for him to come back up. When he got to the kitchen, he quickly bent down and crawled into the den were he took an Uzi out of a cabinet, made sure it was loaded, released the safety catch, and then started back up to the bedroom. "I needed that, babe, I have to stop eating that spicy food." As soon as he reached the bedroom, he lunged into the room, rolling over on the floor and coming to a dead stop on one knee, the Uzi ready to be fired. Without hesitation, he sprayed a barrage of bullets at the double wooden shutter closet door. Wood chips, pieces of clothing, shoes, and blood replaced the front of the closet. When the Uzi was empty, PJ remained on the floor, hoping the would-be assassin in the closet did not have a backup. After a minute or two, PJ kicked away what was blocking the door and saw his would-be killer—a man dressed in black, still holding his Galatz, an Israel sniper weapon. PJ could not make out the man's face since the Uzi reshaped it.

PJ turned to look at Cindy. Her neck was broken. He only hoped she died quickly and avoided much pain. She must have come home early and surprised the bastard, and the stupid son of a bitch tried to make it look like she was in bed waiting for him. PJ figured the second member of the crew was probably staked out at the Golden Nugget watching him so that he could call this piece of shit to let him know when he was coming home. PJ thought to himself, *You better start hiding now, you asshole, because I am gonna find you and make you pay.* He went through the dead man's pockets and found only a cell phone. He was a professional, taught not to carry any identification. But he broke the rules. He had a cell phone. Suddenly, the cell phone started to vibrate. The killer had turned off the sound. PJ answered the phone and whispered, "Hello."

"Is that you, Emil? Did you get him?"

PJ smiled and whispered, "Yeah." There was a pause on the other end of the phone.

"Who the fuck is this? You're not Emil."

PJ didn't reply. Then the call ended. PJ quickly hit the button that would bring up the caller's name and cell phone number. Nick Paraphas. Sounded Greek. PJ made a note of the cell number and name. He would call someone who would give him the caller's address. Right now, he had a more immediate problem. There were two dead bodies in his house. He thought for a minute about taking both bodies out of the house and dumping them somewhere so he would not be involved. But he couldn't do that to Cindy. She deserved a decent burial. They had been together for about six months. It was against his better judgment to let her move in, tonight being a perfect example of why. Cindy's mother lived in Denver and came to Vegas about two months ago to see Cindy in the new Caesars review. That was when PJ met her. How was he going to call and tell her her daughter was murdered because she took off work early? He shook his head in disgust. *"I'm getting too old for this shit,"* he mumbled to himself.

He took out his cell phone and called his friend Sandy Keller, a Las Vegas homicide detective he met shortly after moving to Vegas. "Sandy, PJ. I got some bad shit at my place. Somebody evidently was able to override my security and break into the house. Cindy must have come early, and the bastard broke her neck, then laid her on the bed to make it look like she was waiting for me. The bottom line is I got to him before he got me, and I blew him away. What we have here are two dead bodies."

There was a moment of silence. "Jesus Christ, PJ . . . besides that, how was the show, Mrs. Lincoln?"

PJ had one more telephone call to make before the police arrived. The call was to Clarence Efont in New York City. Clarence worked for the CIA in a special division that traced e-mails, hacked into computers, wormed its way through passwords, retrieved deleted computer files, and got more information from an ordinary cell phone than anyone would think possible. PJ knew him from the days when he was working with the CIA as a "special contractor."

"This call better be pretty freakin' important. Please tell me either someone died or had a baby." It was three in the morning New York time, and PJ knew Clarence was asleep.

"Hey, you mean old bastard. It's me. Do I have any favors left?"

There was a moment of silence on the other end of the phone and then a husky laugh. "PJ?"

"Yeah, it's me. How are you?"

"I'm good . . . hey, I heard about Walter. I'm sorry."

"Thanks. But I have the feeling whoever was responsible for killing Walter also put out a contract on me."

"Holy shit," Clarence said. "What happened?"

"Seems like there was a hitter waiting for me at my house. Unfortunately, my girlfriend came home early, and the son of a bitch broke her neck."

"What do you want me to do?" Clarence asked his old friend.

CHAPTER FOUR

The years 1943 through 1995

In 1943, the largest Jewish ghetto in Poland was in Warsaw. That is where Herman and Ruth Kleinberg lived. They owned a small dress store and lived on the second floor. When Hitler ordered the ghettos emptied and announced that all the Jews be sent to concentration camps, the Kleinbergs, like many other Jewish families, knew that was a death sentence. Ruth Kleinberg was six months pregnant with their first child and was frightened. "What is going to happen to us?" she cried. Herman held his wife close and assured her he would find a way for them to escape and not go to a death camp. However, in his heart, he too was frightened. What was he going to do? He remembered back to 1938 when a boatload of Jewish refugees was refused entry into Cuba, Argentina, Great Britain, and the United States. And as a result, the boat had to return to Germany, and most of the Jewish refugees ended up in concentration camps. Would America open their doors to Polish Jews now? And if so, how would he and his wife leave Poland?

Before Herman Kleinberg could think of a way to escape from his homeland, the men in the ghetto began to resist the German efforts to liquidate the ghetto and started what was to be known as the Warsaw Ghetto Uprising. After twenty-seven days of fighting, the ghetto uprising ended with the death or capture of almost all of its inhabitants.

Fortunately, Herman and Ruth had managed to find safety with a group called Żegota. Żegota was an organization with the expressed purpose of helping Jews in Poland. The help included financial aid, forged-identity documents, hiding places, and, in many cases, a way out of Poland to the United States.

Hiding from the Germans was not easy. Sometimes the group Żegota would move their hiding place two or three times in one month. The hiding and moving from place to place was taking its toll on Ruth Kleinberg. There were no doctors to help her, and she was afraid of losing her baby. Finally, Herman went to the man in charge of their group. "I must get my wife to America. She is six months pregnant and needs medical help."

"I understand," the man said. "And you are in luck. We have a truck moving to the boarder tonight where they will meet up with a group that will take them to the seaport. There is a cargo ship that has agreed to take them to France. From there, we have an underground that will get them to England and then to America." Herman looked at the man.

"Are you crazy? My wife could not survive that type of trip. She would lose the baby, I am sure."

The man put his arm around Herman's shoulder. "I know how you feel my friend, but what other choice is there? The Germans are getting closer and closer to us. I don't know how long we can keep up this cat and mouse game." Herman nodded. He knew the man was right. He had no other choice.

"No, I refuse to leave without you," his wife cried when Herman told her she was to leave that night without him.

"You must go. Think of our baby. Believe me, I will join you as soon as possible."

"But where will I go when I get to America? . . . What will I do? . . . I don't understand why this is happening to us, Herman."

Herman held her tightly and stroked her hair. "There is a Polish relief fund in America who will take care of you until I get there. They will make sure you have a good doctor for our baby. Everything will be all right. You must go. This is our only chance." They lay in each other's arms until it was time for Ruth to leave. As she left with other members of the small group, both she and Herman knew this was probably the last time they would see each other. But she would have their baby. That would have to be enough. The day after Ruth left the Żegota hiding place, the Germans raided the hideout and killed everyone remaining there, including Herman Kleinberg.

By some miracle of miracles, Ruth made it to New York. However, she had lost a lot of weight and was exhausted from the long trip. She was not doing well. The Polish relief fund was able to get her into a small private clinic run by Dr. Yashsa Shomoski, a young Russian Jew who had emigrated from Russia at the start of the war. He was committed to helping as many Jewish emigrants as possible. His problem was constantly trying to raise money to continue to operate his small hospital. The Polish relief fund helped whenever possible; and on occasion, private individuals would make a contribution, but he never had enough money. He didn't know if he would be able to keep the clinic open.

And then one day, he met Arnold Lippincott. He was introduced to him by a mutual friend, a doctor at New York City General Hospital, and he was offered a way to keep the clinic open. The only problem was he didn't know if he could meet Arnold Lippincott's demands. Arnold Lippincott owned a bank in Upstate New York, and numerous other holdings around the country. He was a very wealthy man by anybody's standards. Arnold was in his midfifties and had recently married a young lady from the New York stage twenty-five years his junior. It wasn't until after they were married that Arnold discovered she could not bear children. The doctor who informed them was very discreet. He did not say who was to blame. He just told them she couldn't have children. That was all Arnold needed to know. He would now find a way to correct this problem so that he could have an heir.

So when he met Dr. Yashsa Shomoski, he decided this was his answer. "I want a boy. He must be healthy. No known physical or mental problems. No family. No parents to come forth ten years from now and claim him. An orphan with no known ties. When we take him, it must be like he is our biological child. You can do this, I know. And when you do, I will set up a trust fund for the hospital in the amount of $1,000,000. The fund will be controlled by my bank. You will receive $10,000 a month from the fund for the hospital. In addition, I will pay you $25,000 in cash, which you may do with as you please."

Dr. Shomoski received this offer several months before Ruth Kleinberg came to his hospital. He was not thinking about the banker's offer at the time Ruth was admitted. However, as she entered her ninth month, Dr. Shomoski discovered Ruth Kleinberg was going to have twins, and under no circumstances could she go to term. This meant deciding on a date to take the babies by performing a C-section. This was risky because she was getting weaker by the day. She had already received two blood transfusions and needed a breathing machine. He had to make a decision. There was no family to consult. There was not even another doctor on staff qualified to help him make the decision. On the morning of September 10, 1943, he made the decision to operate. He spoke to Ruth, trying as best he could to explain the risks involved. "Can you save my babies?" she asked in a weak voice, reaching for the doctor's hand.

His eyes were moist. "Yes, I believe we can." She smiled.

"Then do it, Doctor ... don't cry ... I know you will do your best. God bless you."

Before the operation was complete, Dr. Shomoski knew Ruth Kleinberg would not survive. Now his job was to deliver the two babies. And that he did. He took two healthy baby boys from Ruth Kleinberg's stomach as she drew her last breath. Both Ruth and Herman Kleinberg came to this earth, produced two baby boys, and then died. No one would remember them. No one would ever talk about them. No one would mourn them. It was like they were never here. Now there were two new people to replace them. And each would leave their own footprints in the sand of life.

Dr. Shomoski thought long and hard before he called Arnold Lippincott. Once he made the call, there was no turning back. But this was the only way he could keep the hospital open. *May God forgive me*, he thought.

After Arnold Lippincott received Dr. Shomoski's call, he wasted no time in making the arrangements to pick up his new baby. "You will take care of the birth certificate," Lippincott told the doctor. "You will show my wife and me as the parents, and the baby's name will be Walter Arnold Lippincott. Birthplace Buffalo, New York. Religion Methodist. I have arranged for a doctor and a nurse to pick up the child at seven o'clock tomorrow morning. I would prefer if there were as few people as possible around. Is that all right with you?" Arnold Lippincott was telling the doctor, not asking him. What the doctor did not tell Lippincott was that the baby he was getting had a twin brother. Lippincott wanted a baby with no ties. The doctor had made up his mind that this was the only way he could keep the clinic open. One little lie. Besides, it would be almost impossible to find a home for both babies. And the doctor was afraid that if he asked Lippincott to take both children, he would back away and not take either one.

God would forgive him. Since there was only a refugee nurse who had assisted him in the operation, he was not worried about explaining what he was doing. After his call to Lippincott, Dr. Shomoski called the American Jewish Refugee Group. "I have just delivered a baby boy from a woman with no identity. I know she was Jewish. She told me she came here from the Warsaw Ghetto. I was hoping to learn more after I delivered the baby, but unfortunately, she died during childbirth. She was brought in by a woman who told me she found her in an alley." Another lie. Would God forgive him? It was for a good cause. Look at all the lives he could save by keeping the hospital open. And they will find a good home for the baby. "God, please forgive me."

CHAPTER FIVE

During the Second World War, those young men who were not in the service held some sort of wartime defense job. As was the case of Morris Gould, who worked at the Philadelphia Navy Yard. Morris and Edith Gould were your average middle-class American married couple. Morris worked hard at the navy yard, and Edith did her part to help the war effort by doing volunteer work at the Red Cross three days a week. They lived in a predominately Jewish neighborhood in West Philadelphia. They did not want or expect much out of life. They were realists. They were both in their late twenties and married for three years. Their dream was that after the war, they would have saved enough money to open a small grocery store and raise a family. Their biggest disappointment was when they learned that Edith was unable to have any children. Then like their prayers had been answered, they received a call from the American Jewish Refugee Group. They had placed their name on the waiting list when they learned Edith could not become pregnant. "We have a newborn baby boy looking for a home with two loving parents." The woman from the refugee group knew how those words would sound to the Goulds.

Edith couldn't stop crying from joy long enough to ask any questions. Finally, Morris got on the phone. "That sounds wonderful," he said. "What do we have to do to get the baby?" The woman from the agency explained the details to Morris, as well as told him what Dr. Shomoski had told the agency. "That poor woman," Morris said.

"Yes," the agency woman replied, "one person's misfortune is another person's gain."

When the Goulds went to pick up their new baby, they had already decided on a name. Phillip. "I would like to name the baby after my grandfather," Edith told her husband.

"That's fine with me," Morris replied. "And how about we give him a middle name after my grandfather?"

"I like that," Edith said. "Phillip Jerome Gould. Sounds like a law firm." They both laughed. Edith thought for a minute, then asked her husband, "Do you think kids will make fun of his name when he goes to school? You know, like . . . hey, Phillip is a sissy name."

"No way," Morris said; then with a big smile on his face, he said, "How about PJ? What a cool nickname. PJ! I love it." The Goulds could not have been happier. They were on their way to pick up their dream child . . . PJ.

When the war ended in 1945, the Philadelphia Navy Yard began laying off workers. Morris was a skilled electrical maintenance man, but he knew sooner or later, he would be out of a job. In the course of his job, he became friendly with one of the officers at the navy yard. He told Morris he would do whatever he could to see that he kept his job. Then he came to Morris one day and told him he was being transferred to the naval base in San Diego. He also told him that the navy was embarking on a major rebuilding project there and hiring all kinds of people. "That's great," Morris said, "but there is no way I can afford to pick up and move to San Diego."

The officer put his arm around Morris's shoulder and smiled. "That's where I come in. I'm the guy in charge of this project, and I have been authorized to offer contracts to some civilian specialists to help with the project. You are one of those guys. The navy pays to move you, helps you with housing, and you get a five-year contract at about double what you are making now." Morris just looked at his friend, waiting for the punch line. But there was none.

"How can we leave our family and friends? And besides, how about our plans to open a grocery store here?"

"Edith, this is a chance of a lifetime. Believe me, it will be better than a grocery store. Think how nice it will be to raise PJ in Southern California." With that, Morris pointed to the baby playing in the playpen. The two talked about it all that day and halfway through the night. And finally, Edith agreed. It was a good opportunity. And so in November of 1945, Morris and Edith Gould and their two-year-old baby set out for California. They had no idea they were separating their son from his twin brother by three thousand miles.

CHAPTER SIX

Arnold and Grace Lippincott did not deprive their son, Walter, of a single thing. He had a full-time nanny the entire time he was growing up. On his sixth birthday, his parents bought him a horse that he could ride on their twenty-acre estate. When it was time for him to start school, he was enrolled at one of the most prestigious private schools in New York State. Arnold Lippincott had great plans for his son. He wanted him to go to an Ivy League college when he graduated high school, then go to law school. After he passed his bar examinations, he wanted his son to go into politics. First a congressmen, then maybe governor. Then president. Why not? Anything is possible with money. At least that is the way Arnold Lippincott looked at life. Unfortunately, the elder Lippincott would not live to see his dreams come true. Walter had just graduated high school and was accepted to Harvard. To celebrate the occasion, Arnold decided to take him and his girlfriend (of the month) on a cruise. It was a double celebration. It was Arnold Lippincott's seventy-fifth birthday. On the second day of the cruise, Arnold suffered a heart attack and died in his sleep. Arnold's attorney contacted the owner of the cruise line and convinced him to have the ship return to port. Walter was not surprised or impressed by this. He was used to seeing the power of money in action. This is how things were supposed to be. You were rich, and that meant you got everything you wanted.

After the funeral, Walter's mother talked to her son about what his father wanted for him. Walter had this same talk with his father many times, and although he did not entirely agree with him, he never told him so. He felt when the time came, he would make his own decisions.

Now that his father was gone, he saw no reason to keep up the charade with his mother. "Look, Mother, I can't make any decisions now about what I am going to do when I graduate college. I have about six weeks before I leave for school. During that time, I would like to spend as much time as possible in Father's office. I want to know what goes on and who the people are." Walter's mother knew right there and then that no one was going to tell her son what to do. He was his own man. "By the way, Mother, when will the lawyer be here so we can read the will?"

Grace Lippincott was slightly taken aback at her son's question. She had not given any thought at all to the will. "I don't know, Walter. I guess we have to call him."

"Fine, I will do that tomorrow. In the meantime, you and I should talk about how we intend to handle things without Father." Grace Lippincott just looked at her son. At nineteen years old, he was already a man. He was going to take charge.

When Jonathan Andrews, Arnold's lawyer, met with Walter and his mother, he was not at all prepared for the questions that Walter asked. The lawyer had assumed they would depend on him to handle everything and would follow his advice. After all, he had been Albert Lippincott's friend and attorney for many years. And he was one of the few people who knew that Walter was not the Lippincotts' biological child. "With all due respect, Mr. Andrews, I plan to take charge of my father's business. And I need to know everything that you know. I realize I am going away to college, but I cannot wait four years to find out where the money comes from. I would like for you to remain as my counsel. In that way, we will keep a line of communication open. During the summer, I will spend all my time at the office."

Jonathan Andrews immediately knew this young man was not to be denied. The fact that he was only nineteen years old did not matter. He may not have had the Lippincott genes, but there was no doubt that he was his father's son! "There are two men that really run the show," the lawyer said. "There is Ted Daniels, who is president of the bank. And then there is Billy Russell, who is in charge of the real estate company. What you should know about the bank right off is that it has made and continues to make large sums of money from companies your father helped with either start up seed money or, in some cases, operating capital in order for that company to secure an award of business. He made those decisions mainly on his gut. Of course, he made sure the number crunchers did their job; but he would meet with the principal of the borrowing company, and a lot depended on that meeting.

Sometimes he would insist on having a consultant on-site to make sure what he thought was going to happen did as a matter of fact happen. He usually ended up negotiating a piece of that company's ownership in the process. "The reason being your father saw something other banks didn't, but these companies needed seed or operating money, and they had no other place to go. He was a very astute businessman, your father." Walter nodded and smiled as if to say *"Wait until you see me in action."*

Andrews continued, "There are a number of other people who have a lot of responsibility, but these two gentlemen are the key to what happens. If it is your plan to take an active role in the company, I would suggest we arrange to meet with Ted and Billy as soon as possible."

"Good," Walter said, "set up a meeting here at the house. My father once told me that whenever possible, you should meet on your own turf."

The lawyer made a note to remind himself about the meeting; then he went on to explain to Walter and his mother the terms of Albert Lippincott's will. After all of the legal mumbo jumbo, the lawyer got to the important stuff. The two employees the lawyer described to Walter each was to receive $500,000. There were bequests of $100,000 each to six other employees. There were several donations to various charities as well as a sizeable donation to the Lippincott's church. The rest of the estate was left to Walter and his mother, which consisted of more money than they could spend in two lifetimes. The one provision that did not sit well with Walter was that although he had a lot of leverage to operate the company, all of his stock and voting power and money was in a trust until he was twenty-five years old. And Jonathan Andrews was the trustee. After the lawyer finished reading and explaining the will, Walter looked at the lawyer and smiled. "Looks like we will be joined at the hip for some time."

"I don't anticipate any difficulties, Walter," the lawyer replied, knowing exactly how the younger Lippincott felt having his hands tied for the next six years.

When the lawyer left, Walter sat and talked with his mother until late in the evening. "I certainly am impressed at the way you handled things, Walter," she told her son. "Your father would have been proud."

"Thank you, Mother, but knowing you are proud is enough for me." Walter's mother had trouble holding back the tears. She loved her son with all of her being, and for him to say what he did warmed her heart. She thought about the day she and her husband took him from that hospital in New Jersey and wondered if they made a mistake never telling him about his real mother.

But what good would that have done? No, better they never told him. She was able to manage a smile. She gave her son a hug and assured him he would do well. He returned her smile and said, "I never had any doubts about that, Mother."

About a hundred miles south of Buffalo, New York, in a small apartment on the Upper East Side of New York City, Dr. Shomoski sat in his kitchen reading the *New York Times*. He liked to read the social page and then the sports page, limited as it was. Then the national news, all bullshit to his way of thinking. And then the obituary page. That was the most interesting. Some people he knew, some he recognized from their fame, and some were just names. But he felt they all had a story to tell, and they died before their story could be told. And then he saw the obituary for Arnold Lippincott.

> *Buffalo business man dies of heart attack during a luxury cruise. Arnold Lippincott was celebrating his son's acceptance to Harvard College as well as his own 75th birthday. Joining Mr. Lippincott on the cruise were his wife Grace, his son Walter, Ms. Anita Bleat and Mr. Lippincott's personal attorney Jonathan Andrews. Shortly after Mr. Lippincott was pronounced dead by the ship doctor, the ship line ordered the ship back to port. The Lippincott's have requested that instead of flowers, donations be sent to Children's Heart Hospital and the American Red Cross Heart Fund. The Lippincotts will have a private memorial at their church in Buffalo. Only close friends and relatives are expected.*

The doctor read the obituary over and over. *Close friends and relatives. I surely don't fit into either one of those two categories*, he thought. He looked at himself in the mirror. Life had not been good to him. He closed up his clinic approximately ten years ago in 1951. Patients stopped coming, and the neighborhood changed. Gangs would break in to steal the drugs, and many of the patients who came for treatment really only came for the drugs. After he closed the clinic, he went to work at the Jewish hospital in the Bronx. However, he had been suffering with bouts of depression ever since he separated the twins in 1943. He kept arguing with himself that what he did was the right thing, but something in his brain told him he had done a terrible wrong. Separating two children, especially twins. But how wrong could that be? One twin being raised by a wealthy family, and the other with a family who would give him all the love in the world.

After Dr. Shomoski left the Jewish Hospital, he worked part-time at several different hospitals over the next year. Finally, he realized he was no longer able to work full-time. He had trouble getting up in the morning. Some mornings, he would just lie in bed and stare at the ceiling. His bladder would feel full and the demand for relief urgent. He would think about letting go and wetting the bed. That, at least, would give him a real reason for getting up. He let his hair grow long and had a full beard. His appearance made it more difficult for him to get work at the hospitals. When he closed his clinic, the trust that Arnold Lippincott had set up continued to send him money for almost five years before they discovered the clinic had closed. They discontinued sending him money and sent him a letter demanding he return the overpayments. He ignored the letter and never heard from them again. The $25,000 that he received personally was long gone, and so Dr. Shomoski barely was able to pay his rent and buy food. He pondered the thought about becoming a homeless person, and it did not seem to bother him.

In his depression, he rationalized this was God's way of punishing him for separating the twin babies all those years ago. However, he would not be able to revel in the holiness of being totally poor. Some of the money he had received when running the clinic had been invested in an annuity at the suggestion of a friend. The doctor knew nothing about the investment or how it might benefit him. As it turned out, the money grew significantly. Although it took the investment house some time to locate him, when they finally did, they told him he was entitled to $500 a month. This would make him a well-paid homeless person. He had decided he was a martyr, and the money merely helped him survive a little longer.

CHAPTER SEVEN

The Goulds enjoyed living in California. During the past sixteen years, Morris Gould endeared himself to a lot of the people at the navy yard in San Diego, which provided him the opportunity to open his own consulting company. This allowed him and his family to live in an upscale neighborhood and offer PJ some of the nicer things in life. They took vacations in Northern California and motor trips to the neighboring states. Morris Gould wanted his son to come into the business with him after college, but PJ felt his future was somewhere else. One of his high school friends had an uncle who worked at Universal Studios; and during a summer break, when his friend went to visit his cousin in Burbank, PJ was invited to go with him. After the personal tour at Universal Studios, PJ was sure that he wanted to be in the movie business. He didn't know exactly what he would do in the movie business, but what he was sure of was that he did not want to be an electrical engineering consultant.

The news about Arnold Lippincott's death made the San Diego newspaper business section. It was a small article lost among the more important news of the day; however, it caught Morris Gould's eye because he knew that Arnold Lippincott owned the bank where he did business. He remembered when he first started in business and went to the bank for a loan, and the loan officer told him a story about Mr. Lippincott. "Mr. Lippincott's policy is we lend money to the man and the idea, not just the idea." Morris Gould was not really sure what that meant, but the bank was there when he needed them, and he always remembered that. Morris placed the newspaper on the table and thought for a minute.

I think I'm going to send the family a condolence note. Yup, that's what I'm going to do.

When PJ walked into the room, his father was holding the newspaper and seemed to be in deep thought. "Hey, Dad, what's going on? You okay?" Morris looked at his son and smiled. He had been thinking that poor Mrs. Lippincott was left to raise a son just about his own son's age. Sure, she had all the money she could ever need, but this is the time in a young man's life when his father can be so important. Morris Gould could never in a million years have imagined that the young man who had just lost his father was actually his own son's twin brother. Although twins, growing up in different parts of the country and having different lifestyles gave them different appearances. PJ was suntanned and in excellent physical shape. He was a swimmer; he played basketball, golf, tennis, and high school football. His hair was bleached blond from the sun, and he always wore casual clothes. He didn't own a necktie. On the other hand, Walter did not participate in sports; and although he was not really overweight, he appeared "flabby." Because he had always wanted to look older, he grew a mustache in his senior year of high school when he was elected class president. He liked clothes, and the fact that the prep school he attended required a tie and jacket suited him just fine. Probably if the two young men were to stand side by side, you would be inclined to say they resemble each other.

However, living in two different parts of the country and in different financial circles, their paths never crossed.

"Yes, son, I'm fine. Just thinking about what you are going to do about college."

PJ leaned up against the table and smiled. "Hey, buddy, get with the program. We decided, remember? It's USC."

Morris smiled. "Yeah, I know, just kidding around."

PJ leaned over and ruffled his father's hair and then patted him on the cheek. "C'mon, old man, see if you can beat me at some tennis." With that, PJ was on his way out the door before his father was out of the chair. Morris was no longer thinking about the Lippincotts; he was thinking about trying to keep up with his son, and he loved every minute of it.

CHAPTER EIGHT

Several months after he learned that Arnold Lippincott died, Dr. Shomoski made a decision. He was going to call the Goulds and tell them their son had a twin brother. He rationalized to himself that he no longer was bound to secrecy since Arnold Lippincott was dead. He had been living with guilt for over eighteen years. *The twins should know each other.* He would have to find the Goulds. He remembered they lived in Philadelphia when they adopted the baby. And if memory served him, Morris Gould worked at the Philadelphia Navy Yard. The American Jewish Refugee Group was no longer in existence, so he would have to search elsewhere for the Goulds' whereabouts. The following morning, Dr. Shomoski was on a bus to Philadelphia.

When the bus arrived in Philadelphia, the doctor lost no time in going to the bureau of records in city hall. It took him several hours until he found what he needed to track down the Goulds. Their full names, their dates of birth, their social security records; and because Morris Gould had worked for the government, Dr. Shomoski was able to learn they had moved to San Diego. He was very proud of himself. When he left city hall, it was raining. He pulled up the collar of his coat as he started to cross the street. He never saw the city bus as it turned the corner. The last thing he heard was a man screaming, "Look out!"

The ambulance took Dr. Shomoski to the emergency room at Hahnemann Hospital, which was only several blocks from city hall. When the doctor on duty first looked at him, he asked the ambulance driver why he brought him there and not to the morgue. The ambulance driver gave the doctor a dirty look and the finger. Dr. Shomoski was in very bad shape. Before sending him to surgery, the emergency room doctor made some quick notes on the admittance form: "Patient has a severe concussion, two broken legs, internal bleeding, and multiple cuts and bruises. He is bleeding from the mouth and is not responding. Prognosis uncertain."

Dr. Shomoski spent the next two weeks in a coma. When he finally did awaken, he had no idea where he was or what had happened. The hospital was not sure what to do about trying to contact someone. They spoke to the injured man, trying to get some information. Was there anyone in Philly they could call? Dr. Shomoski had no identification on him other than a social security card and the envelope with all of the information he had gotten from city hall. Most of the contents of the envelope were photocopies of old birth certificates and other courthouse records; however, there was a folded piece of paper with Morris Gould's name, address, and telephone number on it. When the doctors attempted to ask Dr. Shomoski who he was and who they should contact, he kept pointing to the piece of paper with Morris Gould's name written on it and mumbled, "Call him . . . tell him it is about his son . . . tell him I must talk to him . . . please . . . it is important."

It took several telephone calls to Morris Gould before the hospital could convince him to fly East. It was during the final telephone conversation when the hospital social service worker told Morris Gould that there were copies of two birth certificates in the envelope. Well, one actual birth certificate and the other a handwritten copy of a birth certificate form with a note in the corner that read File in Massachusetts. The name on that document was Walter Arnold Lippincott. The actual birth certificate photocopy showed the name Phillip Jerome Gould, birthplace New Jersey. Both were boys—same weight, same size, same date, and same time of delivery. With that information, plus the fact the social worker told Morris Gould they didn't expect Shomoski to last the week and that if he wanted to learn what this was all about, she suggested he get his butt out to Philly ASAP.

Morris lied to his wife about going to Philadelphia. "It's some old navy yard business. They are going to pay my expenses. It will only take me a couple days, and then I'll be home." She knew her husband was not telling the truth, but if it was important enough for him to go and not tell her the real reason, that was good enough for her.

"You be careful and remember there are two people back here who love you and will support you whatever."

Morris gave her a hug, smiled, and said, "You're pretty smart."

She lovingly pushed him away and said, "Go."

At three o'clock the next afternoon, Morris Gould was sitting in the office of Bernice Landerman, social service worker for Hahnemann Hospital. Dr. Goldenberg, the emergency room doctor, was also there as was the assistant administrator, Henry Thompson. They all looked very serious and businesslike. There was no attempt at bedside manner here; Morris Gould explained the circumstances under which he and his wife had adopted their child through the American Jewish Refuge Group. He had copies of all the papers, and he had been assured by a local attorney that everything was in order. The hospital social worker agreed. She told Morris she was able to locate someone from the Philadelphia branch of the Allied Jewish Services, a national fund-raising group, and they confirmed that Dr. Shomoski had delivered the baby and what the Goulds had done was legal. They had no knowledge of another baby. They told him that every time they tried to question Shomoski, he shook his head violently and mumbled his name. "So," the social worker said, "now you are here. Why don't we try and find out what this is all about before it's too late."

CHAPTER NINE

After almost two hours of questions, half answers, and more questions, Dr. Shomoski was finally able to tell Morris Gould and the others what happened in his clinic almost twenty years ago. Tears were rolling down his cheeks as he tried the best he could to apologize to Morris Gould. Everyone looked at one another in utter amazement. "At this point, I am convinced he is telling the truth," the assistant administrator said. "I think it is time we contact the Lippincott family?" The room fell silent.

Morris Gould turned to look at Dr. Shomoski. "You are absolutely sure there were two babies, Doctor?"

Dr. Shomoski nodded his head, the breathing tube in his nose almost coming loose. Morris Gould looked at the others and said, "Who is to be the messenger?"

When Jonathan Andrews received the call from the director of Hahnemann Hospital asking him if he could meet with him, he was sure they were looking for a grant of some kind. He received these kinds of calls all the time. However, after the director told him it concerned a very personal matter involving the Lippincott family and something he could not discuss on the telephone, he immediately invited the gentleman from Hahnemann to meet him at the New York Athletic Club the following day. He was not about to sit around and wonder what the man had to say. The director agreed to meet him.

Jonathan Andrews sat across the lunch table from Dr. Wolf, the director of Hahnemann Hospital, and listened to him relate the story that Dr. Shomoski had told his people. "I know this entire matter sounds incredible, Mr. Andrews, but I can assure you we at the hospital believe it to be true." Dr. Wolf was accustomed to meeting with lawyers and other professional people and was not at all intimidated by either the Lippincotts' lawyer or, for that matter, the Lippincotts' money.

When Dr. Wolf finished with his story, the Lippincotts' lawyer took a sip of his coffee and then matter-of-factly asked the doctor exactly what was it that Dr. Shomoski and Gould wanted. The doctor was offended by the question. "What do you mean what do they want? They don't want a thing. We have a situation here where there are a pair of twins who were sent to different families immediately after they were born. One without any legal adoption, I might add. And neither of these two young men have any idea in the world that they have a twin brother. And you have the nerve to ask me what they want? Better I should ask you, what do *you* want?"

Jonathan Andrews smiled. "I apologize, Dr. Wolf. I had to be sure."

"Sure of what?" Dr. Wolf shot back.

"Sure that Mr. Gould was not trying to . . . shall we say, cash in on a very delicate situation."

Dr. Wolf looked at the lawyer for a short time and then leaned toward from his side of the lunch table and very calmly said, "You knew Arnold Lippincott took one of the twins and made it look like he was his own biological child, didn't you?"

The lawyer was not about to try and deceive this man. "Dr. Wolf, you are correct. I did know that Walter wasn't Arnold's child. I am the only person other than Mr. and Mrs. Lippincott who knows that. However, believe me when I tell you that none of us knew about the other child." Dr. Wolf knew that was the truth based on what Dr. Shomoski had told his people.

"Well, what do you suggest we do now?" Dr. Wolf asked.

The lawyer finished his coffee and signaled to the waiter to bring the bill. He knew in his heart of hearts that this day was bound to come. Now that it was here, he dreaded the consequences. "I would like to go back and talk to Mrs. Lippincott before I answer that question," the lawyer said.

The doctor thought that was the right thing to do. "Mr. Gould has remained in Philadelphia. He asked me to call him after our meeting. What do you suggest I tell him?" the doctor asked.

"I would suggest you ask him to remain in Philadelphia until after I talk to Mrs. Lippincott. I would hate to have him fly back to California and then have to come back East again should we all decide that is necessary."

Again, the doctor agreed.

Chapter Ten

After Morris Gould returned to California, he wasted no time in telling his wife what happened. She could not believe what she was hearing. "What a horrible man that Dr. Shomoski is! How could he do such a thing? Morris, what are we going to do? What is going to happen to PJ? Oh, Morris, this is terrible." Morris Gould did his best to assure his wife it would all work out although in his heart, he was not too sure. He was home about a week when he received a telephone call from the Lippincotts' attorney. He told him that Mrs. Lippincott had made a decision. The twins had to be told what happened. In the meantime, Dr. Shomoski passed away. When Morris Gould heard the news, his only thought was, *Thank God he was able to tell us what happened before he died!* Jonathan Andrews suggested that each family tell their son in their own way exactly what happened. After both boys had been told, he asked Morris if he, his wife, and PJ would fly to New York so that they could all meet at the Lippincotts' home. He offered to pay all of their expenses. Morris said that was the least of their concerns.

PJ was planning to drive to school the week before Labor Day so he would have some time to get settled before classes started. His father didn't want to spoil his son's schedule. PJ would be leaving for school in ten days. What had to be done had to be done now. The night that PJ's parents told him he had a twin brother was a night all three would never forget. PJ listened as his father related the entire course of events over the past three weeks. First, the visit to the hospital in Philadelphia where he learned from Dr. Shomoski that PJ's mother had given birth to twins. And then how he gave one of the babies to the Lippincotts.

Then how they adopted him. All the time, both families were under the impression they were taking the only child delivered by some poor Jewish immigrant. PJ and his parents spent hours talking about the ifs and "what could have happened."

"It's only by chance that I wasn't the baby given to the Lippincotts," PJ said. "How did that insane doctor decide which baby was to go first?" Finally, when there was nothing left to say, they all agreed to take the trip East and meet PJ's twin brother. How bizarre!

Meanwhile, three thousand miles away in Buffalo, New York, three other people were having the same kind of discussion. Jonathan Andrews was at the Lippincott home with Walter and his mother, telling Walter that he had a twin brother in California. Walter was more concerned about who his twin was and if there could be any financial consequences than he was about the fact that he had a twin brother. However, like PJ, he was well aware of the fact that it was only by fate that he ended up a Lippincott. He could just as easily have ended up living in California with Jewish parents. When Jonathan finished explaining what happened back in 1943, Walter thought for a moment and then asked his lawyer if he could find out more about his biological mother. "What good would that do?" Walter's mother asked, tears running down her cheeks. Walter looked at his mother and understood her fears. "Because I need to know, Mother. It won't change anything. You are my mother. I am who I am. It's just that I need to know more about who my biological parents were. Please try to understand."

CHAPTER ELEVEN

Summer 1963

There are some moments that hang forever suspended in time. The day that PJ and Walter Lippincott met was certainly one of those. Years later, when they would recall the meeting, each man would have different recollections of what actually was said. When the Goulds arrived in Buffalo, there was a limousine waiting for them at the airport to take them to the Lippincott mansion. When they pulled into the driveway, PJ leaned over to his mother and whispered, "Just think, but for fate, I could be living here."

His mother gave him a love tap and said, "That's not funny."

Inside the house, Mrs. Lippincott, Walter, and Jonathan Andrews were waiting for them in the living room. At first, it was very awkward for everyone. There were polite hellos and handshakes and even a hug between the two mothers. Finally, PJ broke the ice. "Okay, so let us try and figure out how we're all related. We two are brothers. There's no denying that," he said, pointing toward Walter. "And you, Mrs. Lippincott, would then have to be my aunt. And of course, you two," he continued, pointing to his parents, "would then be Walter's aunt and uncle. Now we could say that you, Mrs. Lippincott, or if I may, Aunt Grace, might possibly be my mother's sister-in-law—that is, if we could in some way tie my father in with your family." By this time, everyone was laughing and felt much more comfortable with one another. Walter couldn't take his eyes off PJ. He really liked him. He thought to himself, *Having a twin brother might not be all that bad.*

By dinnertime, everyone was talked out. Any question you might think of had been asked and answered. Both families felt they had been blessed. Although Dr. Shomoski had done a terrible thing twenty years ago, they couldn't hate him now. Mrs. Lippincott said it best when she said what a tragedy it would have been had he taken this secret to his grave.

After dinner, Walter and PJ walked outside and sat on the terrace. "So tell me, PJ, how do you feel about having a brother after all these years?"

"I think it's a good thing, Walter. It's a shame we missed all the years growing up together, but I guess in the end, it all worked out okay."

Walter smiled. "Seems kind of strange. I mean, you being Jewish and me a Methodist."

"I have no problem with that." And with a smile, PJ added, "But you got to remember you got Jewish blood running through your veins."

Walter returned the smile and made a sign in the air with his finger, "That's one for the Jew boy."

They were going to get along just fine. Walter told PJ how he wanted to find out more about their biological parents. PJ told him he was fine with things the way they were but would be interested in anything Walter found out. "What do you plan to do after college?" Walter asked PJ.

"Not sure really. I was thinking about poking my nose around the movie business. I have a friend who knows some people in the business."

"Sounds like that might be fun," Walter said. "But if ever you need anything, you know you can call me. We both know but for the luck of the draw, our situations would be reversed."

"Thanks, I appreciate that, Walt."

"It's Walter!"

PJ was taken aback. "What?"

"My name. It's Walter, not Walt. I don't like to be called Walt."

PJ smiled. Walter was not kidding. Had he drawn a line in the sand? *I am Walter, and you are my poor relation.* No, it was his imagination. "Hey, sorry." They smiled at each other and went back into the house.

Before the Goulds left for the airport, PJ and Walter exchanged telephone numbers, and each gave the other an open invitation to visit at their respective colleges.

During the next four years, PJ and Walter visited at each other's school and kept in touch on a frequent basis. After their sophomore year, Walter invited PJ to take a trip with him to Europe. At first, PJ refused, not wanting to play the part of the poor relative. But Walter insisted. "Shit, half of the Lippincott money should belong to you anyhow," Walter said, trying to convince his brother to take the trip with him.

"Well, in that case, I'll just take the money," PJ joked.

"Forget about it," Walter said. "Just come with me. We'll have a ball."

And so they did. When they returned from Europe, they had really bonded. However, they each had their own personality. PJ was more of a free spirit where Walter was more of a private person. Most of that had to do with their upbringing. And with his mustache and dark brown hair combed straight back, Walter had a look of authority. Whereas PJ, with his hair bleached blond from the California sun and his more muscular build gave the impression that he was someone you would like to know.

More than once, Walter asked PJ to come to work in the Lippincott family business when he finished college. "What? And be a banker?" PJ would say. Walter assured him that Lippincott holdings offered more opportunities than just banking. PJ appreciated the offer but told his brother that after their trip to Europe, he decided he wanted to do some traveling before making any job decisions. His roommate in college was going to Israel after graduation to visit relatives and invited PJ to come along and stay with them.

"Going back to your roots, so to speak," Walter said.

"You might say that," his twin answered.

CHAPTER TWELVE

In May 1967, Egypt and Syria took a number of steps that led Israel to believe that an Arab attack was imminent. On May 16, Nassar ordered a withdrawal of the United Nations Emergency Force stationed on the Egyptian-Israel border, thus removing the international buffer that had existed since 1957. Then on May 22, Egypt announced a blockade of all goods to and from Israel through the Straits of Tiran. On May 30, President Nassar and King Hussein signed a mutual defense pact followed on June 4 by a defense pact between Cairo and Baghdad. Arab mobilization compelled Israel to mobilize their troops. PJ had been in Israel almost two months when the talk of an Israel-Arab war was becoming a reality. His roommate told him that he planned to join the Israel army. "Are you crazy?" PJ asked. "You are an American."

His roommate looked at him solemnly and said, "You are right, PJ, but I am also a Jew."

On June 5, 1967, Israel launched a preemptive strike against Egypt and captured the Sinai Peninsula and the Gaza Strip. Despite an appeal from Israel to Jordan to stay out of the conflict, Jordan attacked Israel and lost control of the West Bank and the eastern sector of Jerusalem. Israel went on to capture the Golan Heights from Syria. The war ended on June 10.

PJ was fascinated by what had happened. A small country like Israel took on the entire Arab world, and in six days, the war was over. The atmosphere in Israel was one of jubilance. It was contagious. You could not help but get caught up in the spirit of the moment. As it turned out, PJ's roommate never did join the army. However, he told PJ that he planned on moving to Israel. He was going to return to the States to get the rest of his belongings, say his goodbyes to his family, and then return. He had rediscovered his Judaism. PJ did not feel comfortable staying with his roommate's cousin while he was gone. He had been dating an Israel girl who lived in Tel Aviv, and she invited him to stay at her house until his roommate returned. "How will your parents feel about that?" PJ asked.

"When my grandparents were seventeen, they were running guns for the underground. And soon, I will be going in the army. Believe me, PJ, Israeli girls are much more independent than American girls, and Israel parents are more liberal. My parents will not object." PJ looked at Ronit and thought to himself, *This is a strong lady.* To PJ's amazement, she was right. Ronit's parents did not object to him staying at their house; they also didn't object to him sleeping in the same room with her. Two days after PJ had moved in with Ronit, her brother, Shomal, came home on leave from the Sayeret Matkal. Her brother was a reservist in Israel's elite and most celebrated commando unit, Sayeret Matkal. The Sayeret Matkal was formed in 1957 by an officer by the name of Avraham Arnan. Its main purpose, to create a unit that could be dispatched to enemy-held territory and carry out top secret intelligence-gathering missions. During its ten-year existence, it became much more.

PJ and Ronit's brother became the best of friends over the next ten days. When it came time for Ronit's brother to return to his unit in Tel Aviv, PJ asked if he could go with him. "Are you crazy? What do you mean you want to come with me?"

"I want to learn more about the Sayeret Matkal," PJ said. "After all, I am a Jew. And since the war, I have that feeling of pride."

Ronit's brother laughed. "Having pride in being a Jew and becoming a member of the Sayeret Matkal are two different things. Besides which, I can get into a lot of trouble for even talking to you about our unit. Most people don't even know we exist. And it is not open to voluntary recruits. I was handpicked by a man named Colonel Pashine, who served in the army with my father. That is the only way to become part of our unit And the training is intense. Not many men make it."

The more Ronit's brother talked about why PJ could not join the Sayeret Matkal, the more he wanted to join. "Please, this is important to me." Ronit's brother agreed to introduce PJ to Colonel Pashine, knowing full well that he violated the group's first rule: secrecy.

The meeting took place at a small café just outside of Tel Aviv. Colonel Pashine was a large man in his late sixties. He had the face of a warrior. His skin was tanned from the elements, and his head full of white hair made his face look even darker. He was visibly upset with Ronit's brother. He looked at PJ with eyes that seemed to pierce PJ's skin. His face showed no emotion whatsoever. "I am meeting with you out of respect for Shomal's father," the colonel said. "And let me assure you, young man, there is no such group as Sayeret Matkal as Shomal has told you. Shomal is in an Israel commando training program. I think his imagination got the best of him. Now I suggest you return to California and forget you ever met Ronit, Shomal, and their parents. Staying in Israel can only cause you harm."

As the colonel stood up to leave, PJ gathered all his courage and said, "Try me, sir. You won't be sorry." The colonel looked at PJ and saw something in his eyes that told him he was right. He would not be sorry.

Four things happened after Colonel Pashine and PJ's meeting:

1. PJ was invited to Join Israel's secret elite commando unit, the Sayeret Matkal.
2. Ronit's brother, Shomal, was transferred out of the elite commando group into a tank unit in the regular Israel army and sent to the West Bank for a two-year tour of duty.
3. Ronit stopped seeing PJ, and he moved out of her parents' home.
4. Colonel Pashine was asked to provide security for Golda Meir, who had been named the first secretary general of the newly formed Labor Party. He would remain with her when in 1969, Prime Minister Levi Eshkol died suddenly; and the seventy-one-year-old Meir assumed the post of premier, becoming the world's third female prime minister.

CHAPTER THIRTEEN

Spring 1967

Walter was glad to be finished with college. He was anxious to direct all of his energy to the Lippincott empire. When PJ called to tell him he was going to Israel with his roommate, Walter told him he was crazy. "Come East and work with me, and you won't ever have to worry about money again."

PJ told him he didn't worry about money now. But he left the door open. "When I come back from Israel, I promise I will come East and visit with you. Let's leave it at that, and we'll see what happens." That was fine with Walter.

But after spending several months in Israel, PJ returned to California, only long enough to gather his belongings, sell his car, and move out of his apartment. He called Walter to tell him he would not be able to visit with him. He had to return to Israel without any delay. "I've been offered a job with a security company in Tel Aviv. I'll be working with American tourists, making sure they stay out of trouble. Sounds like a fun job. I will get to see more of the country, and the money is pretty good." Walter's instinct told him PJ was not telling him the entire story; however, he wished him luck and told him that if he needed anything to "just call." PJ gave his parents the same story. They had no reason to disbelieve him; however, they were disappointed they wouldn't see him before he returned to Israel.

Jonathan Andrews had developed a reporting schedule so that Walter knew everything that was happening at Lippincott International while he was still in college. Lippincott International was the holding company for the bank and all of the other Lippincott interests. In addition, Walter spent as much time as he was able at Lippincott's main office, getting to know the people and "how things worked."

One day, while going through some of his father's personal belongings, he came across a file marked A. L. CONFIDENTIAL. In the file were computer printouts with all kinds of numbers, letters, and strange names. Names like Indian Village Har-soon and SG Chicago Ok. And besides, each name was a percentage number. When Walter asked Ted Daniels and Billy Russell what these were, they both told him this was the first time they saw them and had no clue. Walter asked Jonathan Andrews, who said he really didn't know what it was but was sure it was not anything important. It had no meaning as far as Lippincott International was concerned. Walter was not satisfied with the explanation but decided he would table it for now and look into it more when he finished school. He locked it in what was once his father's desk and forgot about it for the time being.

He was out of college about a month when one day, he remembered the file. His father's office was now his. He was sitting at his desk and looked at the drawers and suddenly realized none of them were locked. It had been a long time ago, but he remembered locking the file in one of these drawers. He looked in every drawer, and the file was not there. He called in his secretary, whom he hired six months before he finished college. He wanted her to be ready to go when he was. "Betty, has anybody been using this office?"

"You mean when you are not here, Mr. Lippincott?" It was a rhetorical question. "No, Mr. Lippincott, that is, no one except Mr. Andrews when he is here."

"How often does Mr. Andrews visit the office, Betty?" Walter had to be careful; he didn't want to send out any bad vibes regarding his attorney. That wouldn't be smart.

"Oh, I don't know, Mr. Lippincott. Maybe three, four times a month. Is anything wrong, Mr. Lippincott?"

"No no, Betty, I was just curious. Thanks." And with that, he ushered her out of his office and back to her desk, all the time smiling, attempting to appear that it was really not important how many times his lawyer used his office. He needed to have a long talk with his attorney.

When Walter called him and said it was important they meet and preferably not in the Buffalo office, Jonathan Andrews could tell from the sound of Walter's voice it would not be a pleasant meeting. "I'll come to New York," Walter said. "How about we meet at the New York Athletic Club on Friday?" Jonathan agreed.

The New York Athletic Club was home to many a meeting, but none more important than when Walter Lippincott and his attorney met on that hot summer day in August 1967. Jonathan was already there when Walter arrived. Although only twenty-five years old, Walter had that look of authority and affluence. He wore an expensive three-piece dark gray suit, a white shirt, and a very conservative maroon tie. His hair was combed straight back, and with a touch of gray in his mustache, he appeared much older than his twenty-five years.

"I took the liberty of ordering a bottle of that Chardonnay you liked so much last time we ate here." Jonathan was nervous. Walter just nodded. The waiter gave them menus, poured them each a glass of wine, and then retreated to a place where they could summon him when they were ready to order. There was a moment of silence; then Walter said, very softly, but with a biting tone, "Where the hell is that file I locked in my father's desk?" This was worse than Jonathan expected. He knew he had to tell Walter what the file contained. What he was about to tell Walter would shatter any illusions he had about his father.

Over the next hour, Jonathan explained to Walter how his father laundered money for the mob. How he lent money to the teamsters' union to build casinos in Las Vegas and in exchange received "points" in each one. How his father was a party to the skimming of money from the casinos in Las Vegas and allowed members of the mob to open accounts in his bank under fictitious names. Walter listened, asking very few questions. Finally, Walter put his hand in front of his lawyer's face as if to say "Enough" and then said, "And that file I found. That was a record of all this shit. And I guess it was some sort of code that you and my father invented."

"Believe me, Walter, I didn't know that file existed until you happened to discover it. But as soon as I saw it, I knew what it was. I don't know why he would have kept such a file."

Walter signaled the waiter for some more wine, then looked at his lawyer with cold eyes and asked, "Okay, where do we go from here?"

Chapter Fourteen

Organized crime is more like a business consortium, the result of underlings' loyalty, neighborhood associations, old-boy networking, and favors—not much different from the way a great number of automobile manufactures became the three giants that controlled the marketplace. Not much different from the price-fixing oil companies or the way any number of enterprises chop up the United States into territories. This was Arnold Lippincott's rationale when he became involved with organized crime. And when his friend Joseph Kennedy introduced him to a lawyer representing Howard Hughes who needed a bank to handle large sums of money, he didn't hesitate to tell him he was interested. He knew Howard Hughes was buying up property in Las Vegas, and he saw this as an opportunity to be a part of this growing phenomenon. Legalized gambling.

When Arnold Lippincott told Jonathan Andrews about this, his lawyer said he didn't think it was a good idea. He told him that once you get involved in this type of thing, you can never get out. "This will just be the beginning, Arnold. Las Vegas is controlled by organized crime. And Howard Hughes, Joe Kennedy, and that entire bunch are up to their asses in dirty money."

Arnold smiled. "Jonathan, the newspapers are full of company executives pumping poison into landfill upon which houses are built and in which families with children live just to raise their profit margins. And CEOs who've managed companies nearly into bankruptcy walk away with golden handshakes worth millions. And how about all those preachers who steal and the cops who murder and the politicians who sit down and eat with the devil? You know, Jonathan, sometimes you can't tell the white hats and the black hats apart. Like the man said . . . everybody does business in one way or another. Who is to be the judge?"

Jonathan thought for a moment and then replied, "Maybe you are right, Arnold. Who is to be the judge?"

CHAPTER FIFTEEN

When PJ returned to Israel, he took a taxicab from the airport to a small motel on the outskirts of Tel Aviv, just as Colonel Pashine had instructed him. From the lobby of the motel, he called a number the colonel had given to him before he left. The voice on the other end of the line told him to wait outside the motel and look for a red pickup truck. "It should be there in about twenty minutes," the voice told him. PJ followed the instructions, and when the red truck arrived, the driver opened the passenger door and motioned for PJ to get in the truck. Neither man spoke. The driver seemed to be going in circles until he finally stopped in front of an old two-story brick house on a deserted road. "You will stay here until someone comes to get you. This is a safe house." They were the only words the driver spoke.

PJ rang the doorbell, and an elderly woman who spoke very little English opened the door and motioned for him to come in. She pointed to a room that looked like it was a living room that had been converted to a bedroom. She pointed to the bed and then left. About four hours later, two men in khaki uniforms arrived. They introduced themselves to PJ and told him they would be driving him to the Sayeret Matkal camp. They also told him that from that day forward, his code name was Averhim.

The Sayeret Matkal training location was kept top secret. When PJ arrived, he was taken to the commander's office where he was questioned for almost two hours and then given an envelope filled with forms that PJ was to complete and return in the morning. He was assigned to a barracks and was told his training would start the next morning. The soldier who escorted PJ to his new home smiled and said, "Get a good night's sleep, my friend . . . it may be the last one you get in a long time."

Once admitted to the unit, recruits train for twenty months, with heavy emphasis on small arms, martial arts, orienteering, camouflage, reconnaissance, and other skills important for survival behind enemy lines. The training regime consists of four months of basic infantry training, two months advanced infantry training, a three-week parachuting course in the IDF (Israel Defense Force) Parachuting School, five weeks of counterterror courses in the IDF Counter-Terror Warfare School, followed by more inner-unit counterterror training. The rest of the training is dedicated to long-range reconnaissance patrol training and especially to navigation/orientation, which is of vast importance in the unit. While most of the orientation training is done in pairs for safety reasons, as in every other unit of the IDF, Sayeret Matkal is one of the handful of IDF elite units that conducts long-range solo navigation exercises. During the entire training period, the recruits are constantly monitored by doctors and psychologists. Their evaluation plays a big part in whether a recruit "makes it." Although Sayeret Matkal has its own insignia, it is one of the few units in the IDF whose soldiers are not allowed to wear it in public due to its classified nature.

On April 10, 1969, PJ, now known as Averhim, stood with twenty other men as they were officially sworn in as members of the Sayeret Matkal unit. When the training period had started, there were sixty men. After the ceremony, PJ was invited to have lunch with the unit commander. As the other men received their assignments and prepared to leave, PJ could not help but wonder what was in store for him. One thing he knew for sure: he was not the same man he was when he entered the program twenty months ago. He was not sure if that was good or bad, but he knew without a doubt that he was now . . . Averhim.

PJ and the commander ate lunch in a room adjacent to the commander's office that was used for meetings. The lunch was very simple, served by one of the commander's staff. When they finished lunch, the commander offered PJ a cigar, which he politely refused. Commander Eliha Sabrek was one of Israel's most decorated soldiers. He was a former Mossad officer, who had been the team leader in more than one assassination plot deployed by the Mossad against Palestinian terrorists. After lighting his cigar, he took out a large brown folder from his briefcase. "Do you know what is in here?" the commander asked while opening the file and separating some of the pages on the table.

"No, I can't say that I do, sir," PJ responded.

The commander smiled and said, "It contains your life, Averhim."

PJ made no comment.

The commander went on to tell PJ how well he did in his training. Not only in the physical part, but also in the psychological testing. "You are going to make a fine soldier, Averhim. I see only good things ahead for you."

PJ thanked his commanding officer but was anxious to know what his assignment was.

"I am assigning you to the Military Intelligence unit of the Sayeret Matkal. This unit reports directly to the director of Military Intelligence of the Israel Defense Force. This unit is responsible for carrying out highly sensitive missions, many of which are ordered by the prime minister and Israeli cabinet's top secret Committee X. The unit's nickname is simply the Unit. Their motto is 'Who dares wins.'"

CHAPTER SIXTEEN

After Walter's meeting with Jonathan Andrews at the New York Athletic Club, he decided he needed to meet these people from Las Vegas that had been doing business with his father. Jonathan agreed. Jonathan told Walter at that meeting that since his father's death, it had been business as usual; but there were many issues that needed to be taken care of, and he was not in a position to make those decisions. Walter asked his lawyer what he planned to do if he had not come across his father's personal file. How long could Lippincott International continue doing business with these people without him knowing about it? "I don't know, Walter. I guess sooner or later, I would have to tell you. It was just that I didn't want to say anything that would make you think less of your father. Believe me, Walter, he was a good man. Back then, that's the way people did business." Walter didn't comment on that.

Jonathan arranged for Walter to meet with Carmen Francosi in Las Vegas. Francosi was a real estate developer who lived in Las Vegas. "Who is this guy?" Walter asked his lawyer.

"He is the guy who knows all the guys who know all the guys. He is the go-between for a lot of the people we are doing business with. He is also a close friend of the Kennedys and a big contributor to both the Republicans and the Democrats. He is no flunky."

The meeting took place on November 22, 1967, the fourth anniversary of the Kennedy assassination, in a private dining room in the Sands Hotel, just off the Strip in Las Vegas. Walter had told his lawyer he preferred not to meet in Las Vegas and certainly not in one of the casinos. Jonathan finally convinced Walter to attend the meeting. Carmen Francosi was a tall thin man, with dark olive skin and gray hair. He was always well dressed and did not look his age. He was seventy-five years old. When Walter and Jonathan arrived, Carmen was sitting on the couch by the window, talking on the telephone. There was a table on the other side of the room with all kinds of hors d'oeuvres. There was also a small bar in the room. The bartender greeted Jonathan and Walter and offered them a drink. Jonathan asked for a scotch and water, and Walter just wanted coffee. At the same time, Carmen Francosi motioned with his hand, indicating he would be off the telephone in a minute. Walter did not like the whole setup. This was not his style. He was a boardroom-type guy. He didn't like meeting on someone else's turf, and he especially didn't like to be kept waiting while the person he was meeting with was on the phone. Francosi finished his call and walked over to where Walter and Jonathan were standing and introduced himself. He apologized for keeping them waiting and suggested they all sit down. As the three men walked toward the window, Walter told his host that he preferred the bartender not be in the room while they were meeting. "No problem, Walter." And with that, he dismissed the bartender.

On the surface, there could have been no more perfect alliance between Walter and Carmen Francosi. The two men seemed to have it all. A little bit of arrogance, ambition, money, and the lust for power. However, beneath the surface, they were vastly different. Although Walter wanted to continue building the empire left to him by his father, he did have a sense of right and wrong. In the case of Francosi, there was no right or wrong way—there was only his way. Francosi had risen from humble beginnings, and now that he had personal wealth and political contacts, he would do anything necessary to keep them. "I knew your father back in the old days, Walter. He was a nice man."

Walter nodded as if to say a thank-you. "I assume you know why we are here," Walter said.

"Well, I am not really sure. Jonathan called and told me you wanted to meet me. Well, here I am."

Walter had no intention of being intimidated by some gangster. "Yes, well, I appreciate the fact that you are here, Mr. Francosi. But there are some serious issues we need to address."

Neither was the "gangster" going to be intimidated by some banker's son. "And what might they be, Walter? And please, call me Carmen."

"First of all, Mr. Francosi . . . Carmen, we have two loans on our books to the teamsters' union. And both are collateralized by the same piece of property, and both loans are in default."

"Well, my suggestion is you get in touch with the teamsters' union and tell them to pay up or else."

"That sounds all well and good, Carmen, except both you and I know it is a little more complicated than that. And since you brokered those loans, I feel you have a responsibility to the bank—"

But before Walter could finish, Carmen interrupted him.

"Just a minute here, Walter. I brought these loans to your father in good faith. I didn't hold a gun to his head and tell him he had to lend the teamsters the money. And besides which, like you say, it's a little more complicated. Best we put all the cards on the table right up front. Your old man knew from the start what was going on. There was a lot of money that changed hands back then, and there were a lot of people involved. Important people. People with names like Kennedy and Howard Hughes and Sam Giancana—yeah, Sam Giancana from Chicago—and a lot more that I rather not mention."

Rather not mention? Walter thought to himself. *Who was left? The president?* Better not ask.

"So tell me, Carmen, what do you suggest we do?"

"We! Who do you mean by *we*?"

"Come on, Carmen. You said we should put all our cards on the table. So let's stop the bullshit. We both have a lot at stake here. If the teamsters don't do something to correct the default, the New Jersey State banking committee will eventually look into these loans, and I don't think either of us want that to happen."

Carmen looked at Walter with a smile. "The flower may look different . . . but the roots are the same."

"I beg your pardon, Carmen."

"I was thinking of something Sam Giancana used to say when he compared himself to Joe Kennedy. You know they were asshole buddies."

"So I am told. But let's get down to business, Carmen. Unless the teamsters can correct the default on their two loans within the next ninety days, for which you received a brokers fee of $1 million, I might add, I want $50,000 a month until the loans are current."

Carmen stood up, went to the bar, and poured himself a drink. "$25,000 and not a penny more."

Walter Lippincott and Carmen Francosi then went their separate ways. And now they are partners.

What Walter didn't know was when his father was alive, he was receiving $100,000 a month in cash from the teamsters' union during any period of time the loans were in default.

CHAPTER SEVENTEEN

In 1972, the Israeli Mossad initiated one of the most ambitious covert counterterrorist campaigns in history. Golda Meir and the Israeli cabinet's secret Committee X devised a campaign in retaliation for the massacre of eleven Israelis during the Munich Olympic Games. Meir tasked the committee with devising an appropriate response to the Munich massacre. The panel concluded that the most effective response was to authorize the assassination of any Black September terrorists involved in the Munich incident. The Mossad assumed the responsibility for implementing the panel's directive. To accomplish the directive, the Mossad developed several assassination teams, each with specific mission parameters and methods of operation. The Mossad headquarters' element developed one team utilizing staff operations officers supported by recruited assets of regional stations and managed through standard Mossad headquarters' procedures. A second unit recruited staff officers and highly trained specialists and set them outside the arm and control of the government. The theory was to support this team financially through covert mechanisms and let them operate with complete anonymity outside the government structure. The assassination team deployed through normal channels failed to complete their mission and publicly exposed the entire operation. The second team, which operated with full decentralized authority and freedom of movement, achieved significant success in fulfilling their operational objectives and never compromised the operation.

PJ was part of the second team. He was back in Israel only a month when Golda Meir asked to see him. He had never met the prime minister, so he didn't know what to expect. And he had no idea why she wanted to see him. When he was shown into her office, there sat a little old Jewish lady behind a large desk. This was the woman who had ordered the assassination mission he just completed. He felt a chill go up his back. He thought to himself, *I'm glad she's on our team.* As PJ walked toward her desk, she got up to greet him. She held out her hand. It was soft and warm. Not the hand of a soldier. "Israel is proud of you, Averhim," she said as she walked with him to the sofa. "I am proud of you. You did good." PJ was embarrassed. "Now I have another assignment for you. The CIA has asked us if they could use one of our top covert operators. Of course, we said yes." She smiled. "And you are the chosen one, my Averhim."

With all of his training, PJ was not prepared for this. All he could manage was, "Thank you very much, Madam Prime Minister."

Golda Meir nodded. "And now the assignment, Averhim. The CIA needs someone who will be able to get into Cuba undercover. But I must tell you that once you take this assignment, Israel can never admit to any knowledge of what you have done."

PJ nodded and then asked, "Madam Prime Minister, can I ask what it is the CIA wants me to do once I infiltrate Cuba?"

"Of course, Averhim. They want you to assassinate Fidel Castro."

CHAPTER EIGHTEEN

After his meeting with Carmen Francosi in 1967, Walter realized that at some point in time, he had to distance himself from Francosi and his associates. In the meantime, he had a business to run. In 1972, Walter met and married Anita Woodland. She was the daughter of Sam Woodland who owned a chain of department stores on the East Coast. Walter was disappointed when PJ told him that he was unable to attend the wedding. Walter had seen PJ only once during the past five years although they spoke on the phone every couple of months. "I am really busy developing my own security business. It's very difficult for me to get away," PJ would tell Walter every time his brother tried to get him to return to the States. When the truth of the matter was PJ, or Averhim as he was known to the people who hired him, was busy being a paid assassin. After his assignment to assassinate Castro was comprised by the CIA and FBI, PJ decided to leave the Mossad and work as a hired gun on his own. He had developed the reputation of being the best political assassin in the business. His one criteria for accepting a hit was that he had to believe the target was deserving of his fate. PJ had made himself judge, jury, and executioner.

In 1976, PJ was again summoned by Golda Meir. No matter where PJ was or what he was doing, he would never refuse her request. On June 27, 1976, a French jet airliner en route from Israel to France, after stopping in Athens, was hijacked by Palestinian terrorists and flown to Entebbe, Uganda. Once at Entebbe, the hijackers freed those of the 258 passengers who did not appear to be Israeli and held the rest hostage for the release of fifty-three fellow terrorists imprisoned in Israel, Kenya, West Germany, and elsewhere. Golda Meir asked PJ to be part of the rescue mission that was planned to free the Israeli hostages. PJ didn't hesitate one second in granting her request.

On July 3, 1976, Israel dispatched four C-130 Hercules cargo planes carrying a squad of 150 Israeli commandos and one paid assassin, Averhim, escorted by six Phantom jet fighters to rescue the 103 Israeli hostages. After flying 2,500 miles from Israel to Uganda, the Israeli force rescued the hostages within an hour after landing. Seven of the terrorists were killed, and eleven MIG fighters supplied to Uganda by the Soviet Union were destroyed; the Israelis lost one soldier and three hostages during the operation. On the return trip, the Israeli planes met an awaiting hospital plane and refueled at Nairobi, Kenya. PJ left the Israeli special forces in Nairobi and continued on his own to Algeria to meet up with a CIA operative. After the hostage rescue mission, PJ began to think seriously about retiring from the "killing" business. It took him another thirteen years to finally make that decision.

In the meantime, over six thousand miles away, Walter Lippincott was building his fortune. In 1980, *Forbes* magazine rated him the tenth richest man in the world. And along the way, he made many enemies. Some of these were the men his father started to do business with many years before Walter took over the Lippincott empire. Although Carmen Francosi had since passed away and Las Vegas was being taken over by the corporate conglomerates, there were still plenty of people who wanted revenge. Over the years, Walter had methodically disenfranchised himself from Carmen Francosi and his associates. Walter now had the money and power to do most anything he wanted, and what he wanted was to have a say in the way the country was run. And the only way he could that was to help pick the next president. As the case was, he traded one group of dishonest and manipulative people for another group of the same kind. The world of big business, politics, and organized crime are so interwoven that like his father once said, "Sometimes it's difficult to tell the difference between the white hats and the black hats."

Walter had always been a Republican. His father was a Republican and once told Walter the difference between Republicans and Democrats is strictly dollars and sense. The Republicans can help you keep your dollars, and the Democrats make no sense at all. That was good enough for Walter. It was the early summer of 1980 when he decided to make his move into the world of politics. He needed to find the right politician who could help him get a foothold. His politician of choice was Paul Laxalt, the junior senator from the state of Nevada. Walter was well aware of the fact that Laxalt's tenure as governor of Nevada in the early sixties was noteworthy for coinciding with the purchase of a large number of hotel-casinos by reclusive billionaire Howard Hughes. And Laxalt was never embarrassed by the character of his financial backers or supporters. His donors were a who's who of Las Vegas and all it represented. In addition to his longtime underwriters Moe Dalitz and the syndicate's Doumani brothers, there were investigative targets Binion, Tobman, and Sachs, mob lawyer Morris Shenker, syndicate front Jay Sarno, casino owner Frank Fertitta, Las Vegas entertainment fixture Wayne Newton, the ever-present Parry Thomas, and a host of other notable Strip figures. Laxalt once said, "For a Nevada politician to refuse a contribution from Moe Dalitz would be like running for office in Michigan and turning down a contribution from General Motors." This was definitely a man that could put him on the fast track. *It would be expensive*, Walter thought. *But isn't that what money is for?*

Laxalt, Nevada's silver-haired, suntanned handsome junior senator, had risen to heights no one imagined only a few years before. The ex-governor and casino owner, who survived business failures and scandal at his Carson City Ormsby House to win his Senate seat by a razor-thin margin after a recount in 1974, won reelection in 1980 by a landslide. "Nothing less than a Laxalt lovefest," one politician called it. Shortly after the election, Walter managed to get an invitation to one of the Laxalt VIP-only celebration parties. At the party, he was introduced to Laxalt by a mutual friend and made it known to the senator that he wanted to contribute a "large sum of money" to his future political campaigns. Laxalt thanked him and, with a sly grin, asked, "And what is it I can do for you, Walter?"

By 1982, Walter had become one of the major contributors to the Republican Party and was on their A-list. Not only was he on a first name basis with several senators, congressman, and the governor of New York, but he had also been a guest of President Reagan at the White House. Walter's friendship with Paul Laxalt had paid off. He made it known that he wanted to be on the "inside." And he was willing to pay whatever the cost. He knew that once he was in the loop, so to speak, he would then have a say in who was going to be the next president of the United States.

CHAPTER NINETEEN

On the flight to Algeria, PJ could not stop thinking about the three hostages and one soldier who were killed during the rescue mission at the Entebbe airport in Uganda. PJ was more comfortable working on his own, not putting anyone else in harm's way. Because of that, he was having second thoughts about agreeing to work with a new task force that had been formed by the CIA and the FBI—its purpose, to go after the Colombian drug cartels. There already were more than fifteen special drug enforcement task forces. Some of them created as far back as 1970, each comprising agents and officers from the NYPD, the New York State Police, the DEA, the ATF, the FBI, and the CIA. However, the decision had been made to form this new group using only specially trained undercover operatives.

When he was first contacted by the CIA, PJ was told they needed him because of his ability to be able to infiltrate any foreign country and gather information. He was to be the front man for this new task force. He had given his word that he would take the assignment. He was not one to break his word. However, when he met his CIA contact in Algeria, he learned there was a little bit more to the assignment. The CIA agent told him there was a Colombian drug lord by the name of Carlos Sanchez who was personally responsible for the execution of three CIA operatives. And the CIA wanted a payback. "I cannot tell you this is sanctioned by the U.S. government," the agent told PJ. "You know our president could not authorize something like this. However, believe me when I tell you that you will have our full support and access to all our resources." Now PJ understood. They wanted him to assassinate Carlos Sanchez.

It was early April 1977 when PJ arrived in Costa Rica. He was to meet with a man known only as the Doctor. The Doctor was a major Cali cocaine associate of Carlos Sanchez, who had been told that PJ was a drug dealer in New York and was looking to buy 750 kilos of cocaine from someone who could also arrange the transportation out of Colombia into New York City once the deal was made. The meeting was at the Camino Realto Hotel, a run-down hotel located in a run-down neighborhood in Costa Rica. When PJ checked into the hotel, he requested a suite. He wanted it to appear to the Doctor that he had backup in one of the rooms. The suite consisted of a small living room with a couch, two chairs, a round table, and two little end tables. The bedroom had only one bed, a nightstand with a lamp, and a bureau. They had not wasted any money on an interior decorator. When the Doctor arrived, he was wearing army boots, dark green fatigues, and an old Yankees baseball cap that could not cover his long shaggy black hair. He was unshaven, but that still didn't completely hide the scar on his left cheek that PJ thought was probably the result of a knife fight. The two men exchanged brief hellos and then sat at the small table facing each other. "So, my friend, you are a friend of Juan Yanez," the Doctor said. Juan Yanez was an undercover DEA agent based in Bogota who had arranged the meeting. He was one of PJ's contacts.

PJ just nodded. He remained expressionless. His instincts told him right off not to trust this man. The Doctor looked at PJ, waiting for him to say something. Finally, the Doctor leaned across the table and asked PJ, "How do I know I can trust you, amigo?"

"You don't . . . amigo, but more to the point, I don't think I can trust you."

The Doctor leaned back in his chair and smiled. "I like you, amigo. I think maybe we can do business. Now . . . you got some money you can show me?" PJ leaned across the table; and without the Doctor ever noticing, he took his handgun from the holster strapped to his leg and reached under the table with it until he had the gun pressed between the Doctor's legs, pushing on his testicles.

"What the hell . . . ?" the Doctor started and then stopped when PJ pushed the gun harder against the Doctor's manhood.

"Look, you asshole, I didn't fly all the way down to this shit hole to get jerked around by someone like you. Now before we go any further, tell that . . . amigo . . . of yours who is standing outside the door to get his ass in here." The Doctor just stared at PJ. How did he know he had someone with him who was standing outside in the hallway? PJ pushed harder against the Doctor's groin; his eyes became watery.

"Okay okay, my friend, please, you are causing me pain . . ."

"Call him," PJ said without changing his expression. The Doctor called out in Spanish for his backup to come into the room. A few seconds later, a tall thin man also dressed in green fatigues and army boots came into the room, with a sawed-off shot gun strapped to his shoulder. PJ instructed the man to take the shotgun off his shoulder and also take the pistol he had in his waistband and put them on the table. The man looked at the Doctor who nodded his head, in effect telling his associate to do what PJ said. After the man put his weapons on the table, PJ told him to sit on the couch. Then he took his gun away from the Doctor's groin. The Doctor let out a sigh of relief.

PJ looked at the Doctor for several seconds, then very calmly asked, "Do we understand each other now . . . amigo?"

"Si, amigo, we understand each other."

"Good, then let's get down to business. I'm looking to buy 750 Ks as a starter. If we can do the right kind of deal and you can guarantee delivery, I could use twice that amount every month. Now I know you got your own organization with distribution cells in New York City as well as other parts of the country, and that's fine with me. We won't be in competition. You guys sell to all the Latinos and blacks around the country. More power to you. My customers are the cokeheads who live uptown in New York and who work on Wall Street. We sell the same stuff, but to different people. Compre!"

The Doctor figured PJ was no two-bit drug dealer. He had big balls and was not someone he could push around.

"Si, amigo, I . . . compre. But to do what you want will take some time to set up. And 750 Ks is a lot of goods. I will have to talk with my associates."

"I understand," PJ said. "How much time will you need?"

"About a week or so. In the meantime, why don't you come to Bogota? You will like it better than this . . . shit hole as you say."

PJ had struck gold. Carlos Sanchez was in Bogota, and the Doctor was going to lead him to him.

PJ arranged to meet the Doctor in Bogota the following morning. The Doctor suggested PJ stay at the Palace De Palma, a new hotel in La

Zona Rosa. As he started to leave, the Doctor turned to PJ and asked, "Amigo, would you really have shot me in the balls if I didn't call Pedro to come in?"

PJ smiled and said, "In a New York minute." The Doctor believed him.

After the Doctor and Pedro left, PJ called his contact at the CIA who was in Mexico City with the fifteen-member task force. PJ told him to go to Bogota with the team. The agent was anxious to know what was happening. "Well, first of all, within the next couple of weeks, I should be able to give you the names and locations of the major players of the Colombian cartel. As far as the target is concerned . . . things are moving in the right direction. That's all I can tell you now." The CIA agent was satisfied with that.

When PJ's plane touched down in Bogota, he had no idea of what to expect. The drive from the airport was his first glimpse of the sprawling Andean city of almost seven million people. He realized his preconceived notions were totally off once his taxi arrived in La Zona Rosa, a chic neighborhood west of the city center filled with upscale shops, wonderful restaurants, and lively sidewalk cafés. While there were armed guards patrolling the streets and large buildings, no one seemed anything less than truly at ease. PJ quickly realized that because so few foreign tourists visit Bogota, the city is not run with outsiders in mind. The first thing PJ did after checking into the hotel was to call Juan Yanez, the undercover DEA agent, to let him know that he was at the Palace De Palma and that he needed some weapons. He also told him he was meeting the Doctor for breakfast the next day in the coffee shop, and he might need backup. "Just in case," PJ said. "Just tell me what you need, Averhim." That was the kind of answer PJ liked. No questions or stupid small talk.

CHAPTER TWENTY

When PJ walked into the coffee shop the following morning, the Doctor was already there seated at a table at the rear of the restaurant. PJ took a quick inventory of the coffee shop and was satisfied the Doctor did not have a backup. He then looked for his backup. He spotted a man in a baggy nylon jumpsuit, headphones, and CD player hunched over a bowl of *mondongo*, the spicy Spanish cow-gut stew. This had to be his man. He walked over to where the Doctor was seated and joined him.

"Good morning, amigo, is a nice hotel, no?"

"Is a nice hotel, yes."

"And you not goin' to put a gun to my balls today, yes?"

PJ couldn't help but smile. "No, I'm not going to put a gun to your balls today . . . yes."

"That's good. So I talk to my people, and they are interested. But, my good friend, they ask me how I know you have the money to pay for all the goods you want."

"And what did you tell them?"

"I tell them . . . I think so. I am right, no?"

"You are right, yes."

"Good. Now like I tell you, we will need a little bit of time to set this up. In the meantime, my associate would like to meet you. I will call you in a couple days and let you know when we can do this. This is okay with you, eh, amigo?"

PJ couldn't believe it. Was the Doctor actually planning to take him to meet Carlos Sanchez? Had he passed the test as a drug dealer? He would have to wait and see.

At six o'clock the next morning, PJ's telephone rang. It was the Doctor. "Be downstairs in fifteen minutes, amigo. We are going for a ride." He didn't wait for an answer. PJ thought to himself, *These guys are no dummies. They don't want me to have time to set up a backup or have them followed.*

Ten minutes later, PJ was in the lobby. No Doctor. Five minutes went by when a little boy came into the lobby and walked directly over to where PJ was standing. "You are Amigo?" PJ nodded. The little boy said, "Take the taxi out front." Without waiting for a reply, he left.

PJ followed the boy's instruction and got into the taxi that was parked in front of the hotel with the motor running. About ten miles outside of town, the taxi pulled over to the side of the road and stopped. "You get out now, amigo." PJ did as he was told. He stood by the side of the road for about ten minutes when another taxi arrived.

The Doctor, who was driving the taxi, looked out the window with a big smile, "You need a ride, amigo?"

Since the late sixties, Colombia has been the home to some of the most violent and sophisticated drug trafficking organizations in the world. What started as a small cocaine-smuggling business has blossomed into an enormous multinational cocaine empire. They have the capital and are gaining the resources to outsmart the most sophisticated equipment the government puts in place to stop the smuggling. PJ knew it cost the cartel $1,500/kilo to process the coke in their jungle labs. The price on the streets of America was as much as $50,000/kilo. Pablo Escobar, a common street thief who masterminded the criminal enterprise that became known as the Medellín, was the first to convince the leaders of the other cartels that they could fly small airplanes directly into the United States, avoiding the need for countless suitcase trips. Although Carlos Sanchez was not as powerful as Escobar, he too was now using both airplanes and boats to get the coke to the States.

PJ got into the taxi the Doctor was driving and prepared himself for the ride. The Doctor maneuvered the taxi on the narrow winding roads in the jungle. They were headed for Magdalena Valley northwest of Bogota. In the valley, there were thousands of Colombian peasants who were on the cartel's payroll as employees on their farms, ranches, cocaine laboratories, and air shipment points. PJ assumed they were getting closer to Carlos Sanchez's fortress when he began to see more and more armed guerillas.

The CIA had briefed PJ on the role of the two main guerilla factions. The Marxists and the more powerful FARC, a leftist guerilla group. They protect the fields and the labs in remote zones of Colombia in exchange for a large tax the traffickers pay to the organization. This situation was a disaster for Colombia—both sides in an ongoing civil war reaping huge profits from the drug industry, which is then turned into guns for further fighting.

After about a thirty-minute drive, they came to an area in the jungle that looked like a large farm. There were guards on horseback patrolling the entire perimeter. They eventually stopped at a large house also surrounded by guards. PJ wondered how they got the material here to build the house. Not his worry. Two guards came over to the taxi, one on each side. They greeted the Doctor and spoke to him in Spanish. "They need to search you, amigo," the Doctor said to PJ, in an apologetic tone.

"No problem," PJ answered, spreading his feet and holding his hands over his head. He had not brought any weapons with him. As the guards searched him, he thought about how he was going to be able to fulfill his assignment. It was not going to be easy.

The two guards ushered PJ and the Doctor into the house where they were turned over to two other guards who motioned for them to follow them. They walked through a large marble hallway into a living room that led to a patio. Standing on the patio, which overlooked a manicured garden, was the drug lord . . . Carlos Sanchez. Standing on the edge of the patio was Sanchez's bodyguard. The bodyguard, who had a gun in his waistband, kept his arms folded and his eyes on PJ. Sanchez was a tall man, maybe six feet. He was built like a light heavyweight. He had straight black hair that partly fell over his forehead and deep-set eyes that seemed to look right through you. "This is the big shot drug dealer from New York," the Doctor said as they approached Sanchez.

"And your name, big shot drug dealer from New York?" Sanchez asked as he held out his hand to shake PJ's hand.

"Vincent Ferriera."

The CIA went to a great deal of trouble to establish an alias for PJ. They created an export company and supplied PJ with corporate IDs and tax identification. "And you have some identification, my new friend Vincent Ferriera?" Sanchez said as they all sat down.

PJ smiled. "As a matter of fact, I do. But where I travel, I don't need any. Like you, Mr. Sanchez." Sanchez knew this new buyer of drugs was flexing his muscles. That was good. He liked his style.

"Would you like something to drink?" Sanchez asked.

"Got any Absolut?" PJ asked.

Sanchez nodded, and the bodyguard went to the cabinet and got a bottle of Absolut. He then poured two drinks and handed one to PJ and the other to Sanchez. PJ glanced at the Doctor who simply smiled as if to say "Drink up, my friend."

"Salute," Sanchez said, downing the drink in one large gulp. PJ tried the same, but halfway finished, he started to choke. "Would you like a straw, my friend?" Sanchez said, motioning to his bodyguard to pour him another drink.

"No, thank you," PJ said with a smile.

"Okay," Sanchez said, "so you want to buy some cocaine. I think we got some to sell. But since we don't know one another and this is the first time we do business, I have to have some guarantees that you are who you say you are. So I would like you to send a family member to visit with us here until we receive payment for the first shipment. When you receive the shipment in New York, your family member will then be free to leave. Of course, if something goes wrong—if you don't pay, if the DEA intercepts the shipment, anything like that—well then, your relative ... shall we say, becomes a cost of doing business." The CIA had briefed PJ on this in advance. They told him it was not that an uncommon of a request, but of course one they could not accept.

PJ was quick to answer. "Okay, my friend, I'll send a relative down to Colombia if you'll send me one in New York."

"I'm sorry, my friend, that's not an option," Sanchez replied. "Two family members cancel each other out. There has to be only one—and it must come from you. I need a guarantee."

PJ moved to the end of his chair. "Yes, I understand," he said. "And I am ready to give you one." Then PJ slowly slid his index finger across his own neck and said, "My guarantee is my life."

It was almost eight o'clock in the evening when the Doctor dropped PJ back at his hotel. As PJ got out of the taxi, the Doctor said with a smile, "Good meeting, eh, amigo?"

"Yeah, amigo ... good meeting."

A very strange thing had happened. PJ and the Doctor had become friends. This was not a good thing. PJ knew this. You don't make friends with people you might have to kill. As the taxi pulled away, PJ knew at some point, he would probably have to end the life of his new friend. That's the way it was.

PJ went into the hotel bar for a drink before going to his room. Sitting at the bar was a very pretty woman who PJ sized up right away as a working girl. She was looking him up and down. He gave her a polite smile as if to say "Not tonight, sweetheart." She continued to look him up and down, squeezing her chin, inspecting him as if he were a horse on an auction block. She had that sexy schoolmarm look. Her long black hair hung loose on her shoulders. Finally, she moved closer to him and whispered so only he could hear, "I am your contact. Make it look like you are propositioning me." She smiled and coyly began to play with the drink mixer in her mouth. PJ figured she was either a good undercover agent or a good prostitute. Either way, it was a win-win!

When they got to his room, she was all business. "My name is Maria. I will be your contact to the special task force. They want you to know they received the information you sent. It has been very helpful. They are now working with the Colombian special forces and feel confident they can break up some of the cartel. They want you to now just concentrate on the target."

PJ looked at her. "Does that mean you don't love me?"

She laughed. She liked him. But this was business. "So how went your meeting with Carlos?"

"You know I was with him?"

"Of course. You think we are amateurs?"

PJ filled her in on all of the details of the meeting. He told her they would have to go through with the first buy in order for him to get closer to Carlos. That was the only way he could gain his confidence. She told him that was not a problem.

CHAPTER TWENTY-ONE

The Doctor called PJ the next day and told him they were going to meet Carlos to finalize the deal. "Meet me at the Pozo Lounge in Quito at noon. There will be a taxi waiting for you outside the hotel at eleven o'clock." Quito was about ten miles north of Bogota. PJ couldn't figure out why Carlos was leaving his compound and why was the Doctor telling him in advance about the meeting. Was this a setup? At 11:00 a.m. sharp, PJ was outside in front of the hotel. A taxi pulled up to the curb. The driver leaned out of the window and said, "You are waiting for me, amigo?" It was the Doctor. The ride took about fifteen minutes. The Pozo Lounge was in a deserted part of town, on a street with only a few other buildings. It was an easy location for Carlos to secure, and had PJ tried to put some of his people there, Carlos's guards would have surely spotted them. This was a test. When they arrived at the Pozo Lounge, they were shown in and taken to a small room in the back. About ten minutes later, Carlos walked in with three of his bodyguards. This time, his jet-black hair was slicked down and parted on the side. Combined with his thick mustache that hung down to his chin, he did indeed look menacing. He walked straight to PJ and shook his hand.

"Buenos noches, amigo."

PJ responded, "Mucho gusto, mucho gusto."

With the greetings out of the way, Carlos began to tell PJ that although he originally talked about transporting the load by plane, he had second thoughts.

"The government got some equipment from your country that can detect even a small plane flying low. And they now have a new shoot-down policy. They will fire on any plane that doesn't have an approved flight plan. So I will change the operation to a boat deal. It may cost you a little more, amigo. But for now, that's the way it has to be."

PJ agreed and wanted to know how soon he would need the money.

"On Friday, the Doctor will call you to set up a meet. If all goes well, you should have your merchandise in New York by Monday."

PJ extended his hand and said, "Okay . . . we are in business."

PJ remained in Bogota until he heard the shipment had been delivered to New York. The DEA was not all that happy about having to front so much money, but PJ assured them it would be worth it. He was sure Carlos would contact him again about delivering more loads, and he was right. On Thursday, the Doctor called PJ and told him Carlos wanted to meet him to celebrate the success of their first shipment and plan for the future. They would meet on Saturday at a place called El Rosa Elegante, which was in Ibagué, a small town about twenty miles west of Bogota. Like always, the Doctor would send a car and driver to drive PJ to the meet.

"I will pick you up at six o'clock, amigo," the Doctor told PJ.

"I look forward to it, my friend," PJ said, knowing full well the Doctor was now in harm's way.

PJ called Maria and told her what he needed. He explained to her the danger involved. "Thank you," she said. "But that is life, isn't it? Danger."

PJ agreed and hung up. The time had come. Payback.

Maria called her friend Lt. Manuel Philapo, who was part of the Colombian antidrug task force. They had worked together in the past. "I need a diversion next Saturday. Like a small explosion. Not a bomb. Maybe a utility pole failure or a gas line."

"I know what you mean," the lieutenant said. "No problem."

Maria gave him the location and the time. Then she made arrangements to send PJ the weapons he wanted, a Desert Eagle handgun and a Barak pistol. Both very deadly weapons. And finally, she arranged to have a helicopter available for PJ after his assignment was completed. Everything would be in place.

When the car pulled up in front of a four-story Victorian house, a gigantic place that took up half of the block, PJ assumed they were meeting at some fine-dining establishment. There were palm trees lined up in front of the house and a canopy that you walked under to get inside. When PJ walked in, a gaggle of adoring women—beautiful, elegantly clad women—greeted him. They were dressed in evening gowns as if they were going to a wedding. A very tall thin tan-skinned woman motioned for PJ to follow her. She escorted him a private room where Carlos, two of his bodyguards, and the Doctor, who had walked in ahead of PJ, were waiting. PJ quickly surveyed the room to make sure there was only the one entrance. He thought for a second and decided he would have to eliminate everyone in the room in order to get out safely.

"How do you like this place, amigo?" There was a half-empty bottle of vodka on the table in front of Carlos. PJ could tell from looking at him that Carlos probably drank the other half.

"Very nice," PJ said. Then looking around, he asked, "Is this a private club of some kind?"

Carlos laughed out loud. "No, amigo, it is the fanciest whorehouse in all of Colombia. They got the best food and the sexiest women." With that, he held up his glass and said "Salute" and downed a large glass of vodka. Evidently, the man could drink.

Working undercover in a foreign country can cause incredible stress, and everybody handles it differently. There were some who succumbed to the booze and broads and others who lost their self-control and compromised their mission. PJ was neither. He was a trained perfectionist. Tonight, he would do the job he was trained for.

PJ chose a chair that allowed him to get up in a hurry. He had to be sure that he was able to act quickly as soon as the diversion occurred.

A scantly dressed waitress came in with a tray of drinks just as they all heard the noise. It sounded like a bomb. Everyone in the room started to get up, but before they knew what was happening, PJ had both of his weapons out and instantly killed the two guards. Then he turned to Carlos who was reaching into his coat pocket for his gun. While his hand was in his pocket, PJ shot him twice in the head. As he fell over, PJ fired two more shots into the back of his skull, splattering his brains on the floor. The waitress was screaming. PJ hit her gently on the jaw, but hard enough to cause her to fall to the ground and stop screaming. The Doctor was in shock. The color drained from his face. When PJ turned to him, all he could manage was, "Amigo." PJ looked at him for a second and said, "Sorry, amigo," and then shot him three times in the heart.

When PJ made his way back out to the entrance, the beautiful girls he first saw when he came in were running around, trying to figure out what happened. There was a lot of noise both inside and outside of the El Rosa Elegante. Once outside, PJ could hear the roar of the helicopter overhead. He half walked, half ran to a predetermined empty parking lot about four blocks from the Elegante. The helicopter was just setting down. PJ ran to the open door, reached for the hand of the Colombian commando who was half hanging out of the door, and lifted himself into the plane. In seconds, the helicopter was sky bound. The commando looked at PJ and smiled. They were in the same business.

The helicopter took PJ to Algeria where he got a ride on a C-47 U.S. military transport to France. From France, he flew commercial to Heathrow in London. He took a cab from the airport to his flat on the Westside, kicked away the mail from inside the door, undressed on his way to the bathroom, and then took a long hot shower. He made sure the telephone ringer was turned off and the blinds closed tightly. Then he crawled into bed and slept for the next thirty-six hours, getting up only twice to pee and once to get a glass of water.

CHAPTER TWENTY-TWO

In June of 1995, with all the fanfare of the Super Bowl, Republican Senator Guy Baxter rolled into Shadow Creek, Steve Wynn's 320-acre, $48-million private golf course in Las Vegas, a guarded preserve where the staff is sworn to secrecy; and the few guest players required to have a minimum line of $100,000 at one of the Wynn casinos are served caviar on the fairway. Arriving shortly after the senator, in his own private jet, was Walter Lippincott. They were there for a $5,000-a-plate luncheon. The VIP guest list read like a who's who of the sports world, show business, big business, and Las Vegas casino owners. Although the election was eighteen months away and there were three possible Republican candidates, Walter Lippincott, who organized the luncheon, wanted to get an early foothold for his man.

Tracking Baxter, the national media was beginning to discover in earnest, if not in some shock, that behind all the highly publicized and bipartisan good fortune that Baxter was receiving, there were enormous stakes. Las Vegas interests were inserting unprecedented amounts of money into the political process all around the country and more particular into his campaign. Corporate casinos boasted heavily staffed "government relations" departments, conducting sophisticated polls on issues and candidates on all sides. Americans were gambling their money as never before—and losing more than $40 billion a year. Uncertain of the present and future controls and restraints that the government may decide to put on gambling, the industry wanted to stay ahead of the curve. Walter Lippincott was aware of this and assured the people in Las Vegas his man would stay friendly to the gambling interests in Las Vegas. Walter was well aware of his man's attempt to get legislation passed to make gambling legal all over the United States. Walter was opposed.

As a result, the two men had some heated discussions over the past several months regarding the issue. At one point, the senator told Walter, "I think maybe after our Las Vegas fund-raiser, we should take a look at where you and I are going." Walter was thinking the same thing. Not only because of the gambling issue, but because of the things PJ had told him about the senator's Las Vegas flings. If that stuff ever got out, he could kiss the presidency goodbye. But for the time being, he was his man. And to get him elected, he needed the financial support of Las Vegas. However, the power brokers in Vegas were not anxious to see sports betting legalized all over the country. If Walter couldn't convince "his man" to change his views on the issue, he might have to consider supporting one of the other candidates. Walter was not personally in favor of legalized gambling nationwide. It wasn't that he was all that virtuous; he simply believed that nationwide gambling would increase the crime rate and make many hardworking individuals compulsive gamblers. That would not be a good thing. He would make his decision after the luncheon.

Senator Baxter and his entourage of three male aids made an unscheduled stop in Las Vegas a month before the luncheon on their way back to Washington from San Francisco. They were staying in a villa at the Casino Royale, the last of the syndicate-owned casinos. The registered name of the owner was the JTC Corp. The JTC stood for Joseph Theodor Cantelli. Cantelli had been investigated numerous times by the Nevada Gaming Control Board as well as Washington's task force on organized crime, and each time, he came up clean. But he knew it was only a matter of time before he would have to leave Vegas. He couldn't compete with the new megamillion-dollar casinos being built by large public companies. The old Vegas is gone. Fourteen of the fifteen largest hotels on the Strip were now owned by two megacorporations. The intimacy of Bugsy Siegel's 147—Flamingo Hotel was replaced by the five-thousand-room MGM Grand. All his old cronies are gone. How in only twenty years Las Vegas has changed. Casino executives today who borrow money to build and expand don't have to meet the wise guys in darkened Chicago hotel rooms at three in the morning and be told they're going to get their fingers cut off. That's why he didn't agree with most of the other casino owners. He wanted legalized sports betting nationwide. Once that was passed, he would be 100 percent legit, and he could operate his sports books without always looking over their shoulder. He did that for almost fifty years. Enough is enough! It was time to move on.

It was only a five-minute walk from the main building of the Casino Royal to the separately secured compound that held the ten villas. One of the senator's aids led Sonny Cantelli into the dining room where the senator was enjoying a sumptuous array of cold food and various iced drinks. All nonalcoholic. He had risen high in the political councils of the nation and was the head of several important committees, and the powers to be thought he had a good chance of being the next president.

Sonny walked over to where the senator was sitting and handed him a large brown envelope. Sonny was the eldest of Joseph's two sons. The old man sent Sonny to Las Vegas after he built the Casino Royal. Sonny had that "Vegas appeal". He was tall, good looking, and very Italian. Whatever success the Casino Royal had achieved, it was because of Sonny.

"A little gift from the hotel, Senator," he said. "Have a pleasant stay. Anything you need just let me know." Sonny was the president of the Casino Royal.

The senator clasped both of Sonny's hands with his. "What a delightful present," he said as he took the envelope containing $5 million and handed it to his aid. "Now can I have a few confidential words with you?"

"Of course," Sonny said.

The senator turned to his aids and told them he needed a few confidential words with Sonny. They nodded and left the room. The senator started to pace the room. He stopped, frowned, and looked at Sonny. "Sonny, I have good news naturally, but I also have some bad news."

"Isn't that always the case?" Sonny said, thinking for the five mil, the good news had better be a hell of a lot better than the bad.

Baxter chuckled. "Isn't that the truth? The good news first. And very good news it is. As you know, I have devoted my attention over this past year in passing legislation that would make gambling legal all over the United States. Even the provision to make sports gambling legal. I know how important that is to you and your father. I finally have the votes in the Senate and the House . . . The money in the envelope will insure some of the votes that are on the fence . . . the money . . . it is five, isn't it?"

"It's five."

"And money well spent, you can be sure."

"I agree. Now what's the bad news?"

The senator shook his head sadly. "The president has told me he will veto the bill."

Sonny was confused. What the hell was Baxter talking about?

Baxter continued, "And we don't have enough votes to override a veto."

Sonny needed time to think. "So the five mil is for the president?" he asked for the lack of anything else to say.

"No no, not the president. He will be a very rich man when he retires into private life. He has no need for petty cash," Baxter said with a grin. "But the vice president, that would be another story. If he was president, I know he would sign the bill."

"So what do we do, sit by and hope the president has a heart attack so we can then deal with the vice president?" Sonny was visibly angry now. *What was this asshole trying to pull? He got our five mil, and he can't deliver.*

"Well, not exactly. If something happened to the president. Something like an accident. I know it sounds heartless, but we are all mortal. Anything could happen. You know what I mean."

Sonny lost it. "Are you out of your fucking mind? You don't go around killing presidents. What's wrong with you, Baxter?"

One of the aids popped in. "Is everything okay, Senator?"

"Yes, fine, Alan. Everything is fine." The aid left.

"Okay, Sonny, relax. I'm not asking you to . . . do what you just said. There may be another way. Walter Lippincott."

"What the hell are you talking about?" Sonny asked, now more agitated.

"The president listens to Lippincott. Believe me, I know what I'm talking about. Lippincott played a big part in getting him elected the second term. And Lippincott has promised corporate Las Vegas that he would not let a bill pass that would legalize gambling nationwide. I know. Lippincott has a lot of power. And now somehow, I find myself joined at the hip with this guy. He is our problem."

"What happens if we just wait until you get elected?" Sonny questioned, all the time thinking about what the senator is asking his family to do.

"First of all, there is no guarantee I will get elected. And secondly, things change. The election could change the composition of the Congress. I may not have the votes I have now. There are many factors.

Believe me, Sonny, timing is everything. Without Lippincott around, I am sure I can get the president to sign the bill. And besides that, think about the message that would send to the president."

Sonny couldn't believe his ears. *This guy wants Lippincott out of the way. And what's this shit, "It would send a message" . . . ? Who the fuck does he think he is . . . the godfather? He is some slick guy,* Sonny thought. The personification of the virtuous all-American politician. Yet he was implying we assassinate his own president. He tells us he has done his part, and now it's up to us to kill some citizen so that he can get the bill passed.

The senator was now picking at the food on the table. "I'm only staying one night," he said to Sonny. "I hope you have some girls in your show that would like to have dinner with me."

Back in his office, Sonny called his father in Chicago. He told him he was flying to Chicago in the morning. He had something very important to discuss that he didn't want to talk about on the phone. His father told him his driver would pick him up at the airport. He didn't ask any questions.

Chapter Twenty-Three

After the episode in 1977 with the Colombians, PJ decided to take on fewer assignments. He remained bothered by having to eliminate the Doctor. He made the mistake of letting it become personal. You don't do that in his business. He spent most of his time in London growing his security business. He hired a fellow Mossad agent who had retired to London, and between the two of them, they built a very large and successful business. About once or twice a year, PJ would take on an assignment. However, by 1986, he was ready to get out of the killing business, when he received a call from Israel's prime minister, Yitzhak Shamir. "We have a very important and secret mission, Averhim. Are you available?" PJ had never refused Golda Meir—how could he refuse Yitzhak Shamir?

On August 15, 1986, PJ and ten other Israel commandos landed by sea in Tunisia. It was nine o'clock at night. It had rained the entire day, and the gray clouds hung low over the deserted area where they landed. They quickly dragged their small rubber dinghies from the water and buried them in the sand. The ten commandos with PJ were from an elite army commando unit directly responsible to the general staff. Their intelligence on the targets' location and movements was superb. Their mission was the assassination of the Palestine Liberation Organization's military chief, who was known to be in Tunisia on that Saturday evening. The commandos made their way to the house where the target was within minutes. Their attack was swift and deadly. Fourteen Palestinian guards and associates of the leader were shot and killed before the commando force stormed the house and killed the PLO leader. Israel undercover agents in Tunisia posing as tourists, who had rented five cars, arrived at the scene just as PJ and his team were leaving the house. They quickly threw their weapons in the trunk of the cars, took off their army boots and battle fatigues, and split up into the five cars. They then drove away just as they heard the sirens of Tunisian police cars. They past the police cars without any incident.

The immediate Palestinian reaction was a burst of rage in the shantytown refugee districts of Gaza where the PLO leader, Abu Jihad, grew up. At least twenty Palestinians were shot dead, and over a hundred more wounded by army gunfire in the bloodiest day of protest in months. The Israeli government said little to dispel the universal belief—voiced not only by Palestinians, but also by the Israel press—that Israel's secret forces carried out the nighttime assassination of the PLO leader. On his return flight to London, PJ read the newspaper account of the raid and decided that was his final assignment. He was retiring from the killing business, or so he thought.

In 1987, PJ was contacted by Security Systems International. They were headquartered in Rome and wanted to establish an office in London. They were interested in buying PJ's security business in order to accomplish that. PJ discussed the offer with his associate, and they both agreed the offer was too good to turn down. PJ's associate agreed to remain with the company for three years at a very lucrative salary while PJ decided it was time for him to move on. He was going to move back to the United States. Between the money Security Systems International was paying him and the money he had accumulated over the past twenty years, most of which were in Swiss banks, he was a very rich man. So on November 10, 1987, PJ moved out of his London apartment, said all of his goodbyes, and boarded a plane for New York City.

CHAPTER TWENTY-FOUR

May 1995

When Sonny arrived at his father's home, he was surprised to find his brother, Andy, and his first cousin Joey Sconsi were there. His father told him he assumed there was something of the utmost importance to be discussed, so he asked Andy and Joey to attend the meeting. There was no food or drinks in the den where the four men met. Dinner would come later. This was the time to hear what Sonny had to say. Sonny gave a detailed account, how he gave the five million to Senator Guy Baxter and then word for word his conversation with him. He told his family that Baxter would stop at nothing to get what he wanted so long as he didn't have to get his own hands dirty. When Sonny finished talking, there was a long silence. The four men looked at one another, each expecting the other to say something. Sonny's brother, Andy, seemed the most concerned. Now that he had his chain of restaurants, he was less inclined to take risks. He was running a very profitable legitimate business. However, he was a Cantelli; and whatever decision was made, he would cooperate 100 percent. You could tell from his face that he was waiting for his father to speak.

Joey didn't wait for the old man to say anything. He was a hotheaded Italian. "That fucking senator is crazy," Joey said. "We should whack him just for being an asshole." The old man did not appreciate his nephew's point of view, and his stare told him so.

Joseph Cantelli was a very hard, stern-looking man. In his younger days, the ladies considered him handsome; the men considered him dangerous. When he dressed to go out, his suits, topcoat, and fedora all matched his dark gray personality. His olive-skinned face had a smooth boxy look. You could usually tell his mood from the set of his jaw. His eyes were black and piercing and very vigorously expressed his authority as a leader of men. In his younger days, his word was law among his peers. But this meeting was with his two sons and nephew. And he was no longer twenty-five years old. At this stage of his life, he wanted easy. He had remained composed while Sonny detailed the account of his meeting with Baxter. He finally spoke.

"Sonny, are you sure that was the message the senator was sending? That we should actually assassinate the leader of our country? One of his colleagues in the government. And if not, then to make this Walter Lippincott disappear?"

Sonny said dryly, "The senator is no dummy. He would never incriminate himself. He just presented the facts. He assumes we will act on it. Believe me, that was the message he wanted me to bring back."

Joey, who was a couple of years younger than Andy, was a hot-tempered and impetuous young man. He worked at the Casino Royal for two years, but Sonny told his father he was too much of a hothead and didn't think Vegas was the place for him. Joey came back to Chicago and was now working for the family in one of their sports betting operations at a relatively unimportant job. Whenever the family was together, Joey always wanted his uncle to talk about "the old days."

"I wish I was there," he would say. "You guys knew how to get things done, not like the mamelukes today." Joey's father was killed when Joey was a baby, and his mother died when he was ten. Joseph Cantelli promised his sister, Joey's mother, that if anything ever happened to her, he would take care of her son. And so Joey had been living in his uncle's house most of his life,

"We should do it," Joey said excitedly. "We can get the whole gambling business legal." Joey was hoping that if that happened, there would be a place for him in one of the legal sports betting parlors. He hated working the shit job his uncle had given him.

Sonny's father looked at Andy and asked, "And how about you, my son? What do you think we should?"

Before Andy responded, he turned to look at his brother. "I'll go along with whatever you and Sonny decide," he said.

"And how about me? Am I chopped liver or something? Don't I get a say in this?" Joey bellowed. Again, he received the stare from his uncle.

"And you, Sonny, tell me how you think we should handle this."

Sonny appreciated his father's confidence. "Well, first of all, assassinating the president is not even an option." Sonny's father and brother agreed. Joey didn't say anything. "There is something else you all should know if we even think about . . ."—Sonny hesitated—"think about doing something to Lippincott." Joey liked that. Sonny was actually considering taking out Lippincott. Sonny continued.

"Before I left Vegas, I checked out Lippincott. It seems he has a brother who was in the Mossad."

"The who?" Joey asked.

"The Mossad. It's Israel's counterterrorism force," Sonny said. "They're a tough bunch of guys. Not many people even know Lippincott has a brother, let alone know he was in the Mossad. And one other thing. I got it from a very reliable source that Lippincott's brother was a paid assassin for the CIA."

"What are you saying, Sonny?" his father asked.

"What I'm saying, Pop, is that if we decide to do something about Walter Lippincott, we need to be prepared to do the same about his brother. Because if we don't, I have the feeling he will hunt down whoever is responsible for his brother's misfortune and won't stop until he gets revenge."

"Do we know who he is, Sonny? We have people in Washington. If like you say he worked for the CIA, we should be able to track him down."

"Not yet, Pop, but I've got some feelers out. But I don't think it makes any difference if we know who he is or not. From what I heard, he is the best in the business. And if he isn't neutralized immediately, well, I think we would have a war on our hands. Like you always said, Pop, it's risk and reward. In this case, I'm not sure the risk is worth the reward."

"Bullshit," Joey said.

"Joey, be quiet!" his uncle shouted. "Let Sonny finish." Joey didn't like being put down by his uncle. He knew the old man thought that he wasn't smart enough to have an important job in the family business. He would have to do something to prove him wrong. Do something that would show the old man he was a real soldier. He had to "make his bones." Then the old man would have to take him seriously.

"That's about it, Pop," Sonny finally said. "It's your call."

"And if it was your call, Sonny, what would you do?" his father asked.

Sonny knew his father valued his opinion and would take it into consideration before he made the final decision. "To tell you the truth, Pop, I don't think there is anything we can do at this point. You want the Cantelli family to be 100 percent legit. So do I. So do we all. Andy here has a big business going with the restaurants, and I think we can find our niche in Vegas. Those are both legit operations. As far as the sports book and the other related gambling interests, we'll just have to bide our time. Maybe we'll get lucky, and Baxter will be our next president." Then he said with a smile, "God forbid. Be careful what you wish for . . . you may get it."

Sonny's father looked at his watch. "It's almost time for supper. But I agree with you, Sonny. There is nothing we can do now. Another thing, I think we should continue our ties with the senator. I don't begrudge him the extra five million, but I take it as an insult that he would think we would kill the president of our country to further a business venture. And as far as this Lippincott person is concerned, I am sure that is personal with the senator. Not our business. He seeks to manipulate us. It is better we stay close to him. Things change. We will see what happens." Everyone in the room relaxed, the tension broken, except for Joey; the Cantelli family was content to wait.

Joseph Cantelli spun many webs during the fifty-plus years he spent in building his family business. But the most extensive was the gambling. The Cantellis were a dominating force in illegal gambling in the United States. They had a serious influence on sports betting of all kinds, and ten years ago, they expanded their gambling empire when they took over a slot machine factory in Reno. The previous owner was a degenerate gambler and owed the Cantelli family more money than he could ever repay. The result, the Cantelli family took over the business. Sports were holy in America, and if gambling was legalized, that holiness would descend on gambling itself. The profits would be enormous. In Vegas, legal betting alone ran up over fifty million for just the Super Bowl. Cantelli knew that legalized gambling would provide his family more money than they could ever spend in five lifetimes.

Joey couldn't wait until dinner was finished so that he could leave. "You got a hot date?" Andy yelled as Joey left.

"Yeah, something like that," Joey answered as he left the house. The Cantelli family lived in Skokie, a suburb of Chicago. It was normally about a forty-five-minute drive to the South Side of Chicago. This night, Joey made the trip in under thirty minutes. He parked his Mustang convertible in front of a dimly lit bar called Sidney's. There were no lights on the *d*, *e*, *y*, and *s* neon sign out front; so the sign simply read Sin. The owner, Sid Mastro, was a small-time bookie who laid off the number and racetrack bets that were too big for him to handle to the Cantelli family. It was part of Joey's job to pick up the betting slips and money from Sid every day. Sid was behind the bar talking to one of the regulars and looked surprised to see Joey. He never came around this late; besides which, he was already here today. He left the regular and walked to the other end of the bar where Joey had taken a seat.

"Hey, whatcha doin' here this time of night? Everything Okay?" Sid tried to think what he might have done wrong that would have prompted Joey to be here.

"Yeah . . . we're cool. Lemme have a beer."

"You got it. So what's up?"

"What has to be up? I came to visit." Sid handed Joey his beer and waited for the punch line. Joey took a large gulp from the bottle, then wiped his mouth with his sleeve.

"Well, there is something I need to talk to you about. Pretty important as a matter of fact." Sid just listened. Joey motioned for Sid to lean closer so that he could whisper.

"The family needs for you to do us a favor." Sid's eyes lit up. Anything that would help his standing with the Cantelli family was fine with him.

"You know if I can, I will, Joey. Just name it." Joey looked around the bar to make sure there was no one within earshot.

"We need you to help us find a guy we can trust to, shall we say, eliminate someone." Joey was surprised the words came out so easily. On the ride to Sid's, he kept going over in his mind what he should say. Now that he started, he liked the part he was playing. Like one of the old-time wise guys. He could feel his juices starting to boil.

At first, Sid thought Joey was kidding; then when he realized he was dead serious, he said with a half smile, "You bullshitin' me, Joey? You want me to help the Cantelli family with a"—Sid looked around to make sure no one heard him—"hit? What makes you think I can do that? Jeez, you guys can do that better than me. I mean . . . no offense . . . you know what I mean, Joey?"

"Yeah yeah, I hear what you're saying, but here's the deal. The old man doesn't want to use any of his own people. So I told him you could help us out. Now you wouldn't want to disappoint him, would you?"

Sid thought to himself, *This guy is really putting the screws on me. If I agree, I could be involved in a murder. If I refuse . . . if I refuse, I don't know what might happen.* Sid thought for a minute.

"No, of course not, Joey. But that's a tough order. I mean, I know some guys, but I don't know . . . I wouldn't want to recommend the wrong guys. You know what I mean, Joey?"

Joey smiled. He enjoyed watching Sid squirm. "Don't be nervous. All I want you to do is gimme the names. I'll do the rest. And, Sid, you don't say a word to nobody. You hear what I'm sayin'? Nobody."

Sid nodded. Then he took a cigar box from under the bar, opened it, and started to look through its contents. Finally, he found what he was looking for. He took out a piece of paper and handed it to Joey. Sid pointed to the piece of paper and said, "This is a guy who used to come in here a lot. He's a friend of Angie. You know, Angie, the guy who used to bet the basketball games with us." Joey nodded. "Well, anyhow, one day, the three of us are bullshittin'—me, Angie, and this guy"—again, Sid points to the piece of paper—"Tozzi. I don't know if that's his first name or last name. All I know is we call him Tozzi." By this time, Joey is really getting impatient.

"For Christ's sake, Sid, get to the fucking point!"

"Yeah, Joey, yeah. Well, in the course of us guys talking, this Tozzi says, 'If you ever need someone taken care of, I'm the guy who can do it.' Christ, I hardly know the guy. Anyways, I guess he figured I know a lot of people. And well, that's the whole thing. This guy writes his name and phone number on this piece of paper and hands it to me. This is the first time I looked at it since then. This is the best I can do, Joey. Honest." Joey smiled and took the piece of paper from Sid.

"Thanks, Sid. You did good. I'll tell the old man."

"Just so you know, Joey, this guy is sort of a weirdo. I think he likes boys and girls."

Joey smiled and said, "I'll try to remember that, Sid."

CHAPTER TWENTY-FIVE

It took Joey several days before he was able to contact Tozzi, the name Sid had given him. When he finally reached him, he was not the least bit interested in what Joey had to say.

"How the hell I know who you are! You could be some undercover guy tryin' to set me up. I don't know what you're talking about . . . taking care of someone. You mean like a babysitter?"

Joey said, "I work for the Cantelli family. You know who they are, don't you?"

"Never heard of them."

"Look, Sid gave me your name and phone number. How would I have gotten it otherwise? He said you, him, and Angie was in his place one night. You must remember that?"

Tozzi weakened. "I dunno . . . maybe I do, maybe I don't."

Joey finally said, "Tell you what. Why don't you call Angie, and we can all meet down at Sid's place? You don't got to say nuttin'. Just listen. If you like what you hear, fine. If not, the drinks are on me. Whadayou say?"

There were a couple seconds of silence; then Tozzi said, "Sid. Sid the bookie? Yeah, sure, I remember now. How is he doin'?"

Joey wasn't sure if this guy was on drugs, a plain dumb ass, or just being very careful. "He's doin' fine. So whadayou say? Wanna set up a meet?"

"Yeah, that sounds cool to me. Tell Angie to call and let me know when you guys want to meet. My schedule is pretty open for the next couple years." *The man has a sense of humor*, Joey thought.

On the night of May 3, 1995, Sid closed his bar early. The only two remaining customers he asked to leave were too drunk for it to make any difference. Joey, Angie, Sid, and Tozzi went upstairs to Sid's apartment. He told his wife to go to the movies with her mother; he had an important business meeting. "Important business meeting," she said. "With who? Your parole officer?"

Sid wasn't happy about having the meeting in his apartment. Five years earlier, he served time for armed robbery and was on parole for two years after his release. His parole officer still stopped by every so often to see how he was doing, and he sure as hell didn't want him to get wind that he was involved in setting up a hit. He explained this to Joey, but Joey insisted on using his apartment. "It's a onetime meet, no big deal," Joey told him.

"Okay," Joey said to Tozzi as the four men made themselves comfortable in Sid's living room, "how do you want to handle this?"

Sid interrupted, "I'm gonna go downstairs while you guys talk this out. I really don't want to be involved. I don't want to know any of the details. You gotta leave me out of this."

Joey shook his head. "Sorry, Sid, but you are involved. That's the way it gotta be. Sorry, pal."

"Jesus Christ, Joey, that sucks. You promised me—"

Tozzi interrupted, "What is this, a Sunday school meeting? I came here to talk business. Why don't we stop all this shit and get to it?"

Sid knew there was no point in trying to get out. He was in the minute he gave Tozzi's name to Joey.

Joey spoke up. "You're right, we're here to talk business. Sid tells me you can do a job for me. Make somebody disappear."

Tozzi was not one to mince words. He looked at Joey and said, "Why don't you just freakin' say it? You want me to knock somebody off. Okay, tell me who and where, and I'll tell you how much."

Joey had anticipated this moment, the time when he would give the order to kill somebody. He was sure that old man Cantelli had given the same order many times although he never admitted it. He looked around the room at the other three men and then spoke directly to Tozzi.

"There is a civilian by the name of Walter Lippincott. He is going to be in Las Vegas next month for a political fund-raiser. We want you to kill him when he returns to New York."

Tozzi stared at Joey for a minute and then started to laugh. "A civilian! What do you think this is, a *Godfather* movie?"

Joey didn't appreciate the humor. "Look, Tozzi, just tell me if you want to do the job. I don't need your wiseass remarks."

"Hey, I'm just kiddin' around. Can't you take a joke?" Joey nodded. "Okay, so tell me more," Tozzi said.

Joey continued, "Like I said, Lippincott will be back in New York the end of the month. He's maybe fifty-five years old, about 190 pounds, about five foot eleven, maybe six foot, with a lot of gray hair. And he's always well dressed. In the next couple of days, I'll have the exact date he arrives back in New York. I know he doesn't fly commercial. He has his own private jet. I'll give you the name of a guy in Newark who will be able to tell you when Lippincott's plane lands. This guy used to work with the air traffic controllers here in Chicago a few years back. He left town because he owed every bookie in town. He was also a big better with us. So he asked us to pay his other debts, charge him the juice, and he would make it good. The poor schmuck didn't know we made a deal with the other bookies for fifty cents on the dollar. It took him almost two years until he finally paid us off. He owes us. He'll find a way to get you what you need."

"No problem," Tozzi said.

"One more thing—and this is important," Joey added, "Lippincott has a brother who lives in Vegas. He used to be a paid assassin for the CIA. He is no amateur. I need the name of somebody in Vegas—somebody good who we can trust—who can take him out the same night. From what I hear, this guy is mean. If he is still around after his brother is aced, we got ourselves a nightmare."

"Holy shit," Sid chimed in, "this is really getting complicated."

Tozzi stood up and walked to the window. He turned around and looked at the other men. "This sounds to me like we got ourselves a big-time job here." He then spoke directly to Joey.

"Tell me again, why you guys don't handle this yourself?"

"Because we don't want this to look like a family-type hit. We're hoping you can do this with a little bit of style. Use your imagination, if you know what I mean."

Tozzi smiled and thought to himself, *Yeah, I'll show you some style. I'll shoot the bastard.*

Joey continued, "Next week, I'll have a picture of this guy."

"You prepared to pay the tab on this, Joey?" Tozzi asked. "This is not a five-, ten-dollar job, if you know what I mean."

Joey knew exactly what he meant. "The money is no problem. The Cantelli family always pays a fair price."

Tozzi looked at Sid, who nodded as if to give his stamp of approval.

Joey knew he was taking a chance. He didn't have the money needed for this job. He was going to have to "borrow" some of the Cantelli collection money. But that was okay. Once the old man knew Lippincott was taken care of, he would become the fair-haired boy. The prodigal son, so to speak. After all, like the old man always said, "No risk, no reward."

Tozzi began pacing back and forth. Then he stopped in front of Joey. Joey could tell he was deep in thought. He began to wonder if this guy could handle this job. If something went wrong, it would be his ass. The old man would chew him up and spit him out. Finally, Tozzi spoke, "This is gonna take a crew of at least four guys in New York. We'll need one guy to watch the airport. Once we know when Lippincott's plane lands, we need to have someone there to call and let us know he is on his way home. And depending on where we hit this guy, we'll need a lookout or a guy to give us cover, And then me and one other guy will do the hit. I know a guy, an ex-Green Beret. He loves to shoot people. As far as the hit in Vegas, I don't know, but I figure you gonna need at least two guys. It will take me a couple of days to get you a name, but I don't see a problem." Then he turned to his friend Angie. "You want in on this?" he asked.

Angie smiled. "You bet your ass I do." He didn't ask Sid; he knew the answer.

"Okay then, Joey, you got yourself a deal. Now the price. We are gonna have a lot of expenses. There's the plane fare for four guys. We need to get a car, stake out the place where we're gonna get this guy. There's a lot of shit involved. The New York hit is gonna cost you, Joey."

"How much?" Joey asked.

"Fifty grand," was the answer.

"Jesus Christ," Joey said, "that's a lot of money."

"Take it or leave it," Tozzi said.

Joey stood up, went over to where Tozzi was standing, and put out his hand. "You got a deal," he said.

Tozzi smiled. "But let me tell you, Tozzi, this has got to go smooth. No fuckups. It has to be a clean job."

"Don't you worry, Joey, I got it covered. You can order his flowers. Now I'm gonna need twenty-five Gs up front for expenses."

Joey was not happy with that. He was thinking how he could skim the collections for the next month to pay Tozzi. He was taking a big chance. But there was no backing down now. He told Tozzi he would have the money to him before the end of the week. Sid just listened. Something told him Joey was doing this on his own. He didn't know why, but it just didn't sound kosher to him. Old man Cantelli didn't operate this way. But what could he do? He couldn't question Joey. He thought about calling the old man, but what the hell would he say? He hoped Tozzi knew what he was doing.

Several days later, Tozzi called Joey with the name and phone number of someone in Las Vegas who could handle Lippincott's brother. "Are you sure this guy can do the job?" Joey asked, remembering what his cousin Sonny had told the family about PJ.

"Yeah. He's the right guy. Listen to this. He used to be a terrorist."

Joey screamed into the telephone, "What do you mean 'used to be a terrorist'?" You either are a terrorist, or you're not! What's wrong with you?"

"Relax, Joey. What I meant was he belongs to one of those Muslim groups. As far as I'm concerned, they're all a bunch of terrorist bastards. But I got this good friend of mine who lives in Jersey City, and he told me this is the guy you want. He's a real pro. But look, it's up to you. You know somebody better, then go ahead."

Of course, Joey didn't have anybody better.

"Okay, Tozzi, thanks," Joey said. "I'll give him a call."

CHAPTER TWENTY-SIX

When Sonny returned to Las Vegas, among a number of other items on his desk were two invitations. One was a large gold-colored envelope with embossed letters that read The Path to Victory Runs through Las Vegas. *What the hell is this?* he thought. He opened the envelope, and inside was a beautiful handwritten scripted invitation inviting him to attend the $5,000-a-plate luncheon honoring Senator Guy Baxter at Steve Wynn's Shadow Creek private and very exclusive golf club on June 19, 1995. The other was a lot less extravagant invitation, also handwritten, but not by a professional, inviting him to a private dinner the night before the luncheon being given for Senator Baxter. The invitation was from Gerald Clayton, a very prominent Las Vegas attorney who represented several of the Vegas casinos. Sonny sat and looked at the invitations for several minutes, trying to figure out was going on. The Baxter invitation was easy. They were looking for another sucker to contribute five grand. The Gerald Clayton invite was a tough one. But he made up his mind. He was going to accept both invitations.

Sonny contemplated calling Baxter since they had not spoken since his recent visit. However, he really had nothing new to tell him. The Cantelli family had decided not to act on either of Baxter's "suggestions." Baxter would figure that out soon enough, and besides which, he was sure he would have an opportunity to talk to him at the luncheon. Like his father told him, "Have patience!" The dinner on June 18 was at Gerald Clayton's club on the top floor of a high-rise office building in back of Fremont Street. Fremont Street is an incredible entertainment and gaming area off the Strip in downtown Las Vegas. Hundreds of millions of dollars in public as well as private funds have gone to rebuild and modernize Fremont Street, and the result is the Fremont Street Experience. It is a five-block-long pedestrian mall (enclosed by two million lights), the city's old Glitter Gulch, including the Horseshoe, California, El Cortez, Four Queens, Fremont, Golden Nugget, and Las Vegas Club. And on each side of the street, there is every kind of gift and food store you could imagine.

From time to time, different real estate developers have tried to purchase the post office block close to Fremont Street Experience—bordered by Stewart Street, Casino Center Boulevard, and Fourth Street—and turn it into an entertainment and retail corridor. However, the Fremont Street Association has always blocked the sale, fearing it would take business from the Fremont Street Experience. "Fremont Street is Las Vegas, and anything that detracts from that hurts all of Las Vegas." That was the association's defense. Little did they know that fifteen years later, the Las Vegas City Council would approve a deal with a California-based developer that would lead to a major renovation project in the Fremont Street area.

Sonny arrived at the club at six thirty, the time specified on the invitation. There were fifteen men standing around the room talking, most of whom he knew. They were owners or chief executives of the major casinos in town. Gerald Clayton welcomed him as he walked into the room, first offering him a drink and then asking if he knew everyone there. After a short time, Clayton suggested they go into the dining room as dinner was being served. Up to this point, Sonny didn't have the faintest idea what the meeting was about. That would change in a matter of minutes. As soon as everyone was seated, Clayton said, "For those of you who have not been privy to some of the meetings I have had with several owners, I would like you to know that we are here to talk about legalized gambling nationwide. If there is anyone here who feels he would rather not participate, I suggest he excuse himself before we start." No one left.

Holy shit, Sonny thought, *where is he going with this?*

Gerald Clayton was a large man, six feet three inches tall and weighed all of 250 pounds. If he was not in court, he very seldom wore a jacket. He always wore a red bow tie, brightly colored suspenders, as well as a thick leather belt with a gaudy silver buckle. He once told someone, "In order to be able to dress like me, you better be a damn good lawyer."

After the waiters took everyone's dinner order, Gerald Clayton continued his speech. "Gentlemen, I want to thank you for coming here tonight. I know you all have busy schedules. As you know, I have lived in Las Vegas for over fifty years. I came here out of the army because my parents lived here. My father worked for Jack Binion in the counting room in his casino right down there on Fremont Street," Clayton said, pointing to the window. Looking down from the dining room, you could see the lights of Fremont Street that looked like a long train all lit up.

Clayton continued, "I owe a lot to him. He paid for me to go to law school, and after I graduated and got my license, he helped me set up an office on Second Street. He also got me my first three clients. The Flamingo Hotel, an upstart young guy by the name of Steve something or other, who was looking to buy some cheap land, and a nice old man who put me on retainer just in case he needed a lawyer. If I remember correctly, his name was Myer Lansky." The men around the table all smiled. "Not a bad trifecta, don't you think?" Clayton asked.

He continued, "Now the reason we are all here tonight. For the past several months I have been meeting with some of you regarding the possibility of gambling becoming legal nationwide. In the past, most of you have opposed this possibility. I can remember back in the old days, all of the casino owners felt that way. When Bugsy Siegel and Myer Lansky came to Las Vegas, there was nothing but sand and a couple broken-down saloons. They had a vision, and we are living their dream. But we must recognize that times are changing. During the last five years, we lost three of our founding fathers—Jack Binion, a symbol of the Old West; Moe Dalitz, the philanthropist; and Hank Greenspun, the wheeler-dealer guardian of Las Vegas civic virtue. Some of you were lucky enough to know these men. There is no evidence that these men saw what was coming or, for that matter, knew much about the sophisticated new machinery of advertising, lobbying, and political manipulation. But they were wise enough to know their fabulous ever-changing Las Vegas was always in the changeless power of the past. And I guarantee you, gentlemen, if they were alive today, they would be the first to realize that eventually, gambling will not be limited to just Nevada. And they would act on that.

"There already are Indian-owned-and-run casinos, I should add in name only, in Connecticut, California, Michigan, Minnesota, Nebraska, and Wisconsin. And some states have permitted gambling on landlocked riverboats. So what does that tell us, gentlemen? It tells us there is a golden opportunity for men like you here today to expand your interests. Build casinos and hotels all over the country. The possibilities are endless. Let's do for America what Las Vegas did for Nevada. Our grand vision should no longer be bounded by the jagged mountains surrounding the Las Vegas Valley. Gentlemen, it is there for you to take."

Sonny was speechless. First of all, this guy sounded like a preacher. And Sonny had no idea so many other casino owners would support nationwide legalized gambling. *But it makes sense*, he thought. Look at the $610 million Steve Wynn spent a couple years ago building the Mirage. People couldn't wait to come and lose their money. What would stop him from building the same kind of moneymaker in Boston or Miami if it was legal? Of course, Sonny's family was content just to have their sports book legalized, but look at the possibilities.

Clayton continued, "Now, gentlemen, I know most, if not all, of you have received an invitation to Baxter's fund-raiser tomorrow at Wynn's country club. I urge you to attend. Baxter is an advocate of legalized gambling nationwide. I think it would be in our best interests to support him in his bid for the presidency. There is a fly in the ointment, however. I don't know if any of you know Walter Lippincott?" Several men nodded. "Well, unfortunately, he is opposed to nationwide legalized gambling. And he is a very powerful man. I have spoken to him several times in an effort to have him change his views on the issue, and I am convinced his reason for opposing legalized gambling is because he believes many of you have opposed it, and he needs your support and money. Now you folks need to convince him you are in favor of nationwide legalized gambling."

When Sonny left the meeting, he was anxious to call his father in Chicago; but with the time differential, he knew he would already have gone to bed. He would wait until tomorrow morning. Sonny thought to himself, *What a lucky bastard that Baxter is. He is going to get what he wants, and nobody gets hurt.* If only Sonny knew.

The next afternoon, as Sonny drove his Mercedes past the security and into the sanctuary of Steve Wynn's Shadow Creek Golf Club, he had to admit, the man had style. The grounds surrounding the building where the luncheon for Guy Baxter was being held looked like a painting. There was not a blade of grass out of place. Although there were no less than twenty car jockeys, most of the guests arrived in chauffer-driven limos. Sonny preferred to drive himself. When the young man opened his car door and welcomed Sonny to the golf club, Sonny jokingly asked, "Is there a VIP parking area?"

The young man responded very seriously, "Every spot is a VIP spot, sir."

Inside the clubhouse, Sonny followed the crowd into the dining room. Looking around at the décor, Sonny was impressed. It was apparent Wynn did not skimp on a single thing. In the dining room, there were twenty round tables, each set for ten people. In the front of the room, there was a head table with six chairs. As soon as everyone was seated, Tony Sali, a singer who was appearing at the Bellagio, asked everyone to rise again while he sang the national anthem. After he finished and everyone was once again seated, he introduced the people seated at the head table: Guy Baxter, Walter Lippincott, the mayor of Las Vegas, an ex-Nevada congressman, the former chairman of the Nevada State Republican Party, and, of all people, Gerald Clayton. There was a mild round of applause as Guy Baxter stood, waved to everyone in the room, picked up his wineglass, held it out toward the people in the room, and shouted, "To Las Vegas . . . salute!"

Seated at Sonny's table was a basketball player from the LA Lakers; two executives from Caesars Palace; Alan Gold, Walter Lippincott's personal assistant (or, as Guy Baxter called him, the token Jew); two directors of a California-based electronics firm, who were strong supporters of Baxter; a very pretty woman who worked for one of the major Hollywood studios; and a retired NFL player. "Quite a table," Sonny said to himself. There was one empty chair. Sonny looked at the place card on the table in front of the chair; it read PJ Gould. Walter had left a ticket for PJ at the front door just in case he changed his mind and decided to attend. Since the meeting with his father in Chicago, Sonny had learned that PJ was in fact Walter Lippincott's brother. He didn't know why they had different last names. He got the chills when he read the place card. *What if . . . ?* he thought. *Wow!* What Sonny didn't know there was a what-if. He had no way of knowing that his cousin Joey had arranged for the murders of both Walter Lippincott and PJ Gould.

During lunch, Guy Baxter made his pitch for being the Republican's candidate for president in 1996. He spoke for all of thirty minutes after which, the mayor of Las Vegas added his two cents. At Sonny's table, the conversation went back and forth between basketball, football, the best shows in Vegas, and what a great president Guy Baxter would make. By two thirty, the crowd started to leave. Sonny watched as Guy Baxter, Gerald Clayton, Walter Lippincott, and a man he didn't recognize walked out of the dining room. His eyes followed them, anxious to see where they were going. He saw them disappear into a small sitting room that looked out on the golf course. There were two security guards standing at the entrance to the room. Sonny smiled to himself and thought, *I guess this is where Gerald Clayton works his charm on Mr. Lippincott.* He looked at his watch and realized it was almost six o'clock back in Chicago, and he still hadn't called his father to tell him about last night's meeting. He would do that now.

Before leaving Steve Wynn's Shadow Creek Golf Club, Walter agreed to meet Gerald Clayton and four of the Strip's largest casino owners the next morning. Clayton told him it was important he meet with these owners before he left Vegas. "I want to get back to New York at a reasonable hour," he told Clayton. "So let's meet for breakfast. You set the place." The lawyer arranged for the group to meet in one of the VIP suites at the Bellagio. Walter remembered a meeting he had almost thirty years ago at the Sands Hotel in Las Vegas. The circumstances were a lot different then.

When Walter arrived at the meeting, only Clayton was there. "The others will be here shortly," he told Walter. "I wanted a few minutes alone with you, if you don't mind?"

Walter said, "Be my guest," and poured himself a cup of coffee.

"Walter," Clayton began, "we are closing in on the new millennium, and I see the twenty-first century as the beginning of unprecedented growth in the gambling industry. Believe me when I tell you, Walter, nationwide legalized gambling is in our best interests. Now I know that Baxter had a bill pass the House and Senate that would do just that. And as we all know, the president has refused to sign it." Then Clayton got up from his chair and walked over to where Lippincott was sitting. "Walter, please don't think I am being presumptuous when I say . . . I think you can get the president to change his mind."

Before Walter had a chance to answer, the others began to arrive. Clayton had accomplished what he wanted. He had planted the seed.

—

June 20, 1995

On the flight home from Las Vegas, Walter sat quietly looking out the window at the dark clouds and thought about what the casino owners told him earlier that day. They made it very clear that they intended to do whatever was necessary to make sure that gambling became legal nationwide. And since "his man" supported that, they would help in any way they could in getting him elected. Of course, he first had to win the nomination. However, as was always the case, the casinos planned to make heavy contributions to both parties. In that way, they would have all their bets covered. That kind of cash and power made Las Vegas a kind of shadow capital in political as well as socioeconomic terms. No matter what happened in the next election, the Vegas connections would win. The power brokers in Las Vegas understood parties and personalities were minor compared with the stakes now shared among the large casinos. Lippincott understood the city's bipartisan politics as well as anybody. They would back a winner, whatever party that may be.

When Lippincott left Vegas, he assured the casino owners he would do his best to convince the powers to be to support their interests. Little did he know he would not live long enough to accomplish that.

Sitting in his apartment in Chicago, Joey Sconsi kept looking at the clock. He knew Lippincott was due to land in New York within the hour. When he spoke with Tozzi earlier in the day, Tozzi assured him everything was in place. "Don't you worry bout a thing, Joey. I got you covered. I'll call you as soon as the job is done. Just relax."

REVENGE

Webster's New World Thesaurus
The act of returning an injury/vengeance, requital, reprisal, measure for measure. Retaliation, getting even.

Wikipedia: The Free Encyclopedia
The retaliation against a person or group in response to a perceived wrongdoing. Although many aspects of revenge resemble or echo the concept of justice, revenge usually has a more injurious than harmonious goal. The goal of revenge usually consists of forcing the perceived wrongdoer to suffer the same pain that was originally inflicted.

Revenge is a dish which people of taste prefer to eat cold.
—from *The Godfather* by Mario Puzo

THE CONCLUSION

PJ GOES ... ALL IN.

CHAPTER TWENTY-SEVEN

Still June 20, 1995

It seemed like forever to PJ sitting in his town house waiting for the police to arrive. And to make matters worse, there were two dead bodies waiting with him. His girlfriend, Cindy, and that asshole who killed her. PJ's friend Sandy Keller, the Las Vegas homicide detective, was the first to arrive.

"You look like shit," the detective said when PJ opened the door.

"Yeah, I know. I had a bad hair day."

"Hey, PJ, I'm really sorry about Cindy. That's a goddamn shame. Do you know who to call? Does she have any family?"

"Yeah," PJ said, "as a matter of fact, I just hung up from talking to her mother. That was a tough call." For the first time since he knew him, the detective saw real sorrow in PJ's eyes. He didn't know what to say. He put his arm on PJ's shoulder and told him if there was anything he could do . . . Why do people always say that? "Whatever I can do, just call me." What the hell does that mean?

The doorbell broke the silence. "Must be the crime-scene guys," the detective said. "Look, PJ, before they get started, I want to take a quick look around."

"Sure, follow me," PJ said as he opened the door for the others and took them all upstairs. PJ watched as Sandy made some notes in a small note pad, going back and forth from one dead body to the other. Then Sandy motioned to PJ, and they moved out of the way of the investigation team.

"PJ, is there anything I should know? Anything you would like to tell me before these guys get into it?" Sandy asked with a very serious tone in his voice.

"Like what? I don't know what you're talking about," PJ said. "Only what I told you on the phone, Sandy. That's it. Is there a problem?"

"Well, PJ . . . not really a problem, but the fact that there is no sign of a break-in and no shots being fired by the guy you shot and your girlfriend with a broken neck, if it wasn't you, I would be suspicious as hell as to what actually happened here tonight."

"Are you fucking kidding me?" PJ half shouted, causing some of the others to turn and look at what was going on.

"PJ, relax, I'm a cop. I'm just telling you the way other cops are going to look at this. I am sure we will find enough evidence to corroborate your story."

"Jesus Christ," PJ said in disgust. Then as if remembering something very important, he said, "Something happened in New York today that you should know—that is, if you don't already know."

Sandy shrugged his shoulders as if to say "I don't know."

"You know I have a twin brother who lives in New York."

Sandy nodded. "I knew you had a brother. I don't remember if I knew he was your twin. I also know he's very rich. I often wondered why you weren't in business with him."

PJ thought to himself, *I wonder what Sandy would say if he knew what I really used to do.*

"Could you see me in a three-piece suit every day, Sandy?"

"No, I guess not," the detective said.

"Well, as I started to say . . . and I don't know if there is any connection to what happened here . . . my brother was murdered earlier today outside of his apartment." After saying the words out loud, PJ felt a strange feeling come over him. After all, this was his twin brother he was talking about. But they had such completely different lives, it was almost like he was talking about a stranger.

"Jesus Christ!" Sandy said.

Sandy appeared more upset than PJ. "I got a call from Johnny King when I was playing cards at the Nugget," PJ said. "I tried calling his wife before you got here, but no one answers the phone. It must be crazy back there, what with cops and media people all over."

"I don't know what to say, PJ. You know you have my sympathy. Do you know how it happened?" Sandy asked.

"It seems a couple guys ran over to his car just as the driver pulled up to his apartment house. There was a neighbor looking out the window, and she saw the whole thing. She probably wasn't close enough to be able to identify them." Sandy just shook his head.

"The weird thing is, he was just here in Vegas. And as it worked out, I never got to see him." Maybe that's what bothered PJ the most. He had the opportunity to see his brother one last time before he died, and he didn't do it.

"I am really sorry," Sandy said.

By this time, the Las Vegas crime-scene people were all over the town house. They were taking pictures, dusting for fingerprints, and drawing lines on the floor where PJ had shot the intended assassin. Just about the same time, Sandy's partner, Josh Hayward, arrived. He looked like a Josh Hayward. He was in his late twenties, six feet tall, blond hair; and you could tell he worked out every day. He was on the Las Vegas police force all of five years when he got his gold badge. Sandy was sure he had some kind of pull in order to get his detective badge in such a short time. He was a real eager beaver. As far as Sandy was concerned, he was a real pain in the ass. He was going to law school at night, and after getting his degree, he wanted to join the FBI. He nodded to PJ and then spoke to his partner. "Hey, Sandy, sorry it took me so long to get here. I was all the way on the other side of town when I got the call."

"No sweat," Sandy said. Then pointing to PJ, he continued, "Do you know PJ?"

"No, don't think I do," his partner said. "Nice to meet you. Sorry under these circumstances."

PJ nodded and shook hands with the eager beaver. "Nice to meet you," PJ said. "While you're taking a look around, do you mind if I talk to your partner for a couple minutes?"

"No, not at all," the young detective answered while, at the same time, taking out his detective paper and pencil so he could take notes. PJ put his arm around Sandy and walked him out of the bedroom.

Once in the hallway, PJ said, "I realize this is not your normal crime scene, and I know you have a job to do. But I need you to do me a favor, Sandy."

"Like what?"

"First of all, I have to be sure you will keep what I tell you strictly between the two of us."

"C'mon, PJ, we go way back."

"Okay. I already told you how I was able to get to this guy before he got me. What I didn't tell you is I went through his pockets looking for some sort of ID. The only thing I could find was his cell phone. And between you and me, Sandy, I think this guy is a pro. First of all, did you see the piece he had on him? A Galatz. That's an Israeli sniper weapon. Your average shooter doesn't use a gun like that. And not carrying any ID is more than a coincidence. Pros are trained not to carry any ID. But that's all besides the point. While I'm holding this guy's cell, it rings. A voice says, 'Emil . . . did you get him?' I answer yes, hoping the caller will give up a little more information. But he knows I'm not Emil, and he hangs up. I pushed the Recall button, and the name Nick Paraphas comes up. I have no idea who that is, and I have less of an idea why someone would try to kill me. And I am sure this was not an attempted robbery."

Sandy interrupted him, "How would you know something like that?"

PJ said, "Believe me, I know. Now I plan on leaving for New York early tomorrow, so I need you to do something for me. What I'd like you to do is check out this Paraphas, and let me know what you can find out about him. Who he is, where he's from, you know the drill." Sandy stared at PJ for a few seconds before saying anything. He then put his hand on PJ's elbow and ushered him downstairs away from the Las Vegas investigation team. By this time, two Las Vegas police ambulances had arrived to take away the dead bodies.

"PJ, are you out of your freakin' mind? Do you have any idea what you're asking? First of all, you can't go around taking evidence from a crime scene. And secondly, what do you mean find out who this guy Paraphas is and let you know? Why? What do you think you're going to do once you know? This is a police matter, PJ. And another thing, how did you know that gun was a Galatz? And while we're on the subject of guns, why would you keep an Uzi in your house? That's not the kind of weapon people keep around. And where do you come off saying this guy is a pro? How would you know about something like that? I don't know what the hell is going on here, PJ. But if what you say happened happened, then let the police handle it. This is out of your league, PJ. This is serious stuff. I can't screw around with evidence. Now if you don't mind, I'd like you to give me the cell phone so I can tag it."

PJ stared at his friend with a look the detective had not seen before. He felt a chill go up his back. For a few seconds, PJ didn't say anything. He just looked at his friend as if to say "Pay close attention to what I am going to say because I am only going to say it once."

"I can't do that, Sandy. I am giving it to somebody I know who will get more information out of it than you could ever imagine. And believe me when I tell you this, Sandy, do not underestimate what I can or cannot do. My girlfriend and my brother have just been murdered, and if not for my instinct, I too would have been murdered. I really don't give a shit how it looks. I told you exactly what happened. Whether or not you believe me is up to you. Now I'm asking you not to say anything about the cell phone or Paraphas. Maybe someday, I will be able to explain. But for now, I'm asking you to trust me. I know what I am doing. And I intend to find the people who are responsible for this. And neither you, your partner, or anybody else is going to stop me. When you play Texas Hold'em poker, Sandy, and you have a hand that you know can't lose, you bet all of the money you have on the table. That's called *going all in*. Sometimes a person will bluff and go all in, hoping no one will call him (pay to see his cards).

"Sandy, I am going all in on this, and I'm not bluffing. And it is not a game. It is what I do. And I don't intend to lose. Now I'm going to New York in the morning. I'm not sure where I'll be staying, but when I do, I'll call you. In the meantime, you have my cell phone number. I need that information, Sandy. And one way or another, I will get it. Once again, Sandy, you have to trust me on this one."

Sandy knew right then and there that his friend was more than just a poker player. But who was he?

Sandy's partner called down from upstairs for him to come up to the bedroom. There was something important he needed to show him. Sandy was annoyed. "I'll be right there!" he shouted. "I am sure whatever it is you want to show me isn't going anywhere."

PJ said in a monotone, "Well, Sandy, what's your answer? Your partner is waiting."

Sandy looked at PJ. "Like I said, PJ, I'm not sure what the hell is going on here. But it must be pretty goddamn important to you. And to tell you the truth, it scares the shit out of me. I don't know why, but for now,

I'll go along with you. But you know, at some point in the investigation, Paraphas's name is bound to come up. If and when that happens, I don't want to get caught standing there holding my you know what. And I have to tell you again, I think you're taking a hell of a chance by not letting us handle this. Without the call on the cell phone that helps to prove this guy broke into your joint to do you harm, it's just your word. I got no problem with that, PJ, but the DA might not agree with me. You could end up in hot water, PJ."

PJ listened and nodded his head as if to say "I understand."

"One last thing, PJ, no one can ever know that I was party to a cover-up." PJ nodded again. "And I beg you, PJ . . . don't leave me out to dry on this one. I'm a good cop. I'm not a cowboy, and I sure as hell don't want to get involved in something that can cause me grief. I have a wife and two kids, and someday, I would like to retire with a pension. Don't fuck me up."

PJ put out his hand to the detective and said, "I wouldn't do that, Sandy, and you know it."

The two men understood each other. Sandy went back upstairs, and PJ tried again to call his sister-in-law.

"What the hell is so important that it couldn't wait until I was finished talking to PJ?" Sandy started mumbling the question to his partner even before he was back in the bedroom.

His partner was accustomed to Sandy's sarcasm and paid no attention to it. "Look at this," Josh said to Sandy, pointing to the dead man's arm who was lying on the stretcher, waiting to be taken to the morgue. He was as excited as if he just found the crown jewels. Not that they were missing.

"Look at what?" Sandy asked, not anxious to look at what was left of Emil.

"Look at that tattoo on his lower arm." The medic had wiped away the blood so that Josh could get a better view.

Sandy looked at the tattoo, not aware of its significance. "So he has a tattoo, so what? My wife has one on her butt, and that doesn't mean anything either."

Josh was now the one who was irritated. He gave his partner a look and said, "This tattoo is the trademark of an Islamic cell here in Vegas that has known ties to Osama bin Laden's Al-Qaeda network. After the

1993 car bombing at the New York Trade Center, the FBI sent out all kinds of information regarding Islamic and militant Middle East cells in the States, and the one thing I remember is this tattoo design. The FBI included a picture of it in the report. I know you must have read it. And listen to this, Sandy. There was an attack on a prominent businessman in New York earlier today, with no apparent motive. It came over the wire. What if these two murders are connected? Sandy, we could be sitting on top of some sort of conspiracy or multiple assassination plot. That is, assuming your good friend PJ isn't the one who killed the girl and then killed this other guy in a cover-up." Josh was becoming more excited as he spoke.

Sandy said, "Give me a break, Josh. First, you tell me the dead guy is some sort of terrorist, and then you have him in a love triangle." Having said this, Sandy really had no idea what happened here tonight. He wished he knew what the hell was going on. What was PJ up to? What was it he didn't know about his friend? More importantly, what was he getting himself into? Then he very matter-of-factly said to his partner, "The guy in New York was PJ's brother." Josh dropped his arms to his side and just stared at Sandy.

It was two thirty in the morning. Josh and Sandy were sitting in a Dunkin' Donuts restaurant somewhere between PJ's town house and the police station. They had been there for the past two hours talking about the events of the past evening at PJ's town house. They compared their notes to make sure their report would include everything. They also speculated on the possible motives for the attempt on PJ's life. Neither one felt it was robbery. And Josh wanted to know more about PJ. Why would he have that kind of weapon in his house? And after listening to PJ's account of what happened, the way he was able to go back downstairs, get his weapon, and blow the guy away, there had to be more to the story. Although Sandy didn't encourage his partner, he had the same questions. They also talked at length about Walter's murder in New York. Was there some connection? It sure was a strange coincidence—one brother shot and killed, and the same night, an attempt made to murder the other brother. Josh told Sandy he wanted to contact the FBI and compare notes. "They need to know what happened here tonight," he told Sandy.

"Why don't we leave that decision up to the captain?" Sandy insisted.

Before the two detectives left PJ's town house, Josh made it a point to tell him that he should not leave town. After all, he shot and killed a man; and even though he claimed the man allegedly broke into his house, there was no sign of forced entry. Also, there were no shots fired from the dead man's gun. He was sure the DA would insist on a grand jury investigation. "We need to wait and see if the DA intends to file charges against you," Josh said.

Of course, this was pretty much what Sandy told him, but he still was upset. "Are you kidding me?" PJ said, beginning to lose his cool. Sandy assured him it was just routine, and he shouldn't get excited. Josh was not pleased with Sandy's downplay of PJ's involvement. Sandy told Josh he would take full responsibility for allowing PJ to travel to New York for his brother's funeral. Josh just shook his head. PJ simply smiled a thank-you and thought to himself, *As if they were going to stop me.*

CHAPTER TWENTY-EIGHT

June 21, 1995

PJ spent most of the next day helping Cindy's parents make arrangements to fly their daughter home. They flew into Las Vegas early in the day. He did the best he could to console them. Before he left, Cindy's mother gave him a kiss on the cheek and said, "It's not your fault that she was murdered PJ. You know she really loved you." PJ had no response.

The following day, PJ was on the first flight out of LAX to New York. Before leaving California, he finally was able to reach his brother's widow. During the twenty-three years his brother was married, PJ saw his sister-in-law all of a half-dozen times. However, the few times they did, they enjoyed each other's company. The former Anita Woodland once told PJ, "Knowing you is like seeing Walter as if he were someone else. Someone more daring, more . . . can I say, exciting?" He thought she was flirting, but he never pursued it. When PJ called to tell her he was flying into New York, she insisted on having her car pick him up at the airport. "We are family, and I want you to stay at the apartment," she said. PJ agreed to the car but told Anita he preferred to stay at a hotel. He wondered if he should tell her about the attempt on his life, but he decided against it. He would tell her when he got to New York. He promised to call her as soon he arrived in New York.

June 22, 1995

When the Boeing 707 landed at JFK, PJ was still sleeping. The stewardess nudged him gently as the plane taxied to a stop at the gate.

"We're in New York, sir, it's time to get up." She was very pretty. Another time and PJ might have tried to hook up with her. But there was more important business today.

As he approached the main terminal, PJ spotted Anita's driver holding up a sign that read Mr. Gould. It wasn't often that people used his last name. Over the years, he had simply become PJ. He made eye contact with the driver, and when he got close enough, the driver introduced himself, "Hello, Mr. Gould, my name is Jacob. Do you have any luggage?" PJ told him that he didn't have any, just what he carried on.

They walked outside of the terminal, and parked directly in front of the entrance was a Rolls-Royce limousine. It was parked in front of a sign that said No Stopping. A New York cop was standing ten feet away and made no attempt to tell the driver to hurry up and get out of there. PJ thought to himself, *About the only thing money can't buy is poverty!*

After they were in the car, the driver told PJ that Mrs. Lippincott gave instructions to drive him to her apartment. PJ smiled. She sure was insistent. *Why not?* he thought.

"That will be fine, Jacob," PJ said as he leaned back and contemplated his next step. It had been almost seven years since PJ was last in new York. As he looked out the window of the limousine on the ride to Walter's apartment, it hadn't seemed to change very much. He glanced at the newspaper Jacob gave him when he got into the limo. In large headlines on the front page was the story about Walter being shot.

MILLIONAIRE BUSINESSMAN SHOT AND KILLED
IN FRONTOF HIS LUXURY APARTMENT HOUSE

When the limo pulled up in front of the Lippincotts' apartment building, PJ realized this is where the shooting took place three days ago. Was this the same car? And the driver, was this his first day working for Anita? Before the driver got out of the limo, PJ leaned forward and said, "Pardon me, Jacob. Do you know if this is the car my brother was in when he was shot?"

"No, sir, this is a new car the dealer sent to Mrs. Lippincott yesterday. I believe the police have the other car."

"Oh . . . thanks. I don't mean to be inquisitive, but have you just started to work for Mrs. Lippincott?"

"No, sir. I've worked for the Lippincotts for over four years. I know what you're thinking. The limo driver was also shot and killed the other night. There are two of us . . . I mean there *were* two us. Mr. Lippincott wanted a driver to always be available for Mrs. Lippincott in the event one of us was driving him. We have a town car that we keep in the apartment house garage. However, we always use the stretch for the airport. There but for the grace of God, it could have been me the other night."

PJ knew firsthand about fate. There had been many times in the past when the difference of an hour or a day meant the difference between life and death. When he got out of the limo, he stood for a minute and tried to imagine how the shooting took place. He looked up at the apartment house next door. He guessed that was where the woman lived who saw the shooting. According to the newspaper account of the shooting, Walter's assistant was still in the limo when he was shot, and the driver was lying in back of the limo in the street. Why did they kill everybody? If Walter was the target, what happened that caused them to kill the driver, Walter's assistant, and the doorman? It didn't make any sense. The doorman approached PJ and offered to take his bag. PJ said, "No thanks," and followed him into the apartment house. He wondered if he was making a mistake staying here. *Well, too late now*, he thought. *Let's see what happens.*

Coincidently, about the same time that PJ was reading the headline in the New York paper, four other people in three different cities were also reading about the shooting. In Skokie, Illinois, the affluent suburb of Chicago, Joseph Cantelli read the account of Walter's murder for the second time.

He couldn't begin to think who did it. During the past year, there had been several mob killings, both in Boston and in Philadelphia. And this definitely looked like a mob-style killing. But how could Walter Lippincott be involved in that sort of thing? Even though the old man was not close to the crime families in Boston and Philadelphia, he pretty much knew what was going on. And he never heard mention that Lippincott was involved with either family. He thought about what Senator Baxter said to Sonny in Las Vegas, that it would be easy to get the nationwide gambling bill passed if Lippincott was out of the picture. Just then, the telephone rang.

"Hello, Pop, how are you?" It was Sonny calling from Las Vegas.

"Sonny, I am good. And you?"

"Good, Pop. Have you seen the paper today?"

"Yes, Sonny. I don't know what to say. I think this is a bad thing that happened. What have you heard?"

"Nothing more than what I read in the paper. Pop, do you think Baxter had anything to do with this?"

The old man thought for a minute. "I don't know, Sonny. I will make some calls today to see what I can find out."

"There's something else, Pop, that you don't know."

"What is that, Sonny?"

"There was a shooting at Walter's brother's apartment two nights ago. The same night Lippincott was killed. The papers didn't have too much information, but I was able to find out that Walter's brother surprised a burglar in his place and shot and killed him. And that's not all. It seems the robber killed his girlfriend. Some showgirl who was living with him. I don't understand why there wasn't more in the papers. Evidently, it didn't make the national news."

"No, it didn't, Sonny. Not good . . . not good."

"Yeah, I know what you mean, Pop. I think I should come home so we can talk more about this. What do you think?"

"Good idea, Sonny."

"Okay, good. We'll talk more when I'm there. Call me after you make your calls."

"I will . . . and, Sonny, you be extra careful. I want you to have one of your security guards, somebody we know real good, go with you if you leave the hotel."

"Pop, what are you saying?"

"I am just saying . . . be careful."

"Okay, Pop. Talk to you later."

Meanwhile, on the South Side of Chicago, Sonny's cousin Joey was sitting with Sid in his bar. Both men were clearly unnerved by the way the shooting was reported in the newspaper. "What the fuck is wrong with those guys?" Joey said, downing his fourth shot of bourbon, followed by a beer chaser.

"Jesus Christ, the old man is going to blow his stack when he reads this. Four fucking people dead for no reason! Jesus Christ!" Sid just kept shaking his head. He had been right all along. Killing Lippincott was Joey's idea. How did he let Joey talk him into this? Shit!

"And here it is, two days, and I haven't heard a goddamn thing from this guy in Vegas who was supposed to take care of Lippincott's brother," Joey said, continuing his bourbon and beer chaser routine.

"You ain't heard nothing at all from the guy you hired to do the job?" Sid answered for the sake of something to say.

"What's wrong with you? Are you deaf? I just told you I haven't heard anything. And there's nothing in the paper." Joey was getting drunk, and the more he drank, the meaner he got.

"Why don't you try calling him?" Sid asked, hoping that was a good idea.

"Because I don't think I should. I got a bad feeling about this."

Sid simply nodded. He had a bad feeling about this whole business from the very start.

Joey had no way of knowing the man he hired to kill Walter Lippincott's brother had failed in his attempt and instead was the one who was killed. And the intended killer's cell phone was now in the possession of PJ, the same cell phone that Joey called when he hired Emil Sudhan. When Tozzi gave Joey Emil Sudhan's name and phone number, he was reluctant to call him. A terrorist. Shit, what the hell was he getting himself into? But he had no choice. He had to make sure that Lippincott's brother was not around after he was killed. And he didn't know anybody else he could call to do the job. Joey waited a day and then called . . . the used-to-be terrorist. Like Tozzi, Sudhan first told Joey he had no idea what he was talking about. He didn't admit to knowing either Tozzi or Tozzi's friend in Jersey City. Joey finally told him to call the person in Jersey City and then call him back. Without waiting for a reply, Joey gave him his cell phone number before Sudhan disconnected.

The next day, Sudhan called Joey and was ready to talk business. "I will need someone to work with me on this," he told Joey.

"That's up to you. Just so long as you get the job done on the same day," Joey told him.

"How am I going to get my money?" Sudhan asked Joey.

"I don't know," Joey said. "I can't come to Vegas. Is there anybody in Chicago I can pay?"

Sudhan laughed. "What do you think I am—a chain store?" Joey didn't appreciate the humor. "I will fly to Chicago the day after I do the job," Sudhan said. "We will meet at the airport. And, Mr. Joey . . . if you don't, me—"

Joey interrupted, "You'll get your money. Don't worry."

"Mr. Joey, I am not worried . . . I make other people worry."

Very funny, Joey thought. They agreed on a price of $20,000. Joey thought that was a bargain compared with what he was paying Tozzi.

And in the nation's capitol, Senator Guy Baxter was sitting in his office reading about the Lippincott murder in disbelief. Was it at all possible the Cantelli family was responsible? The *Washington Post* made the murders sound like an old-fashioned Mafia hit. WAS THIS THE START OF RENEWED VIOLENCE BETWEEN THE REMAING MAFIA FAMILIES? was the paper's headline. The *Post*, more than most of the other papers, talked about Lippincott's relationship with the present administration, his opposition to the pending legislation regarding legalized gambling, and his friendship with several Las Vegas casino owners.

Baxter put down the paper to answer his private telephone line. It was the White House press secretary. "Senator Baxter, the president instructed me to ask you if you would make a statement to the press on behalf of the White House regarding the death of Walter Lippincott."

Baxter hesitated a moment, then asked the press secretary, "What does he want me to say?"

The press secretary responded, "He said that if you asked, I was to tell you it was up to you."

Baxter hung up the phone and thought to himself, *That son of a bitch Lippincott won't leave me alone, even when he's dead.*

CHAPTER TWENTY-NINE

June 22, 1995

It was past midnight when Joey finally left Sid's bar. Sid tried to convince him to stay the night. He thought he was too drunk to drive. "You can sleep it off on my couch," Sid said, but Joey was drunk and stubborn, a bad combination.

When Joey opened the door to his apartment, he could hear his telephone ringing. He reached in his pocket for his cell phone, flipped it open, and held it to his ear; but the ringing continued. It took him several seconds to realize it was his landline that was ringing. He made his way to the couch, sat himself down, then picked up the telephone on the end table, and managed a hello between hiccups. "Joey, where the hell you been? And why didn't you answer your cell? I've been trying to call you for the past two hours."

Joey stared at the phone for a second before politely asking, "Who the hell is this?"

"Jesus Christ, Joey, this is Sonny, you drunken bastard!"

"Who the hell you calling a bastard? I know it's you. I was just pulling your leg." Joey tried to get his wits about him.

"Yeah yeah, I bet," Sonny said, pissed off at his cousin. "I need to ask you something, Joey. Are you sober enough to talk?"

Joey shook his head, trying to clear the cobwebs, wishing now that he hadn't had so much to drink. "Yeah, I'm fine. What's on your mind?"

Sonny thought about waiting until morning when Joey was in better shape to talk, but he decided now was as good a time as any. "You didn't answer me, Joey, why didn't you answer you cell?"

"I never heard it ring. I think maybe I need a new battery."

"Yeah, maybe. Joey, let me ask you, did you know Walter Lippincott was murdered a couple days ago?" Joey was sobering up very fast. He needed time to think. "Joey . . . you there?"

"Yeah yeah, I'm here. Who was murdered?"

"Walter Lippincott, the guy we talked about at Pop's house last month."

"Why would I know that? You saying I had something to do with it? Whatayou . . . crazy?"

Listening to Joey, Sonny knew he was right. His cousin was somehow involved with Lippincott's murder. Why didn't he just answer the question? Why was he so nervous? Maybe Joey was the setup guy. For all he knew, he could have taken part in the actual shooting. And how about what happened in Vegas at PJ's? Was it possible Joey was that stupid? Who else could it have been? He eliminated Guy Baxter; he was too smart. Maybe some common enemy of the two brothers. Impossible, that was too far-fetched. Most people didn't even know they were brothers. He kept thinking back to the meeting at his father's house with Joey and his brother. He remembered Joey saying Baxter's idea to eliminate Lippincott was a good idea and after dinner when Joey couldn't wait to leave. Where was he going in such a hurry? And how many times did Joey say to him that he wished he could do something to make the old man proud of him? Show him that he was a real stand-up guy?

"Joey, you need to tell me what happened. How were you involved in this?" Joey started to ramble about how he was crazy to think he was involved when Sonny shouted into the phone, "Stop jerking around, Joey! You're in deep shit!"

"Now start telling me the truth. No more of your fucking lies!"

There was a moment of silence; then Joey said, "It was for the family, Sonny. I did it for you and the old man. I know how important the gambling bill is to us—"

"To us!" Sonny yelled into the phone.

"Hey, Sonny, I'm part of this family. I do my share . . . I do more than my share."

"Be careful, Joey . . . watch what you say here."

Joey could feel the sweat running down his back.

Sonny decided it wasn't a good idea to talk about this on the phone. He told Joey he was taking the red-eye that night to Chicago and would call him when he got in. In the meantime, he told him not to talk to anybody.

"And I mean anybody and everybody. Get a battery for your cell in the morning, and then get your ass home and stay there. And remember, don't talk to anybody until I call. Maybe there's some way I can save your ass on this one, Joey, but I ain't making any promises."

Joey was now sober. "What the hell are you talking about . . . ? What do mean save my ass?"

Sonny interrupted, "We'll talk about it when I get there. I'll call you from the airport."

Sonny knew it was too late to call his father. He would call him from the airport in the morning. It was not going to be a call he wanted to make. Sonny tried to make some sense of what his cousin had done. Was he really that stupid to think he would be rewarded for doing something like this? And if he set up the New York murders, there was no doubt in Sonny's mind he was responsible for the attempt on PJ's life and the killing of his girlfriend. "Jesus Christ," he said to himself, "this could be a nightmare!"

The Las Vegas papers didn't make the shooting at PJ's house front-page news. It just so happened there was an attempted robbery at the MGM Grand Hotel and Casino that same night where two of the attempted robbers were shot and killed in a running gun battle on the casino floor. There was also a hostage standoff in the parking lot, which was finally resolved when the Las Vegas SWAT team shot and killed the other two bad guys and rescued the hostages. To make the story complete, MGM security had gotten wind of the attempted robbery that morning after questioning two casino employees on an unrelated incident. That was all front-page stuff and made the national news. The killings at PJ's house were on page 3. No pictures, no mention of a possible tie in to the Lippincott shooting in New York.

CHAPTER THIRTY

June 22, 1995

When the elevator stopped at the thirty-sixth floor, PJ hesitated a moment before getting out. His brother's penthouse apartment took up the entire twenty thousand square feet. PJ had known for a long time how rich Walter was, but seeing the apartment reinforced it. The door to the apartment was half open. Walter's widow, Anita, greeted him with a smile as he entered the apartment. "You should be careful leaving the door open," he said, returning her smile. "You never know who might come in."

Anita, dressed in a white silk blouse and gray slacks, walked over to him and kissed him on the cheek. "They called from downstairs to tell me you were on your way up. Besides which, we don't allow undesirables in the building."

PJ liked her. She was funny. She was beautiful. She was very rich. And oh yes, by the way, she was his brother's widow.

"Would you like something to drink?" Anita asked, taking PJ by the hand and walking him to the sofa.

"Just something cold," he said. Anita called the housekeeper and asked her to bring in a tray of iced tea and cookies. *How cute*, he thought.

"So," Anita said, "it took Walter being shot to bring you back to New York." PJ frowned. "I guess that was mean," she said.

PJ grinned. "Well, not really. It is the truth. You know, I was never real good at this kind of thing."

"What kind of thing is that?" Anita asked, knowing full well what PJ was talking about. Then reaching out to take his hand, she said, "I do know what you mean, PJ, and I appreciate you being here. I've had enough of this media circus, the police, and lawyers to last me a lifetime. I can't wait until this is all over."

PJ just nodded and said those famous words, "You know, if I can do anything, all you have to do is ask."

He got up from the sofa and walked to the window. "You have a great view from up here," he said without turning around.

"Thank you," she said and got up from the couch to join him. He remained silent.

"Is everything all right?" she said, sensing there was something wrong.

"As a matter of fact, everything is not all right, Anita . . . The same night that Walter was shot . . . someone broke into my apartment."

"Oh," she said, waiting for the rest of the story.

"And that's not all. When I got home, he was still there. To make a long story short, I was able to get to him before he got to me."

"Get to him?" she asked.

"I shot him, Anita. I not only shot him, I killed him."

"Oh my god," she said putting her hands to her cheeks. "I don't understand. You shot him? You keep a gun in your house?"

"Yes, I keep a gun in my house. But that's not the whole story. It gets worse. There was this girl who was living with me." He half laughed. "This girl, her name was Cindy. She didn't deserve what happened, Anita." PJ put his hands on her shoulders. "The son of a bitch strangled her."

"Oh, PJ, that's terrible. You never said anything when we talked on the phone. I didn't know you were living with someone. Oh, PJ, I'm so sorry. That is horrible."

They walked back to the couch and sat down.

"Yes, it is . . . she didn't deserve to die that way."

"Oh, PJ, how horrible. What can I say?"

They held out their hands to each other, and for a split second, he felt a chill come over his body.

"PJ, do you think this has anything to do with Walter being shot?"

"I'm not sure, Anita, but I intend to find out."

"What do you mean . . . you intend to find out? This is a police matter."

He realized he said the wrong thing. "Yeah, that's what I meant, Anita."

"PJ, let me ask you something. Walter once told me that you worked for the CIA. When I asked him what you did, he was very vague. He said it was nothing real exotic. I didn't believe him, what with your being in Israel and London and who knows where else. Tell me the truth, PJ, does all of this have anything to do with what you were doing for the CIA?"

"No, Anita, believe me. First of all, it's been almost ten years since I worked with them. And when I did, Walter was right. It was never anything real exotic. It was security background checks and stuff like that. And getting back to your question, we don't know if what happened at my place really has anything to do with Walter being shot."

"PJ, I am not some dumb blonde. What are the odds that twin brothers in different parts of the country—"

PJ interrupted her. "I know, Anita, you're right. I didn't want you to worry. I didn't want you to think this was some kind of conspiracy. But you are right. There has to be some connection. But at this point, I really don't know what it is. However, I do know some people who may be able to help solve this thing. I know this is a police matter, and believe me, I will not do anything to interfere. I'm just going to ask you to trust me on this one, Anita. There's a lot I can't tell you now. Maybe someday, but not now. Give me some time. As soon as I know what's going on, I will let you know."

She looked at him with sad eyes. "I hope you know what you're doing, PJ."

"I do, Anita, believe me."

"Then will you promise me one thing?"

"What's that?"

"Please be careful."

"I promise," he said. They sat in silence, looking at each other. PJ didn't know what was happening. Here he was with his brother's widow for less than an hour, and he felt like he had known her his entire life. But he didn't have time to think about it any more; the housekeeper announced that dinner was being served.

During dinner, Anita and PJ talked about their past, with PJ being very careful not to say too much.

"How come you never married?" Anita asked.

"Nobody ever asked me," he replied.

"Oh, I can't believe that. You probably have to beat them off with a stick," she said as she finished her fourth glass of wine. *Is she flirting?* PJ wondered. *Not at a time like this.* Time to change the subject.

"I've lost track, Anita. Is Walter's mother still alive?"

"No, she passed away about two years ago. She continued to live in that big house in Buffalo all those years. Walter tried to get her to move to an apartment in New York, but she wouldn't hear of it. She was very set in her ways. I liked her. She was a nice woman." PJ agreed.

They finished dinner, and the maid began to clear the dishes from the table. Anita suggested they have their after-dinner drinks in the library. "This was Walter's favorite room," she said, waving her arms around as if to show off the thick paneled walls and shelves full of all kind of books. PJ agreed. It was impressive. "Would you like a brandy?" she asked, opening the liquor cabinet. PJ smiled a yes and allowed her to fill his glass.

"PJ, you and Cindy . . . was it serious?"

PJ had to think. *Was it serious?* "I liked her a lot, Anita. I guess maybe if we had more time, who knows?"

"I see. I am very sorry, PJ. it is a terrible thing."

Outside, it had begun to rain, and the sound of the raindrops on the window almost sounded like a musical instrument. Anita made herself comfortable, safely settled against the pillows on the plush leather couch. "Come sit beside me," she said to PJ in a coy tone of voice. "I won't bite."

"Is that a promise or a threat?" he asked, immediately regretting that he said it.

"It's a promise," she said, holding out her empty brandy glass for him to refill.

"I guess you're wondering why we never had any children," she stated as he poured another shot of brandy.

"To tell you the truth, I really never thought about it. But now that you mention it, how come you never had children?"

"Because I couldn't," she said. "Isn't it strange? Walter's mother was not able to have children. That's why they adopted Walter. But you know that of course." It didn't require an answer; he simply nodded.

"When Walter found out that I couldn't have children, our relationship changed. It was almost like he blamed me for something that I had no control of."

PJ wasn't sure he wanted to hear this. "Anita, you don't need to explain anything to me."

"I know, PJ, but I want to. You know, Walter was never the kind of man who showed his feelings. Both in business and in our personal life. Oh, don't misunderstand me. He was more than generous. But that was with things. Not with his feelings. You know he had a mistress?" PJ didn't answer.

"No, there is no way you would know that. He told me that if I wanted a lover, he wouldn't mind as long as I was discreet. Believe me, I thought about it more than once, but never had the guts. And then out of a clear blue sky, at any given time, Walter would say to me, 'Let's get away somewhere. How would you like to go to Paris or the French Riviera?' And so we would go somewhere for a week, and he would be the perfect husband. Then we come home, and he becomes the same old Walter. But I shouldn't complain. He always gave me the feeling of security and would never have done anything to embarrass me. And in his own way, I believe he loved me as I did him in my own way. Surprised?"

PJ didn't know what to say. "I've embarrassed you, haven't I?" she said, reaching out for his hand. "I'm sorry. How about we change the subject?" She got up from the sofa, refilled her brandy glass, and then sat down again. She curled her feet up under the pillows and laid her head on the arm of the sofa. "Tell me, are your parents still living?" she asked him. PJ felt a sigh of relief.

"My father is. He lives in a retirement community in Palm Springs. He's seventy-eight and still going strong. My mother died about six years ago."

"Oh, I'm sorry, I didn't know that," she said politely.

PJ looked at his watch. It was almost midnight. A decision had to be made. This was not a casual dinner date. This was his brother's widow, and the body was still warm.

"I have to be up early tomorrow," he said. "And it's been a long day."

"Of course," she said, getting up from the couch and reaching for his hand. "Come, let me show you to your room." Her hand was warm. He had the urge to pull her closer and kiss her. What the hell was he thinking?

"I enjoyed myself tonight," she said. "You're very good company." She kissed him on the cheek and told him she would be up early and join him for coffee before he left. "You can use one of the cars tomorrow. The driver will take you wherever you need to go," she said. "Sleep good. I'll see you in the morning." He watched her walk away, knowing full well that she was aware he was watching her.

There was something about her that intrigued him. It certainly was not her looks alone. He had known many beautiful women over the years. She seemed to have something more appealing than beauty. She was intelligent and had a sense of humor. After spending just this one evening in her company, his feelings about her were confused. His last thoughts before falling asleep were of Anita. She was standing in the doorway wearing only a flimsy nightgown. Was it only in his mind, or was it real?

In her room, climbing out of her clothes and into her pretty flannel nightgown, Anita wished the evening with PJ had continued. She felt comfortable with him. In a way, he looked like Walter; and as a matter of fact, they had some of the same mannerisms, but they were two different people. She stopped brushing her hair and stared at herself in the mirror of her dressing table. Her face, wiped free of makeup, seemed pale to her. There were shadows under her eyes and a few faint lines at their corners. She was forty-seven years old, and the idea of not loving someone filled her with dismay. Though perhaps lacking in passion, her life with Walter had an emotionally stable quality that she enjoyed, a sense of belonging. Now that Walter was gone, she didn't like the prospect of being alone. She had grown up in a small but loving family, and after her parents died, he was really her only family. What was the plan for her future? Would she marry again?

As she moved from the dressing table to the bed, she continued to think about PJ. She felt guilty thinking about him. Walter was not in the ground yet. What was wrong with her? But she did not allow her mind to travel too far along that line. What was the point? Always more a pragmatist than a dreamer, used to setting goals she had a good chance of achieving, she thought it useless to try to imagine a relationship with Walter's brother. She pulled the covers over her shoulders, turned off the lamp on the night table, and closed her eyes. It would take a while before sleep would come.

June 23, 1995

PJ had just finishing showering when Albert, the day houseman, knocked gently on the bedroom door. "Mr. Gould, Mrs. Lippincott wants you to know that coffee is ready when you are. She is on the terrace."

It had stopped raining, and although a little bit damp, it was a very pleasant morning.

"Tell her I will be there in a couple minutes," PJ replied, sticking his head out of the bathroom door, not really sure who might be in the room, the image of Anita standing in his doorway still in his head.

"Good morning," he said as he walked on to the terrace.

"Good morning," she said, her mouth full of a piece of danish pastry. She was wearing a cashmere jumpsuit in a shade of emerald green that complemented her eyes, made her skin glow, and brought out the gold in her hair. "I hope you slept well," she said, managing a couple swallows of coffee.

"Like a baby."

"Good," she said while pouring him a cup of coffee. Then in a more serious tone of voice, she said, "PJ, I hope you will forgive me for last night. I think I had too much brandy."

PJ smiled. "Last night? What happened last night?"

"Thank you," she said. "You are a true gentlemen. Now I know we haven't talked about it, PJ, but you know Walter's funeral is tomorrow." He simply nodded. She continued, "I told you on the phone that Walter's wishes were that he be cremated. When I spoke to the funeral parlor yesterday, they told me they have been receiving calls every day since the death notice appeared in the paper. People wanting to come to the funeral service. I couldn't handle a large crowd of people, most of whom I don't know, just wanting to be seen at Walter's funeral. So I decided it will be a very private service. A couple of Walter's associates and several of our close friends. That's it. Do you think I'm doing the right thing?"

"There is no right or wrong thing, Anita. It's what you feel in your heart. And if that's what you want to do, you have my support all the way."

She smiled and reached across the table to put her hand on top of his. "Thanks, PJ, you don't know how much that means to me. So tell me, where are you going today?"

"I'm going to visit with an old friend of mine from London. We haven't seen each other in years."

She smiled. "You are such a good liar, PJ."

Anita's driver took him to the Plaza Hotel. He told the driver he would be about three or four hours and would call him on his cell when he was ready to be picked up. The driver gave him his cell number and drove off. PJ went into the hotel, looked in one of the stores for about ten minutes, then looked out at the limos parked across from the hotel, making sure his driver had not parked nearby. Then he left, using the entrance on the other side of the hotel. He got into a cab and gave him an address on West Thirty-ninth Street. When the cab pulled up to the address PJ had given him, he saw it was an old warehouse that had a For Sale sign on the front door. He turned to PJ and asked, "You sure you got the right address, buddy?"

"Yup." He paid the driver and got out of the cab and waited until he drove away. Then he crossed the street, turned the corner, and went into a bookstore that was hardly Borders. It was dark and gloomy and very uninviting. "Can I help you?" the voice came from an older man sitting on a lounge chair in the rear of the store.

"Yes, I'm here to buy a copy of *The Old Frontier*."

"Do you know the author?" the old man asked.

"No, I don't, but I know you have it in stock because a good friend of mine bought a copy."

That dialog was the code for non-CIA people.

"And your name, my good man?"

"None of your business, you son of a bitch." A roar of laughter came from the man in the rear of the store.

"PJ, you old damn fool!"

The old man got up from the chair and walked to the front of the store. "I'll be a son of a bitch! I thought you were dead."

"Not exactly," PJ said, exchanging a hug with his old friend.

"You still remember the code," the old man said.

"I'm surprised you still do," PJ said, half laughing.

This was where the CIA operated their special decoding facility. There were only three people here, all experts in being able to retrieve information from computers, cell phones, tape recorders, you name it.

"I guess you want to see Clarence," the old man said.

"You got it, Cirus. Hope he's here."

"Where the hell do you think he would be? Follow me." Cirus took PJ into the rear of the store and pushed a button; and one of the storage shelves swung open to reveal a room full of all types of electronic equipment—video cameras, computers, and a table piled high with cell phones.

"Good luck," Cirus said as he went back into the bookstore and returned the shelf to its proper position.

Clarence Efont was a former New York State Police detective whose forte was busting identity thieves. People who used stolen credit cards, bought things on the Internet using other people's bank accounts, stuff like that. He was recruited by the CIA about fifteen years ago and never looked back. He was so stocky and thick, people would say that you could break a bat over him, and the bat would splinter. He always wore a very serious expression beneath a full head of thick grayish hair that he pushed straight back. In that dark gray mop, there was a streak, like a bird feather, of white gray.

Clarence always spoke in a gruff voice—that is, when he used it, which was rare. He was a man of very few words, but he wasn't anybody's fool. He'd graduated from Fordham University where he was a member of the hockey team and was an excellent student. Now he was a dedicated family man and a CIA group supervisor, and he took his job very seriously.

"So what kind of trouble did you get yourself into this time?" Clarence asked PJ, never looking up from what he was doing.

"Good morning to you too," PJ said with a smile.

Clarence continued with what he was doing and, at the same time, reached out his hand and said, "Let me see the cell phone." PJ handed him the phone and waited. "What a piece of shit," Clarence said, looking at the phone.

"I need whatever information you can retrieve . . . from that piece of shit."

Clarence looked up at PJ and smiled. "You look good for an old fart."

"Thanks. Coming from you, I take that as a compliment," PJ said.

PJ walked over to where there was a pot of coffee, helped himself to a cup, and then found a chair. He watched as Clarence played around with the phone, then put some sort of magnet on it, and attached it to a small recorder. He waved his hand, inviting PJ to come closer. Clarence put on a set of headphones that were attached to the recorder, listened for a couple of seconds, and then started to write some telephone numbers on a pad. After about ten minutes, he took off the headphones and handed the pad with the telephone numbers to PJ.

"The list on top are all the incoming calls for the past two weeks. Most had been erased, but I was able to get them back. The numbers on the bottom of the page are the numbers he called for the last fifteen days. It will take me a little time to retrieve older calls. This cell is an old model and automatically erases calls after a period of time. I may not be able to get the dates, but I think I can get the numbers. How far back do you want me to go?"

PJ thought. "I dunno . . . maybe thirty days."

"Thirty days it is. What I'll do after I get the numbers, I'll give them to Herman over there," he said, pointing to a man on the other side of the room who looked like an unmade bed! He was in need of a haircut and shave, and his clothes looked like he had slept in them. "He'll be able to get you names and addresses for the numbers. Or at least most of them. Depends a lot on where the call came from or where he called. But we'll play around with it and get you whatever we can. In the meantime, I'll give him this list to work on. He should have some names and addresses for these in a day or two. Gimme a number I can reach you." And with that, Clarence returned to what he was doing before PJ came in.

"Thanks, old friend, I really do appreciate it," PJ said as he started to walk away. Clarence didn't look up; he simply waved his hand over his head as if to say goodbye.

CHAPTER THIRTY-ONE

As soon as Sonny's plane touched down in Chicago, he called his father. He spoke to him before he left Las Vegas and told him about his conversation with Joey. "What a *puto*," his father said. They agreed to wait until they were together before talking about it any more.

"I just landed, Pop. I don't have any luggage, so I should be at the house in the next hour or so."

"Good, I'll wait for you."

When Sonny arrived, his father and brother were just finishing breakfast. "Did you eat?" his father asked.

"Yeah, had something on the plane. But I'll take some coffee."

The three men took their coffee and went into the living room. They sat down and for the next couple of seconds just looked at one another.

"Is not a good thing, my sons. Your cousin has done a very stupid thing."

They spent the next couple of hours trying to understand Joey's motives and the possible consequences of his actions. How could he have been so stupid? When the housekeeper came in with a tray of hot coffee and biscuits, they had run out of things to say. The old man poured himself a fresh cup of coffee and sat in silence.

"So, Pop, what are we going to do?" Sonny asked.

The old man put down his cup of coffee and took out a cigar from his jacket pocket. He didn't offer one to the boys, knowing that they didn't smoke. He gently rolled the cigar around in his hand, then slowly put it to his lips, and wet the cigar with his tongue. Both Andy and Sonny were used to this ritual. The old man had gone through the same routine many times when they were just boys. After lighting the cigar, the old man looked at both of his sons and asked, "Do we want to save his life, or do we throw him to the lions to be slaughtered?"

Andy looked to Sonny for the answer.

"I don't know, Pop. He is family," Sonny said. "How can we not save his life? The question is how. And to tell you the truth, I'm worried about you and Andy. From the stories I've heard about this PJ character, I don't know how far he will go to satisfy his thirst for revenge."

"And I too worry, Sonny, both for you and Andy. Ah, but if I was fifty years younger—"

"I know, Pop, I know," Sonny interrupted and then turned to his brother. "Andy, what do you think? After all, you got a lot at stake here."

Andy poured himself a cup of coffee and said, "I would like to strangle that cousin of ours, that's what I'd like to do. But whatever you and Pop decide is fine with me. The only thing I can say is we need to be careful. We need to find out exactly what Joey has done. You know what I mean. How many people are involved in this. We have a lot at stake here."

"I agree, Andy," Sonny answered and then turned to his father. "Okay, Pop, it's your call."

The old man took a long puff from his cigar and looked at his two boys. It seemed his thoughts were focused on their future. He continued with long puffs on his expensive cigar crunched between his teeth. When he finally spoke, the cigar never left the center of his lips.

"Well, first things first, I have decided Joey will have to leave the country. That is the only chance we have of saving his life. We will send him to our cousin's home in Palermo. He should be safe there. I do not think this PJ will find him there. And then I will find a way to deal with this man who has now become a nail in our shoe."

Sonny looked at his father. "How will you do that, Pop?"

"I will know better when I finish this cigar," the old man said with a smile. Could his father really find a way to neutralize PJ? He would have to wait and see. In the meantime, he would meet with Joey and tell him what they decided. He knew the clock was running, and he didn't have a whole lot of time.

It was early evening by the time Sonny arrived at Joey's apartment.

"Where the hell you been?" he screamed at Sonny. "I've been gone nuts sitting here waiting for you!" Sonny could see his cousin was really stressed out. How was such a *stronza* (turd) like him able to set up two murders? Well, at least one they were sure of.

"I was with Pop all this time. You sure screwed up big time, Joey."

Joey was unable to sit still. He was agonizing over what he had done, wishing to himself that he could undo it. But of course, that was not going to happen.

"What did Uncle Joe say?" Joey asked, constantly moving back and forth on the couch.

"Jesus Christ, sit still, will you? You're making me crazy jumping around like that."

"I know, I know, I'm nervous, Sonny. What am I gonna do? What's gonna happen to me?"

For a minute, Sonny felt sorry for his cousin. He was acting like a scared child. He never saw him like this before. "Okay, Joey, calm down. I think Pop has worked out something for you, but first, I have to know exactly what you did. Who you spoke to about this, who else knows about this, where you got the crew to do this—everything. And while we're at it, where did you get the money to pay these guys?"

A smarter guy would have been ready for what was happening. But Joey was a victim of his own bravado and stupidity. He felt the world was closing in on him.

"C'mon, Joey, start talking!" Sonny was getting impatient.

"Okay, Sonny. But before I tell you, you gotta believe me when I tell you I did it for the family. After that night at your father's house, I knew somebody had to do something, or the gambling bill wasn't going to pass—"

Sonny interrupted him, "Joey, Lippincott was going to tell the president to sign the bill. All the casino owners are in favor of nationwide gambling now. They know it's going to happen sooner or later, so they don't want to miss the boat."

"Shit, Sonny, I didn't know that! Why didn't somebody tell me?"

Sonny just shook his head. "Okay, Joey, forgetaboutit. Just tell me what happened. But first, tell me about the money. I don't know how much this sort of thing costs, but whatever it is, I know you don't have that kind of money."

When Joey told Sonny that he was skimming the numbers bank in order to get the money to pay the hit men, Sonny lost it.

"Faccia di merda! (You son of a bitch!)," he screamed. "Are you crazy? You stole from Pop! What did you think was going to happen when he found out? How did you expect to pay it back? . . . Jesus Christ, Joey . . . tell me . . . how much?"

"A lot, Sonny."

"How much is a lot?"

"Fifty grand, but I only gave this guy twenty-five so far. I still owe him the balance. I know If I don't pay them the balance, Sonny, they'll fucking kill me."

"Not if I kill you first, you dumb son of a bitch! So the bottom line is you took twenty-five Gs. I don't know what Pop is gonna do when he hears about that. You're in deep shit, Joey!"

"C'mon, Sonny, stop talking like that. You gotta help me! You gotta!"

Sonny went to the liquor cabinet in Joey's living room and poured himself a glass of scotch. Joey started to get up to join him when Sonny shouted, "Just sit the fuck still!" There was fire in Sonny's eyes. This was a different Sonny. Not the happy-go-lucky casino owner. For a second, Joey thought his cousin was serious about killing him. Sonny downed his drink and then walked back to the couch and sat down next to his cousin. He took out a pen and a piece of paper and looked straight ahead. He didn't want to make eye contact with him. Then very calmly, he said, "Okay, Joey, first, the names of the guys in New York you hired to kill Lippincott who, by the way, killed three innocent bystanders. And then the name of the guy in Las Vegas. He really fucked up." Joey still didn't know what happened in Las Vegas.

"What are you talking about? What guy in Las Vegas? And who fucked up? I don't know what you're talking about."

"Joey . . . stop lying to me! We know you set up the hit on Lippincott's brother. Now tell me who and how much. We know you did it, so stop screwing around! You're just wasting time."

Joey just looked at his cousin. His mouth started to move, but nothing came out. His silence spoke volumes. That was enough for Sonny. He knew he did it.

"C'mon, Joey, now!" Sonny yelled, at the same time pushing him back against the sofa. Joey put both hands to his face and shook his head back and forth.

"Sonny, I haven't heard from the guy in Vegas since the first time I talked to him. I swear on my mother's grave. I got his name from the guy who was gonna take care of Lippincott. His name is Emil Sudhan. We made the deal on the phone. It was twenty grand. He was supposed to call me after . . . you know after."

"After he killed Lippincott's brother," Sonny said sarcastically.

"Yeah, but I never heard from him. I don't know what happened, Sonny. Really, I never heard from him. Did he kill him?"

"You really don't know, do you?"

"No, I swear."

"You stupid son of a bitch!" Sonny said, looking at his cousin in disgust. "Okay, Joey, give me the names of the guys in New York—and don't leave anybody out! Then I'll tell you what happened in Las Vegas."

Joey thought for a second and decided not to tell Sonny about Sid. *I'll just give him Tozzi and Angie.*

After Sonny told his cousin what happened in Las Vegas, he didn't know what to say. And when Sonny asked him if the guy in PJ's apartment had an accomplice, he said he didn't know. "I really don't know, Sonny. He said he might need somebody to help him, but I told him that was up to him. I don't know what he decided. Like I told you, Sonny, I only spoke to this guy one time. He was supposed to call me after he did the job. When he didn't call, I started to worry. Man . . . I'm really sorry," Joey said.

Sonny said, "There sure are a lot of things you don't know, Joey. Why didn't you call him?"

Joey just shrugged his shoulders as if to say "I don't know."

Then Sonny dropped the bomb. He told him he had to get out of the country. At least for now. That was the only way they could protect him. If he stayed here, PJ would surely find him . . . and kill him. This was the only solution. They would make arrangements for him to live with his second cousin in Palermo. Joey went crazy. "You just can't ship me off to Italy like some bag of shit! I'm a person!" he bellowed. "You can't do this to me! What am I gonna do in Italy? Shit, I hardly speak the language! C'mon, Sonny, there has to be some other solution."

In a way, Sonny felt sorry for him, but he was the one who caused all this trouble. He was lucky his father didn't kill him. Then Sonny thought about the money Joey had skimmed from his father's collections. Maybe his father would kill the poor bastard. After several hours of the same thing over and over again, Sonny finally told his cousin to just sit tight. He promised him he would talk to his father again to see if maybe there was some other solution. In his heart of hearts, he knew there was no other way. If Joey remained in Chicago, PJ would find him and kill him. It was as simple as that. There was no doubt in Sonny's mind about that.

What really worried him was if PJ thought the Cantelli family was behind this. But what could be their motive? But then again, what was Joey's motive? Like his father said, "This is not a good thing!"

When Sonny left, Joey thought more about what he told him. "You have to go live in Palermo." He thought to himself, *What kind of bullshit is that?* Suddenly, he jumped up from his chair and stood there looking at his front door. *Holy shit,* he thought, *they're gonna fuckin' kill me!* He slowly sat down again and started to pick up the phone. *They ain't gonna send me to Italy to hide. They're sending me there to kill me. I would disappear off the face of the earth.* He thought about calling his uncle. But what would he say? He knew he had to get out of his apartment and hide somewhere. But where? Sid's place. Yeah, Sid's place. He didn't tell Sonny about Sid. That's a safe place. Then he thought, *Shit, when they find out it's Sid's collections I've been skimming, they'll be all over him. But they wouldn't expect me to go back there. That's a good idea? Maybe not.* He was sweating all over and began to shake. *Jesus Christ, I'm making myself crazy. I have to start to think straight.* Then he began to think about Tozzi. What was he going to do about him? Tozzi told Sid he was going to Atlantic City with Angie for a couple days, and when they got back, he expected the rest of his money. *Good thing my cell phone wasn't working,* Joey thought. *I sure as hell didn't want to talk to him.*

Then it came to him. Maria. Maria Falcone. He dated her before she moved to New York. "She really liked me," he whispered to himself. He had her number somewhere. She had a loft on West Fourteenth Street. *That's perfect,* he thought. *Nobody knows about her. I'll stay there until this whole thing dies down. After a while, I'm sure Uncle Joe and Sonny will understand.*

CHAPTER THIRTY-TWO

June 25, 1995

It was the day after Walter's funeral. PJ was sitting with Anita in her kitchen, having coffee. "I'm glad that's all behind us," she said, talking about the funeral.

"I think you held up very well," PJ said.

"You're much too kind," she said, sipping her coffee.

"So tell me, PJ, what are your plans now?"

"Well, I'm waiting to hear from a friend of mine. As soon as I do, I'll know better. But I've been thinking, Anita, since I really don't know how long I'll be in New York, I think it's best if I go to a hotel."

She put her coffee cup down and stood up. "No such thing, PJ. You can stay here as long as you want. It's ridiculous for you to go to a hotel."

"Anita, please . . ."

"No, PJ, I won't hear of it. Besides which . . . I don't want to be alone now."

They looked at each other for several seconds; then she said, "Okay, PJ, now that's settled, why don't you tell me what the hell you are up to."

"I told you, Anita, nothing. I have some personal things to take care of."

"Bullshit," she said, surprising herself as well as PJ. "I want to know. You can trust me." He never confided in anyone before about what he did. It was not the kind of thing that made for good dinner conversation. Why was he even thinking about confiding in her? He never told anybody that he was a paid assassin. But for some strange reason, he wanted her to know. Was it because he wanted her to know that he was different from Walter? More of a man than Walter. Walter was dead. There was no competition. He didn't like the feeling of indecision. She kept looking at him. "Well, PJ, let's hear it," she said, half smiling.

"I don't know if you're ready for this. And if I tell you, I'll have to kill you."

"Very funny," she said. "Believe me, after what I've been through this last week, I'm ready for just about anything."

He got up from the kitchen table and walked to the other side of the room. "You going somewhere?" she asked. He turned and looked at her. *God, she is gorgeous*, he thought. The tight fit of her one-piece jumpsuit showed off her long legs and narrow hips to the fullest. She was in great shape for her age. For any age. And her face, skin as smooth as a rose petal. Eyes . . . he had never seen eyes quite that color before—so pale and brilliant a blue, like bits of colored glass, like perfect turquoise stones.

"You are very beautiful, you know," he said.

"Thank you. I'll hold that thought," she said and began to blush. She was irritated with herself. She had not blushed in years. "You're not so bad looking yourself," she said, thinking that she was sounding and acting like a schoolgirl.

But she was right. He was good-looking. Good-looking in a different way than Walter was. He was just over six feet, with broad shoulders; and even at fifty-five years old, he had the physical appearance of an athlete. His brown eyes seemed to look straight through you. His face was appealing, and his smile was wonderful; and there was about him a vitality, an aggressive self-confidence, a suggestiveness that hinted subtly at sex.

"What are you thinking?" he asked, still standing on the opposite side of the room.

She smiled and said, "I'm thinking you should tell me what the hell is going on."

"First, I need to answer this call," he said, taking his cell from his pocket.

"Coward. I'll give you some privacy," she said as she got up from the kitchen table and started out of the room. Then she added, "But we'll continue this conversation later."

The call was from Sandy Keller, his detective friend in Las Vegas.

"PJ, how you doing?"

"Good, Sandy, how are things out there?"

"Well, I've got some good news for you."

"Really? I could use some good news."

"Believe it or not, this guy Nick Paraphas turned himself in this morning."

PJ was shocked. "You are shittin' me," he said.

"Nope. He called early this morning and asked to talk to the detective in charge of the shooting at your apartment. They tracked me down and transferred the call to me. I arranged to meet him at the station. We just finished taking his statement. The bottom line is he was afraid that if the investigation somehow led to him and we eventually tied him into the murder, things could really go bad for him. He figured he was better off turning himself in and try to make a deal. He has a record a mile long. Listen to this.

"At age thirteen, he and his older brother were arrested after a spree of vandalism, knocking out signals on the streetcar system in New Bedford. By the time he was seventeen years old, he led a gang that broke into homes and small businesses, stealing money, jewelry, you name it. When he was eighteen, he was sentenced to the Concord Reformatory for five years. After serving about eighteen months, he led a wild breakout. They beat up people and robbed the bars in Boston's Scollay Square. Over the next twenty years, he was in and out of jail nine times for everything from armed robbery to assault with a deadly weapon. He showed up in Vegas about two years ago.

"The interesting thing, he's never been involved in a murder. In his statement, he said he was just a lookout on this job. His job was to call Emil when you left the casino. He said Emil told him some guy from Chicago wanted you roughed up. He swore Emil never told him he planned to kill you. Of course, he's trying to cop a plea. I told him that will be up to the district attorney."

"Wow, hard to believe, Sandy. Sounds like the gang that couldn't shoot straight. Did he tell you who the guy is in Chicago?"

"No, what he said was Emil told him they were doing the job for some big-time crime family in Chicago. He said it was like Emil was bragging that he knew somebody in organized crime. He was always mouthing off about the people he knew. He claimed he once belonged to a terrorist organization that planned to overthrow the government. We asked the FBI about him. They told us he's a real nutcase. They've had him under surveillance for years. He is a real nobody. He was a member of an Islamic cell for a while until they threw him out. They didn't even want him. I haven't talked to my captain about what his plans are to track down the Chicago caller. Between you and me, I would like to close the case here and let the FBI do their thing, but I don't know if he's going to feel the same way. We have no other leads at this point.

Just so you know, my partner can't understand why we didn't find any cell phone on Emil. Paraphas claims he called him when you left the casino. He called him again about an hour later, and somebody else answered the phone. My partner can't understand that. The FBI also wants to know if we found his phone. When they learned about the call from a supposed member of a Chicago crime family, they became a lot more interested in the shooting. They think both shootings are related. The one here and the one in New York. They asked a lot of questions about you, PJ. I wouldn't be surprised if they contact you. Just wanted to give you a heads-up."

"I appreciate that, Sandy. And I'm really sorry if I've put you in a bind."

"Yeah, that's okay. I'll handle it. But like I said, PJ, I don't know how far the FBI plans to go with this. So if I were you, I would be very careful."

"I hear you, Sandy, and thanks for your concern. Tell me, am I cool with you and your guys? I mean, am I still a suspect in the shooting at my place?"

"Not as far as I'm concerned, you're not. Now that we got Paraphas, there shouldn't be any problem. He will confirm your story, so you are okay. I have to tell you though, before this guy turned himself in, the DA wanted an inquest. But I'm sure that's all academic now."

"Thanks again, Sandy . . . and Sandy . . . I owe you."

"Yeah, I guess you do. Let me know when you're back in town, PJ. You can buy me a cup of coffee."

"That's a deal, pal. Talk to you later."

PJ put his cell phone back into his pocket and stood in the kitchen, staring at the wall. A crime family in Chicago gave the order to kill him? He racked his brain but couldn't think of anything in his past that might have triggered that. He needed that list of names and addresses from Clarence. There had to be a record of the call Emil got from Chicago.

Anita walked back into the room. She could see PJ looked disturbed. "Are you okay?" she asked.

"Yeah, I'm fine." And then for some strange reason, he felt he owed her an explanation. "Anita, there are a lot of things I would like to tell you. But unfortunately, I can't do it now. This call was from the detective in Las Vegas who is in charge of the shooting at my house. There was a second guy involved in the shooting who just turned himself in, but there are still a lot of blanks I need to fill in. For me to do that, I have to go to Chicago for a couple days. I know I keep saying this, but just trust me and give me a little time. I need to take care of this, Anita. I hope you can understand."

He never had to explain his actions to anyone in the past. He did what he did and answered only to himself. Now he was asking her to allow him to do whatever it was he did. Was he asking her to wait for him? That was stupid. In the twentysome years they knew each other, they barely got past the hellos and goodbyes; and now after a week together, he felt like he owed her an explanation for what he did. What he really wanted to do was put his arms around her and press her warm body against his.

Anita looked at him without saying a word. It was like she was reading his mind and understood what he was thinking. She walked over to where he was standing and gently kissed him on the cheek. Had she stood there another second longer, he would have grabbed her and kissed her and then who knows what. But that didn't happen. As she turned to leave the room, she said, "When you come back, and I know you will come back . . . I will be here."

As soon as Anita was out of the kitchen, PJ called Clarence.

"PJ, I was just about to call you. We were able to retrieve most of the information from that guy's cell phone. And while I'm thinking about it, the goddamn cell has been ringing on and off all damn day."

"Yeah, that doesn't surprise me," PJ said. "It's probably the FBI trying to get someone to answer so they can find out where the cell is."

"Oh," Clarence said. "Should I be concerned?"

"Nah," PJ said with a laugh, "you know those FBI guys. They're not half as smart as you CIA guys."

"Cute," Clarence said. "Do you want to pick up the list, or can I drop it off somewhere for you?"

PJ thought for a second. "I'll pick it up in about an hour."

Then as an afterthought, Clarence said, "I put a little icing on the cake for you. After the kid got all the names and addresses, I had him run them through our mix-and-match program. This kicks out any known criminals or people we are watching. And guess what? One of the names on the list is Joey Sconsi, nephew of Joseph Theodor Cantelli, reputed member of organized crime in Chicago."

"Bingo!" PJ shouted into the phone.

CHAPTER THIRTY-THREE

When the average person thinks about the mafiosi, they think about serious, no-nonsense, hardworking racketeers, and killers. The kind of people you won't find being interviewed on *60 Minutes* or helping Al Ruddy make *The Godfather* movie or talking to Gay Talese so he can write *Honor Thy Father* or Nicholas Pileggi for his *Wiseguy*.

That was the Mafia that once was. The old images now seem like a caricature—the aging dons living behind high-walled estates, taking part in the shadowy world of secret rituals, swearing vengeance on their enemies, dispatching hit men to end the lives of rivals. It was the stuff of novels and movies—and it was all real.

But in the past few years, the bosses and underlings of organized crime have been buffeted by the onslaught of federal crackdowns. A procession of turncoats and government agents that has infiltrated the Mafia's inner sanctums has crippled its leadership and inflicted damage that was never deemed possible just a few years earlier.

The underworld's most intimate secrets of how it operates have been laid bare as at no time in the past. Today, the Mafia is divided by an old and new generation and is torn asunder by different ideals. The new breed mafiosi, native Americans for the most part, are no longer willing to live and work by the standards of a bygone era. They want to be underworld yuppies with their hands in the corporate world of the 1990s.

But one thing stays unchanged: the culture of organized crime. Mob members call each other wise guys, and so-called wise-guys rules define a strict code of conduct. For example, a member who vouches for someone who may in time betray the organization takes the hit—usually before reprisals are taken against the stoolie. Also, a fixer taking a payoff for the job must produce exactly what he promised the mob; he can't offer excuses or refunds.

Those are only two of the many old values that are still in vogue. Many of the others have been put on the back burner because of the new "elitist" mafiosi. The mob has finally begun to go back to the old ways that were so successful in the past. However, some of the older dons who now have sons and daughters in successful legitimate businesses are content to be done with the violence of the past. And like Joseph Cantelli, they hope that legalized gambling nationwide will make their now-illegal business legal.

PJ was aware of this, and that was why he was having such an enormous problem in believing Joseph Cantelli would order a hit on both him and Walter. What was his motive? Was there something in Walter's past that could be the motive? He didn't think so. He knew the Cantellis owned the Casino Royal in Vegas. He couldn't remember ever even being there. That had nothing to do with all this. After Clarence gave him the list with Joey's name and phone number on it, he was able to find out that he worked for the Cantellis as a collector in Chicago. That was about all he could find out about him. The big question was this: had Joey acted on his own, or did his uncle command the killing? But once again, what was the reason? The more he thought about it, the more he was sure of one thing: Joseph Cantelli had no hand in the killing of his brother and the attempt on his life. PJ believed in fate and sometimes in coincidence, more often than not when it served his purpose. This was neither fate or a coincidence. Joey Sconsi was the person responsible. He didn't know why, but he intended to find out. After that, he would kill him.

CHAPTER THIRTY-FOUR

When Joey called Maria Falcone, she was more than surprised, considering she hadn't heard from him since moving to New York almost five years ago.

"Joey, how are you? I don't believe you still have my phone number."

"Are you kidding me? I think about you all the time," he lied. "It's just that I've been so busy . . . you know what I mean? Anyhow, I'm gonna be in New York on business, and I really want to see you. And since I don't have a place to stay, I was thinking of bunking in with you for a while."

Maria was taken aback. "Gee, Joey, I don't know. I'm kinda seeing somebody. It may be kind of awkward."

"Hey, Maria, whatayou talking about? I thought we had something for each other."

Maria had to laugh. "Joey, it's been like five years. I mean after all . . ."

Joey didn't like getting the brush-off, not even if it was from someone he hadn't seen or spoken to in five years. "C'mon, Maria, it will only be for a couple days. I really want to see you."

"Really, Joey, do you mean that?"

"Sure I do. Whatayou say?"

"Okay, Joey, I guess it will be all right. When are you planning to come to New York?"

"How's about tomorrow?"

Maria was a tall good-looking grabber who wore clothes with the assurance and style that Marilyn Monroe did when she wanted to show off her ass. She was a Sicilian and had the sexually inquisitive eyes of a Bedouin woman. She knew from the time she was twelve years old that she wanted to be a model. She loved the fact that she was born a female. Before moving to New York, she lived with her father and her sister, Teresa, on the South Side of Chicago. And as soon as she was old enough for it to make a difference, she hated every minute of it. Her mother had died when she was only six years old, and all she could remember of her childhood was that she had to help take care of her father and her sister.

She had her first clear shot at Joey at her sister Teresa's seventeenth birthday party. He was there with his cousin Andy. The party was at the American Legion Veteran of Foreign Wars hall, and Joey had promised her he would come because her sister didn't know enough people to invite. There was a four-piece band of either bald or white-haired World War II veterans who played for free at all the parties at the VFW hall. After the band played "Happy Birthday," they would play old dance music. Maria made sure she was standing next to Joey when the dance music started, so all she had to do was grab his arm and say, "C'mon, let's dance." She was only nineteen at the time and was still a virgin. After the party, they went into the coatroom to make out.

"Do you have a rubber?" she asked Joey when the petting got hot and heavy.

"No, but I promise, I'll pull out."

Before she had a chance to say no, he was deep inside of her and never kept his promise.

"Jesus, Joey, suppose I become pregnant?"

"Don't worry," he said. "I know where you can get an abortion."

Now he was coming to stay with her in New York.

The same day that Joey left for New York, Tozzi called Sid.

"Where the hell is that *stugotz* Joey?" Tozzi screamed into the phone.

"I don't know," Sid told him. "I ain't seen him in a couple days. Where are you? You back from Atlantic City?"

"No, we're still here. Angie got real lucky at the craps table, so we're gonna stay another day. But never mind that, I've been trying to reach Joey for two days, but he don't answer his cell. What the fuck is going on?"

Sid wished he could turn the clock back and make all this go away. "I don't know what to tell you Toz. He ain't been around."

Tozzi was getting more angry by the minute. "Okay then, tell me how I can get in touch with somebody from the Cantelli family. I'm comin' home tomorrow, and I want my money. I got these two guys in New York breathing down my back. They wanna get paid. I only gave them each half, and they ain't the kinda guys you fuck with."

Sid didn't know what to do. He didn't want to give him Cantelli's number, but if he didn't, Tozzi would know something was wrong. Shit, he had vouched for Joey, and now he wasn't around.

"C'mon, Sid!" Tozzi shouted again. "I ain't got all day."

"Look, Tozzi, I just deal with Joey. I don't know the Cantellis' number."

Tozzi was not a complete idiot. "Well, if Joey ain't around, who's making the collections for Cantelli?"

"It's a guy named Vinny. He covers for Joey when he's not around."

"Something's not kosher here, Sid. What's going on?"

"Look, Tozzi, I'll try to find out for you by tomorrow. In the meantime, you guys have a good time in AC."

"Whadayou, the fuckin' Chamber of Commerce?" Tozzi said sarcastically and hung up the phone.

Sid sat behind the bar looking at his cell phone as if it would tell him what to do. Should he call the Cantellis? Suppose they really did order the hit? It would not be cool, calling to tell them Tozzi wanted his money. Where did he come off telling them something like that? And if Joey did it on his own, shit, he was in a no-win situation.

Where the hell was Joey? He had to find out before Tozzi came back to Chicago.

Chapter Thirty-Five

June 30, 1995

Joseph Cantelli lived in the same house in Skokie, Illinois, for over fifty years. At one time, he owned ten acres of ground around the house, including two smaller homes on the same property. Those were in the days of the Mafia wars and behind the wall strongholds. Over the years, the Cantelli family sold off some of the property surrounding the house and eventually tore down the two smaller houses. They no longer felt the need for all of the security measures they once maintained. After his mother died in 1985, Sonny tried to convince his father to move to Las Vegas; but the old man had his roots in Chicago, especially in this house. Every room in the house was decorated the way he remembered the furnishings of his parents' home in Sicily. He could remember every room as if he were looking at a set of photographs. While the furnishings in the house were not modern in any way, they were rich, if a little worn—fringes, velours, and gilt-framed pictures everywhere. This was his home. This is where he wanted to spend his remaining days.

There were two men who lived in the house with him. Sal "Sally" Constego, who was his driver and former bodyguard, and Tommy Mansino, who was the cook. The three had been friends for over fifty years. Although he seldom left the house, he kept in close touch with the people who worked for him, running his gambling empire. He wanted Andy to take over that part of the family business, but he had made the decision to go into the restaurant business instead.

More than once, he told Andy that when gambling in sports became legal in all the United States as it was now legal in Nevada, he would not be able to count the money fast enough. But Andy had made up his mind, and nothing either Sonny or his father said could change his mind.

It was just past eight o'clock, and the old man was sitting in his favorite chair in his den, gazing dreamily at the TV. Sally had already gone to his room, and Tommy was in the kitchen, drinking coffee and reading the newspaper. As he did so often, he thought about the old days. He remembered how at the age of only seventeen, he became a "qualified" man in one of Chicago's toughest crime neighborhoods. And now he sat and watched TV. But life was good, and except for the problem his nephew had caused, he had no worries. Suddenly, he felt a hand on his shoulder. He looked up and saw a tall stranger, wearing black pants and a black sweatshirt, standing beside his chair.

"Who are you? How did you get in here?" Cantelli asked.

"I think you know who I am," PJ said. "And as far as how I got in, it was really very simple."

"So . . . I would guess you are the one they call . . . PJ," Cantelli said. "You know if this was fifty years ago, you would be a dead man now."

"With all due respect, Mr. Cantelli, if this was ten years ago . . . I think you know what I mean," PJ answered.

"Yes, I think I do. You know, it's a shame we were not born at the same time. You would have made a good . . . shall I say . . . adversary . . . is that the right word?"

PJ walked across the room so that he was facing Cantelli. "May I sit down?" he asked.

Cantelli pointed to the chair opposite him and said, "You know, you could have called and made an appointment, Mr. PJ. It was not necessary for you to come in this way."

"I wanted to make a point," PJ said with a smile on his face.

"Well, Mr. PJ, you have made your point. Now why don't you tell me why you broke into my house."

"Again, Mr. Cantelli, I think you know why I am here. But I will tell you anyhow. I am here because of what your nephew has done. However, to show my respect for who you are, I wanted to talk to you first before I settled the score with a member of your family. Your nephew is responsible for killing my brother, three other innocent people, and a beautiful young girl who had not yet experienced life."

Cantelli did not become the man he was by being intimidated or threatened. He had fully expected that sooner or later, he would have to deal with what Joey had done. However, he had to be sure of his options before he made any decisions on what to do.

"Mr. PJ, you speak like someone who is prepared to act like the police, the jury, and the executioner. If my nephew has done the things you say he has done, then you should go to the police and let them handle it. I have faith in our legal system, Mr. PJ. I think you should do the same." PJ had not expected the old man to fold up like a cardboard box when he approached him, but by the same token, PJ had to allow the old man to play out his part. Give him the respect he deserves.

"Unfortunately, Mr. Cantelli, I cannot depend on the system in this case. I know in your business, you always said things should never get personal. However, in this case, it is personal."

"Mr. PJ, you said . . . my business. And what is my business?"

"Well, you own a casino in Las Vegas and a chain of restaurants on the East Coast. And I am sure a man of your experience has ventured into other areas of business."

"I see," Cantelli said. "Mr. PJ, why don't we get to the point here. I appreciate your coming to see me first before you—what did you say?—settle the score. But we are talking about my nephew. He is the only son of my sister. How can I be sure he did the things you say he did?"

PJ knew the old man was looking for a reason to give up Joey.

"Mr. Cantelli, I have the cell phone from the man who broke into my house and killed an innocent girl. There are calls on that phone to and from Joey. Also, there was a second man in Las Vegas who was a lookout. He turned himself in and gave a statement to the police. He said a Chicago crime family ordered the hit." Then PJ added his own postscript. "He also told the Vegas police the caller from Chicago got Emil's name from the guy who was doing the New York hit. It doesn't take much to put two and two together. That's enough for me to know your nephew was the guy behind this whole thing. What I don't know is why. I don't even know your nephew." PJ was taking a chance. He didn't know what Joey told the Cantellis.

The old man listened, trying to piece together what PJ was telling him and what Joey told Sonny.

"Mr. PJ, please tell me, do you think someone ordered Joey to do what you say he did?"

PJ looked at the old man without blinking. It was like he was looking into his soul. All of his training and experience was on the line here. He had to be right. This was a bluff he had to win. "What I am saying, Mr. Cantelli, I believe your nephew told the people he hired they were doing the killing for . . . for you."

"And you, Mr. PJ, what do you think?"

This was his all-in bet. "I think he was doing it on his own, Mr. Cantelli. But like I said, I don't know why. But regardless why he did it, he must be held responsible. There is no other way, Mr. Cantelli. I am sorry, but this is the way it has to be."

The old man had spoken these same words more than once in the past. He knew what it was to take revenge. He also knew there was little room for mercy, but he had to try. Joey was family. He looked at the man sitting across from him and saw himself when he was much younger. But before he could respond to what PJ said, Tommy appeared at the door, holding a shotgun. He spoke in Italian, asking Cantelli what was going on. Who was this man? How did he get into the house? What did he want him to do? The old man raised his arm as if to tell Tommy not to do anything. At the same time, PJ, very matter-of-factly took a Luger automatic handgun out of his waistband, stood up, and held his hand straight out, pointing it at Tommy. Without taking his eyes off Tommy, he said to Cantelli, "Tell that foolish old man to put away that shotgun and come sit down before I have to blow his head off." Before Cantelli could said anything, Tommy put the shotgun down and raised his arms.

PJ said, "Tell him to put his damn arms down and come sit down before he has a heart attack." PJ put his own gun back in his waistband and sat down. He looked at Cantelli and said, "You were about to say something, Mr. Cantelli."

CHAPTER THIRTY-SIX

July 1, 1995

When PJ checked into the Ambassador Hotel, he didn't know how long he would be staying in Chicago. It depended on what happened after he spoke to Cantelli. Now the morning following his visit with Joseph Cantelli, he was having breakfast in the coffee shop, replaying in his mind what the old man told him. He wanted to make a deal. He would tell PJ everything his nephew told him if he would spare his life. At first, PJ told him he couldn't do that. He said that even if he didn't tell him, he would somehow find out. It might take him a little longer, but he would find out what he needed to know. The old man did not waiver. He told PJ he would have to retaliate if something happened to Joey. "What good would it do for you to kill him? I can punish him in such a way he might wish that I allowed you to kill him."

PJ liked Cantelli. What he didn't like was the fact he was permitting the old man to stay in the game. The longer they talked, the better the chance there was for the old man to win.

PJ finally agreed. "I trust you, Mr. Cantelli. And if you tell me you will punish your nephew, then I believe you. Like I said before, if this was ten years ago, we would not be having this conversation."

The old man smiled. "Mr. PJ, you have made the right decision."

"We'll see. Now suppose you tell me why your nephew did such a stupid thing." PJ asked, "What was his motive? In my mind, it had to have something to do with you. In some way, he thought he was helping you, but how? I can't figure that out."

"You are a very smart man, Mr. PJ. Joey did think he was helping our family. It is a little complicated. But for a long time, our family, like some other casino owners in Las Vegas, have supported legalized gambling throughout the country. Senator Guy Baxter has been trying to get a bill passed that would allow this to happen."

"Do you know that piece of shit? If you will excuse my expression," PJ interrupted.

"Yes, we do. We have contributed to his campaign for years in the hopes that someday, he would be president."

PJ smiled and said, "Money brings power."

The old man corrected him. "It is the other way around, my friend. Power brings money." PJ shrugged his shoulders as if to say "Okay!"

"Anyway," the old man continued, "your brother was opposed to the bill passing, and he told the president this. Your brother was a very powerful man, Mr. PJ, but you already know that. Then one day, the senator was talking to my son and said if it wasn't for your brother, the president would sign the bill. Please don't misunderstand me. The senator was not saying someone should kill either your brother or the president. That would be ridiculous. But as fate would have it, the night my son was telling this story, my nephew happened to be here.

"When my son spoke to Joey, he told him that was the reason he hired someone to kill your brother. He thought that would help us. In his mind, without your brother around talking to the president, the gambling bill would pass. He never spoke to me about this." The old man was very careful so as not to implicate the senator.

PJ was speechless. "Is he some kind of a moron? What the hell is wrong with him? And why me? What did I have to do with all this?"

"Evidently, someone told him you were Walter Lippincott's brother. And if something happened to him, you would take revenge. So, my friend, Joey made the decision to have you killed. I am very sorry, Mr. PJ."

"Well, he was right about one thing. I sure as hell will take revenge for my brother's murder. And with all due respect, Mr. Cantelli, that may be what Joey told your son. But there has to be more to the story. You don't order the murder of two people just because you think it will please someone."

"Accept it for what it is, my friend," the old man said.

PJ nodded. For the time being, he would. But his mind was racing a mile a minute. Was it possible Senator Baxter had more to do with this than just making a casual comment to Sonny Cantelli? If he was involved, he too would pay.

When PJ asked Cantelli where Joey was, the old man told him he had disappeared. "After my son spoke to him, he vanished. We have not heard from him since that night. I cannot tell you why. We, of course, are looking for him. And I am sure he will turn up. When he does, I will find out as much as I can for you, Mr. PJ."

Cantelli gave PJ the two names that Joey gave to Sonny. PJ told him he needed more information. Joey had to tell him where he could find Tozzi and Angie. Cantelli understood and said he would do everything he could to find out where these two *stronzas* (pieces of shit) were.

Tozzi came into Sid's bar loaded for bear.

"Okay, you son of a bitch! Either you tell me where I can find Joey, or you tell me how to get in touch with his uncle. One or the other. No more screwing around. I got two hotheads in New York who want their money by the end of the week or else. And the *or else* is your ass. And believe me when I tell you, you don't want to be messin' around with them! Those two freaks can be mean. So you better figure out some way for me to get my money so I can pay these guys. Either you put me together with this asshole, or I'm holding you responsible."

"Tozzi, be reasonable. You told me to give your number to anybody who was looking to get someone aced. That's what I did."

"Yeah, but I didn't expect you to hook me up with a pussy. Now let's hear it. Joey or his uncle."

Sid had no choice. He didn't know where Joey was, so he had to talk to the Cantelli people. "Okay, wait here," Sid told him. "I'm gonna try to get in touch with Vinny. He'll tell us what to do."

"Good, go do something! Before you go, pass me that bottle of gin, will ya?" Sid slid the bottle across the bar and went into the back room to call Vinny.

"What the fuck you mean you need to talk to Mr. Cantelli? Nobody talks to him but us," Vinny said. "That's why he's got us. Has this got something to do with Joey? Because if it does, you better start talking to me now."

Sid had made up his mind. He was not going to talk to a flunky. He was in enough deep shit. He wanted to make sure the Cantellis got the right story, not a secondhand version from some cowboy who wanted to

Harry Brooks

be a hero. "Can't do that, Vinny. I need to talk to somebody who has the old man's ear. If he finds out you wouldn't help me . . . well, you know what's gonna happen."

"Prick!" Vinny hollered into the phone. "Okay, stay put. Someone will call you later today."

Sid got crazy. "That's not good enough, you asshole! I got somebody on my ass who needs answers now. And yes, it is about Joey, and I know you guys are looking for him. I gotta talk to someone now."

Silence, then, "All right, all right. I'll get somebody to call you in the next tem minutes."

Tozzi hollered to Sid from the bar, "What's goin' on?"

"Everything's cool, Toz. I got somebody from the Cantelli family calling me back in a couple minutes. Have another drink . . . it's on the house."

In less than ten minutes, Sid received the call he was waiting for. The man spoke in a deep voice that had a serious tone. Like a lawyer maybe.

"Mr. Mastro, my name is Phil Cantor. I work for Mr. Cantelli. I understand you have some information for him regarding his nephew."

"Well, yeah, but it's a little more complicated than that."

"I have time, Mr. Mastro."

"Hey, look, you're making me nervous. Call me Sid. Everybody calls me Sid."

"Okay, Sid, now why don't you tell me what you want me to convey to Mr. Cantelli. I promise you I will repeat it to him as close as I can, word for word."

Sid looked through the doorway to make sure Tozzi couldn't hear him. He was content for the time being drinking the free booze.

"Okay, here goes. A couple weeks ago, Joey comes into the bar and tells me he needs the name of a guy who can . . . you know, somebody who can . . . you know what the hell I mean."

Phil Cantor said, "No, I'm not sure I do, Sid. Why don't you just tell me?"

Sid didn't like the way this guy talked. "How do I know you're who you say you are? How do I know you're not a cop tryin' to trap me?"

"Good thought, Sid. You're a cautious man. But didn't you tell Vinny you wanted to talk to somebody up the ladder? Well, that's me, Sid. So why don't we stop the bullshit and get to it?"

174

"Okay, okay. Joey comes in and wants the name of a hit man. He says the Cantellis want to hit a guy but don't want to use their own people."

"Joey said that?" Phil asked.

"Yeah, he did. I told him I didn't know anybody, and I didn't want to be involved in that kind of shit. I take the numbers and horse bets, that's it, but Joey keeps pushin'. Then I remember this dude who used to come in the bar. He said if anybody was ever looking for a guy to make people disappear, I should give them his name. So I give Joey the guy's name. Next thing I know, Joey sets up a meeting in my place with this guy Tozzi and a guy named Angie. Joey and me know Angie. I try to get out of the meeting, but he insists I stay. Anyhow, Joey tells them the Cantellis want to get rid of this guy Lippincott. That's the guy they shot in New York."

"Yes, I know," Phil said.

"They plan the job, you know set the date, and all that shit. And Tozzi says he needs two more guys to help on the job."

"Do you know who they were?" Phil asked.

"Yeah, Tozzi told me. A guy by the name of Sal Morreti and another guy who Tozzi said was an ex-Green Beret . . . I think his name is Carl something . . . yeah, that's it, Carl Wilson. They called him the Sharpshooter. Both those guys live in New York. Well, the bottom line is, Mr. Cantor, Joey only gave Tozzi half the money. The deal was fifty grand. Joey gave him half up front, twenty-five Gs, and then he disappears. Now Tozzi says I'm on the hook. I ain't got no twenty-five Gs to give him. And I sure as hell don't want to hear from those two kooks in New York. So since the word on the street is you're also looking for Joey, I figured to call you, and maybe we can help each other."

"Let me ask you something, Sid. Don't you think you're an accomplice to these murders? After all, you're the one who gave Joey Tozzi's number."

"Oh shit, you are a cop, ain't you?"

"No, Sid, I'm not a cop. But I am a lawyer, and I work for Mr. Cantelli, just like you do in a way. And I want you to know that you are in a very delicate position. And I think I can help you. However, in order to do that, you have to trust me. You have to tell me everything you know about this."

"Okay, maybe I believe you," Sid said reluctantly. "So what happens now?"

CHAPTER THIRTY-SEVEN

When Phil Cantor told Sid the Cantelli family was going to make good on the twenty-five Gs that Joey owed Tozzi, he couldn't wait to hang up the phone and tell him. Tozzi in turn called the Sharpshooter in New York. "I'm gonna have the money tomorrow, Carl," he told him. "I think I'm gonna go back to Atlantic City after I get the money. I'll call you so we can figure out how I can get your share to you."

The following day, July 2, Sid was sitting in Phil Cantor's office in downtown Chicago. The lawyer told him to be there at ten in the morning, and he would have the twenty-five thousand dollars to give to Tozzi. Sid asked him why Tozzi couldn't go and get the money himself. Why did he have to go? "Because you do," Cantor told him. "Take it or leave it." Sid was not happy about being the bagman, but he wanted this whole thing to be over.

Phil Cantor first went to work for the Cantelli family in 1985 when he was hired to defend Eddie Seccio, the man who was in charge of the Cantelli numbers bank. He was a high-profile Chicago criminal defense lawyer. Although the district attorney thought he had an airtight case against Seccio, after six weeks of pretrial motions, evidence of witness tampering, and having more than half of the State's evidence thrown out, the judge dismissed the case and reprimanded the district attorney's office for lack of preparation. Cantelli was so impressed with him that he put him on an annual retainer and used him to help with a variety of matters. Today, he was handling a very sensitive matter. The old man was paying the balance of the money Joey owed a hit man, plus he had a plan in mind to find the killers he hired. Phil Cantor would know how to handle this.

It was almost eleven o'clock when Phil Cantor's secretary finally ushered Sid into his office. He was on the phone when Sid came in; he put his hand over the mouthpiece and told him to sit down. He pointed to a chair in the front of his desk. The chair faced the window, and the curtains were open just far enough so that the sun was partially in Sid's face. Cantor was a large man, over six feet tall, and he weighed close to two hundred pounds.

He was only fifty years old but looked much older because of his full head of white hair. He sat behind a large desk, the top of which was made from an old church door, mounted on a heavy carved marble base. To make it look even larger, the entire desk sat on a six-inch wooden base, which gave the impression that Cantor was always looking down at whoever was sitting in front of the desk. The setting was designed to intimidate the person sitting there. In Sid's case, he was fully intimidated.

"Good morning, Sid, sorry to keep you waiting. Would you like some coffee?" the lawyer asked while, at the same time, looking for something under the pile of papers on his desk. Sid shook his head no. He just wanted to pick up the money for Tozzi and get the hell out of there. Finding what he was looking for, Cantor smiled and held up a manila envelope for Sid to see. Then he cleared away some of the papers on his desk and placed the envelope in the middle of the desk just out of Sid's reach. Sid didn't have a clue as to what was going on. Cantor picked up the phone and dialed his secretary. "Janet, will you please bring in the $25,000 for Mr. Mastro. And oh yes, bring me the release form he needs to sign. Thank you." He hung up the phone, leaned back in his chair, and stared at Sid. "You okay, Sid?" he asked with a smile.

"Yeah, sure . . . shouldn't I be? Something goin' on I don't know?" Sid asked, now visibly very nervous.

"No, not at all," Cantor said.

Then Sid asked, "What kind of release I need to sign? All I want to do is pick up the money for Tozzi. Why I got to sign a release?"

"Sid, relax. It's just a formality. After all, we're turning over a lot of money to you. You can understand that, can't you?"

"Yeah yeah, I guess so," Sid answered, sorry now that he agreed to be the bagman. Shit, how did he let himself get so involved. That goddamn Joey; it's all his fault.

Cantor leaned forward in his chair, reached for the envelope he had put in the middle of his desk, opened it, and said, "Tell you what, Sid, how about we play a little game while we're waiting for my secretary to bring in the money?"

"What kind of game?"

"One where you can take home $10,000 for yourself. How does that sound?"

Sid was really nervous now. What the hell was going on? Something wasn't right. He wanted to get up from his chair and get the hell out of there, but he was too scared to move. He was out of his league here.

"Okay, Sid, here's how it works. To start with, the $10,000 in this envelope is yours. I'm giving it to you." Cantor showed him the money in the envelope. "Now here's the tricky part. I'm going to ask you a couple questions. If you give me the right answers, I won't take back any of your money. However, if you give me the wrong answer, I'll take some money away from you. How much I take depends on the question. Sounds easy, Sid?"

Sid nodded.

"Okay then, let's get started. First question. How would you like to help clean up this mess that Joey caused, which includes finding Sal Morreti and Carl Wilson, the other two men in Tozzi's crew?"

Sid was confused. "Whadayou mean 'help clean up this mess'? And find those two guys? I don't know where they are. I only know they're from New York. How can I help?"

"Wrong answer, Sid. That cost you $1,000," the lawyer said as he took $1,000 from the envelope.

Sid summoned up all his courage and said, "I don't know what kind of game you're playing, Mr. Cantor, but I don't like it. Now why don't you give me Tozzi's money and let me get out of here?"

"You can leave anytime you want, Sid. But you don't get Tozzi's money until we finish our little game."

Sid leaned forward in his chair. "Okay, Mr. Cantor, what is it you want me to do? Just tell me."

The lawyer smiled, put the $1,000 back in the envelope, and tossed it to Sid. "That's more like it," he said, at the same time calling his secretary and instructing her to bring in the $25,000 for Tozzi. "Now here is what we want you to do."

CHAPTER THIRTY-EIGHT

Driving home, Sid thought about what Cantelli's lawyer said to him: "You need to find out exactly where and when Tozzi is going to meet Morreti and Wilson. You also have to find out where he plans on staying when he goes to Atlantic City. Whatever you hear about Joey, you pass on to Vinny. He's going to call you tomorrow and ask you some questions about Angie. Give him straight answers. Tell him whatever he wants to know. Now the Cantellis are going to give you a bonus. You know about Lippincott's brother. How Joey told you that he would take revenge for his brother's murder. Well, Sid, like it or not, you are on his short list. Now so long as you help us get what we need, we believe we can get you a 'pass.' Don't ask me how. You don't want to know. These two shootings have taken on a life of their own, and since you are the one who gave Tozzi's number to Joey . . . well, I'm sure you understand. One last thing, Sid, just in case you get any crazy ideas about talking to the authorities, you and I now have an attorney-client relationship. That means this conversation doesn't leave this office."

The more he thought about it, the scarier it got. How were they going to get him a 'pass' with Lippincott's brother? What was the connection. And why did they want to know all this stuff? He knew damn well why. They were going to whack these guys. That had to be it. And he was going to be the guy setting them up! "Jesus Christ!" he said out loud as he ran a stop sign. *That's all I need now is to get stopped by a cop*, he thought.

CHAPTER THIRTY-NINE

It was July 4. PJ had been in Chicago almost a week, and he still didn't have any more information then the day he arrived. As far as he knew, Tozzi was still out of town; and he didn't know how to find his partner, Angie. He decided he would call Joseph Cantelli after breakfast. Unless he had some more information for him, he would return to New York and go to work on finding the other two shooters. This was not like in the past when he knew the location of his target. Back then, he had the benefit of both the CIA and Israeli intelligence agencies.

When he came out of the shower, his cell phone was beeping, letting him know he had two voice mail messages. One was from Anita. She just wanted to know how he was. He had not spoken to her since he left New York. When he heard the sound of her voice, he realized that he missed her. That was a good thing . . . he thought. The other message was from Phil Cantor. The message simply said, "We have a mutual friend in Chicago who asked me to call you. I have the information he promised you. Please call me at 312-555-6500."

Two hours later, PJ was sitting in a restaurant at the foot of the Chicago River. When PJ returned his call, Phil Cantor suggested they meet there for an early lunch. When the lawyer arrived, the owner greeted him with a hug and showed him to PJ's table. It was not quite eleven o'clock, and they were the only customers.

After the lawyer sat down, the waiter handed them menus, asked them what they wanted to drink, and then left. Cantor introduced himself to PJ and thanked him for coming on such short notice.

"I have some good news for you, Mr. Gould," Cantor said.

"My father is Mr. Gould," PJ said with a smile. "Please call me PJ."

The lawyer nodded. "First off, I want you to know that our mutual friend appreciates your understanding regarding a certain young man."

"Have you heard from him yet?" PJ asked.

"No, but we would expect to hear something soon. He is bound to need money wherever he is."

The more PJ thought about it, the less he liked the fact he agreed to give Joey a pass. One of the first things he learned when he joined the Sayeret Matkal was that everyone was responsible for their actions. And when revenge was taken, it was taken against everyone who played a part in the wrongdoing. In this case, Joey was directly involved. He gave the order. When PJ agreed not to take any action against Joey, his rationalization was he was getting the four men who actually did the shooting in exchange for allowing Joey's uncle to punish him accordingly. No matter, he wished he hadn't agreed.

The lawyer continued, "Now to continue with the good news. Do you know a man named Sid Mastro?"

"No, I don't think I do. Why?"

"He owns a bar on the South Side. He also operates a sports book, and he lays off most of the bets he takes with our friend. We have learned he was the one responsible for giving the names of the shooters to our friend's nephew."

"Well, there's another name to add to my list," PJ said with absolutely no emotion.

The waiter brought coffee, and the two men waited until he left before continuing their conversation.

Cantor took a sip of his coffee and then leaned over the table. "It's not going to be that easy, my friend." PJ knew he wasn't going to like what he was about to hear. Cantor continued, "He is also the one who came to us with the information you want."

"And why would he do that?" PJ asked.

Cantor then went on to tell PJ about Sid's call to Vinny and what happened after that. "So you see, PJ, we have already made a deal with him. And between you and me, the poor bastard really had nothing to do with this. He was put in a no-win situation by our missing young man." PJ was becoming irritated with the way this guy was pussyfooting around, not using any names.

"Look, Phil, you and I are both professionals. We're in different professions, but nevertheless, professionals. If you're worried that I'm wearing a wire, you can relax. I'm not."

The lawyer smiled. "You come right to the point, don't you?"

"I thought it best we clear the air. And while we're at it, there's something else bothering me. I'm not accustomed to making deals about who lives and who dies. I do what I have to do and let the chips fall where they may. Now with all due respect to our . . . mutual friend, he seems to want to make those decisions. I agreed with Joey. I don't know that I can agree to let this Sid character off the hook. I need to hear what he has to say before I give you my answer."

Phil Cantor took an envelope out of his pocket and handed it to PJ. "After you read this," he said, pointing to the envelope, "I am sure you will agree our friend Sid has given you the information you are looking for."

CHAPTER FORTY

Six o'clock, July 5, 1995, Saturday night

The first target on PJ's list was Angie.

Angie had returned home to his small apartment on State Street at five thirty. He had to get dressed in a hurry for his Saturday night job as a waiter at Scilolia's, an Italian restaurant in Old Town. One of his buddies, also a waiter there, was picking him up at six fifteen. This was a routine Angie followed every Saturday night—and it was a ritual PJ was well aware of after studying Sid's notes. He had given PJ the layout of Angie's digs; and PJ found it would be no problem scaling the vertical ladder, which dangled from the fire escape to the alley alongside the three-story tenement, then climbing to the third floor and surprising Angie in his "boudoir."

And that was precisely what PJ did. He caught Angie, with his bow tie on and his pants down. He was standing in front of the dresser mirror in his shorts, combing his hair, when PJ sneaked up the fire escape and approached the window of Angie's bedroom. Crouched on one knee, he peeked into the room. Angie was trying to make his part as straight and perfect as he could. Several times he combed out his hair and started over.

He raised the loaded .38-caliber revolver in his hand and brought the sight up to his eye. Through the closed window, he aimed the barrel carefully at the center of Angie's chest. He squeezed the trigger. The bullet tore into Angie's right breast and spun him around. PJ could hear him cry out in pain and shout, "Son of a bitch!" PJ hit him with a second shot in almost the same place. Angie fell to the floor without making another sound. PJ put the .38 back in his pocket and made his way down the ladder. He walked the two blocks to where he parked the rental car, looked around to make sure no one saw him, then got in the car, and drove to the airport. One down, three to go.

CHAPTER FORTY-ONE

On the plane ride from Chicago to New York, PJ once again looked over Sid's notes. He did a good job. Not only did he describe each of the four killers, he also outlined their daily habits. Evidently, after he gave Tozzi the money, he was able to get him to talk about Morreti and Wilson, the two shooters who lived in New York. It was like he was bragging about how much he knew about them. He told Sid how he planned to "break the bank" in Atlantic City. "I think I'm gonna move there. I like the beach and the ocean," he said to him. He told Sid whatever he wanted to know. As far as Angie was concerned, Sid knew him well enough that he didn't need anything from Tozzi. Sid made sure to mention Tozzi told him Wilson and his friend Morreti were very weird guys. Whatever that meant. PJ smiled to himself. *Thank you, Sid.*

He folded the notes and put them back in pocket; then he leaned back in his seat and tried to sleep.

When the plane touched down at JFK in New York, PJ was sleeping. The pretty young stewardess who had been trying to get PJ to ask her for her number gently tapped him on the shoulder. "Mr. Gould, we're here." PJ opened his eyes and gave her a smile. "Thanks," he said

Then she leaned over and whispered, "We lay over here until tomorrow night. I don't have any plans—"

Before she finished, he put his hand on her arm and said, "Any other time, I would have asked you to marry me by now. But unfortunately, I'm on a tight schedule. So I'm going to have to take a pass. Believe me, it's my loss."

The stewardess smiled and said, "You are a very sweet man. She is really lucky to have you." And then she went about her business of telling people to put their seats in an upright position and stow all of their belongings. All PJ could do was smile and think what could have been.

He thought about calling Anita to tell her he was flying in, but he knew she would have insisted that her car pick him up and that he stay at her apartment. This was not the time. Right now, he was in a different "zone."

After picking up his rental car, he drove out of the airport on to the Long Island Expressway and headed for New York. By the time he got to the Plaza Hotel, it was past midnight. All he wanted to do was shower and get into bed. And that's exactly what he did. His cell phone woke him up at eight o'clock. It was Phil Cantor.

"Good morning, PJ, hope I didn't wake you. But I have some information for you."

"No, that's okay. What's up?"

"We heard from Joey. That is . . . our mutual friend heard from him."

"Oh, where is he?"

"He's in New York. He wouldn't tell us exactly where. He did tell us he's staying with some girl. We couldn't get much more out of him."

"Why did he call?" PJ asked.

"Well, first of all, he said that he wanted to apologize for the trouble he caused. Then he told our friend he planned to stay in New York for a while. He didn't ask for money, so whoever he's staying with must be footing the bills."

"Unless he took some petty cash with him when he left," PJ said.

"Good point. But that's not our problem. I just thought you would want to know we heard from him."

"Thanks."

"By the way, if I can ask, where are you these days?"

"You can ask, but I think it's best if you don't know," PJ said.

"That's fine. Keep in touch. And, PJ . . . good luck."

He then called room service and ordered breakfast. They said it would take about forty-five minutes. That was fine. He had time to shave and shower.

Room service knocked on his door just about the same time he came out of the shower. He put on the Plaza Hotel terry cloth robe and opened the door. The coffee smelled good and made him think about Anita. He didn't know why. Maybe because it was a nice peaceful smell.

PJ looked at his watch, 9:15. *Too early to call Anita? What the hell.*

Chapter Forty-Two

Anita told PJ to meet her at Le Cirque for lunch. She was attending a charity auction a block away from the restaurant and would be there no later than twelve thirty.

"If you're tied up—" PJ started when Anita interrupted him.

"Are you out of your mind? You be there or else," she said with a giggle.

"You got yourself a date," he said.

PJ arrived at Le Cirque at twelve o'clock. He was glad he called her. Now that he was going to see her, he realized how much he missed not seeing her. He told the maitre d' who he was meeting and was greeted with an expansive smile, then escorted to a table in a quiet corner of the restaurant. Before leaving, the maitre d' recommended the venison with berries. PJ thanked him and sat down to wait for Anita. He looked around the restaurant, which was full of fat men in suits and ties and fancy women dripping jewelry. It took him a minute to focus. And then he thought about the reason he was in New York in the first place. It was to kill two men. He bet there wasn't another man, or woman for that matter, in the room who could ever imagine doing something like that. He was only there a few minutes when Anita arrived. The maitre d' greeted her with a polite hug and ushered her to his table. She didn't look like the other women who were there. She was dressed in a Chanel two-piece tailored suit with a fluttery pleated skirt and a coral crepe de chine jacket over a tank top in beige and gold Lurex that showed off her womanly figure. The only jewelry she wore was a small diamond bracelet and a single strand of pearls. She was a beautiful woman.

"Hello, stranger, I thought you lost my number," she said as the maitre d' pulled out the chair for her.

He put two menus on the table, then asked them what they wanted to drink. They both wanted coffee. "Right away," he said as he signaled the order to the waiter and then left.

"You look very nice," PJ said, trying not to be too corny.

"Thank you," she replied and then felt herself blushing. She hoped that was not going to be a habit when she was with him. "So tell me, what have you been up to, or shouldn't I ask?" she said, cupping her chin in her hands with her elbows on the table.

"Nothing you would be interested in," he said just as the waiter delivered their coffee.

"Oh, you would be surprised what interests me."

The waiter stood nearby, waiting to see if they were ready to order.

"Tell you what, how about we order lunch, and then I'll tell you anything you want to know?" PJ said with a smile.

"Why don't I believe you?" she said, opening the menu.

He watched her eat. She had ordered the beef in sour cream sauce, with dumplings and cranberries on the side. "You like your food, don't you?" he said approvingly.

And then it happened again. She felt herself blushing. She put down her fork and leaned over the table and said, "Okay, let's get this over with."

PJ looked at her. "Get what over with?" he asked with a puzzled look on his face.

"This thing you have about you that makes me blush like a schoolgirl. Is it some sort of magic power? Come on, let me in on it."

PJ started to laugh. She was fun to be with. He hated for the lunch to end. But he had work to do, and until that was finished, he would have to put his feelings for Anita on hold. Anita knew without asking that whatever it was he was doing, she could not be a part of. She only hoped that he would be safe.

The busboy arrived to clear their plates, sparing both of them the temptation to say out loud what they were thinking. As soon as the busboy finished clearing the table, the waiter came to take their order for dessert. Anita asked to see the trolley.

Anita chose a piece of chocolate gateau while PJ settled for the apple tart.

By the time the waiter had, with great flair, served their choices of dessert and delivered them cups of steaming dark coffee, they had talked about everything from their childhood to current politics. The one thing PJ made sure not to mention was his secret past. A professional assassin.

Talking to her was easy. She told him about the summers at her grandfather's farm, about the chickens and the fruit trees and how she learned to milk a cow. He told her that was difficult for him to picture. She said, "Take me to a farm. I'll show you." They both laughed. Neither of them had any illusions at this point in their relationship. They had just become good friends. Or at least that was what they told each other.

When they left the restaurant, he kissed her on the cheek and once again asked her to be patient and trust him. She wanted him to hold her and tell her that he didn't want to leave her. But that was not going to happen. At least not today.

The doorman signaled to Anita's driver who had parked the black Mercedes sedan nearby. The driver moved quickly to open the door, no waiting for taxis. PJ watched as she got into the car. She turned toward him and said, "You do have my phone number, don't you?"

"Now you're going to make me blush," he said and threw her a kiss. The doorman closed the car door, and PJ watched the limo disappear in traffic. *Another opportunity lost*, he thought.

CHAPTER FORTY-THREE

July 10, 1995, Wednesday night

During the next four days, PJ staked out the apartment where Carl Wilson and Sal Morreti lived. It was on the lower West Side, on Eighth Avenue between Twenty-ninth and Thirtieth streets. It was on the second floor overhead of a fruit and produce store. The neighborhood was inhabited by pimps, both male and female prostitutes, lesbians, transvestites, and a few scattered drug addicts and child molesters. The New York City Police could operate a full-time crime cleanup program here for the next ten years and still not clean up all the shit in this twenty-square block area. He kept referring to Sid's notes. The description of the two men he wanted helped enormously. Between that and asking around, it wasn't too long before PJ had the two men in his sights.

About nine o'clock when it began to turn dark, PJ went to the building where Wilson and Morreti lived. It was a smelly neighborhood, and their particular building smelled like broccoli. And PJ hated broccoli. He looked at the diagram he had drawn one last time. He wanted to make sure he got it right.

He entered the building where his two targets lived and waited in a dark corner near Wilson's apartment door. About twenty-five minutes later, the two men came down from Morreti's apartment above and walked straight to Wilson's apartment. PJ had to hold his breath so the two men wouldn't know he was there. Wilson was tall and looked like he was in good shape. He had on one of those muscle shirts that showed off his biceps, in his case, full of tattoos. Morreti was a little shorter and much thinner, and they both appeared to be under the influence of something other than warm milk.

A few minutes later, they came out of the apartment with a mahogany-colored child. She was wearing a pink nightgown that was torn in the rear. She had a Kewpie doll face and seemed still half asleep as she was led to the stairwell. PJ was almost sick to his stomach. He wanted to blast them right there but didn't want to frighten the child.

The three moved in orderly fashion very much like a ritual. PJ shook his head in disgust. He could wait no longer. He walked up to the two men. He flashed a laundry ticket and his gun. "Excuse me, gentlemen, I'm from the Treasury Department. I wanna talk to you. It's nothing serious, so don't try anything or make me shoot you for no reason. Let's all stay calm."

Morreti and Wilson were in another world. Their eyes were glazed, and their pupils dilated.

"Where the hell you come from?" one asked, startled.

"Please walk upstairs quietly. It'll only take a minute. I think you have some money coming to you. Have you applied for assistance lately? I'm from the Treasury Department." PJ wanted them calm, so he repeated himself.

"Treasury Department?" one of them asked. "We never applied for any financial assistance. Okay, what the fuck do you wanna know about our financial status? We ain't no damn fools, so get on with it."

"Lets just go to your apartment and talk about it. I have a couple of checks made out to you."

"Sounds good. How much money is involved?"

"First, why don't we send this little kid back to her apartment?" PJ said as he took the little girl's hand and gently moved her away from the two men. "Now you go back to bed, sweetheart. Everything will be okay. Good night." Without saying a word, the little girl smiled at PJ and walked back to her apartment.

"What the fuck is goin' on?" Wilson shouted as he attempted to grab the little girl's hand but was blocked by PJ.

"Relax, pal. That's not going to happen," PJ said, pointing to the little girl.

The drugs were still working their magic for Wilson and Morreti, which made it easier for PJ to nudge them toward the stairs. "Okay, guys, up we go," he said, and they started mechanically up the stairs.

He followed them to their apartment, holding his automatic by his side.

"Hey, you got some pad. It's beautiful in here," PJ said, casting an icy smile around the room.

Suddenly, he saw another person, moving around in the back near the bedrooms. It was a girl who looked like a guy. She seemed very nervous. She was black with her hair shaved close to her head.

Shit, PJ thought, *I had not planned on this.* Then the idea began to take shape in his mind that they were bringing the mahogany child for this black butch to play with. Slowly, his blood turned to vinegar.

The two men were beginning to sober up. "He ain't got no goddamn welfare money for us," Wilson said. "Okay, man, what's this all about? What kind of questions you want to ask us? And who the fuck are you?"

PJ quickly checked all around. He had been forced to devise a new plan of action. He pointed his gun at the two men and ordered them to sit down on the couch. Then he told the transvestite to come join the two men on the couch. She moved very slowly, cursing at PJ in a low voice as she made her way to the couch. She was stoned out of her mind. The two men didn't understand what was happening. The butch's eyes seemed to spread wide with fear. PJ made his decision. Get rid of these two scumbags and get the hell out of there. He looked at the transvestite. What was he going to do about her? Could she identify him? *Not in a million years*, he decided.

PJ grabbed Wilson by the neck and shoved him toward the bedroom. With his gun in hand, he ordered Morreti to get up and follow his buddy. As the two men got near the bed, very quickly and unexpectedly, he placed his gun against Wilson's neck and pulled the trigger. Wilson fell facedown on the bed, and in seconds, the bed was covered with his blood.

Morreti turned around to see what was going on. PJ got up close, pointed the gun to his chest, and fired two quick shots. Morreti's eyes rolled white in his head, and he fell to the floor. PJ wiped the gun clean of his prints and then placed it in Morreti's hand first and then in Wilson's hand. Then he threw it on the floor. Let the cops try and figure how this one went down.

PJ walked into the living room and saw the black butch lying on the couch, a dirty hypodermic needle still halfway in her arm. She had overdosed. No need to worry now if she could identify him. He had really wanted to ask her, "What were you going to do with that kid? She's only maybe ten or eleven years old. What is wrong with you people?" But it was over. PJ was sick to his stomach. He had to get out of there.

When he got to the first floor, he saw the mahogany child sitting on the floor outside of what he assumed was her apartment. Then he realized, the door was locked, and she didn't have a key. He walked over and bent down next to her.

"What's your name, honey?"

"Melody."

"Is this where you live?"

She nodded yes.

"Is your mother home?"

"My mother is dead," she said with tears in her eyes.

"Who takes care of you?"

"Uncle Carl."

PJ had to hold his breath to prevent him from vomiting right there. "Those dirty sons of bitches," he said under his breath.

Then he took the little girl's hand and said, "Why don't we get you dressed, and you can come with me? We'll find you someplace nice to live. How does that sound?"

She smiled.

PJ looked at the apartment door and decided a good kick would knock it open. He was right. He couldn't believe what he saw. Empty beer bottles, trash all around, dirty dishes in the sink. The place smelled so bad, he had to hold his breath. He asked Melody where her clothes were. She took him into the bedroom and pointed to an old bureau. The drawers were half open, and different articles of clothing were half in and half out. He told her to get dressed as quickly as she could so they could leave. She obeyed like a robot. *What a life this kid has had*, he thought. When he left the apartment building with Melody, he thought to himself, *Where the hell am I going to take her?* There was only one place.

CHAPTER FORTY-FOUR

That same night

It was close to midnight when he called Anita. He told her he was on his way to her apartment, and he had a little girl with him who needed a place to stay tonight.

"I don't understand, PJ. Where did you find this poor child? Where are her parents?"

"I'll explain when I get there. Leave word with the doorman to let me in." How was he going to explain? *"I just killed two men and saved this child from being raped and sodomized by a doped-up black transvestite."* That should pretty much sum it up.

When they arrived at her apartment, Anita greeted them dressed in a silk robe, her hair tied up in a bun. No matter what she wore, she looked beautiful. "This is Melody," PJ said as he ushered the little girl into Anita's apartment. She had fallen asleep in the car ride over and had trouble even now keeping her eyes open. Anita took the little girl's hand and walked her to the sofa, not saying a word about the way she looked or the color of her skin. *How many women would do that?* PJ wondered.

"Are you hungry, sweetheart?" Anita asked while brushing the little girl's hair back with one hand and holding her shoulder with the other.

"No, thank you, but I do have to pee," Melody said.

PJ looked at Anita who looked back and then started to laugh. "Well, I guess you better show her where the bathroom is so she can pee," he said, starting to feel a little better about what was happening.

Anita showed Melody the bathroom and then returned to the living room. PJ was sitting on the couch, his head resting on the pillows.

"Looks like you had a rough night," Anita said, standing with her arms folded in front of her.

"You should see the other guy," PJ answered.

"I bet."

"I really appreciate this, Anita. I didn't know where else to take her."

"Are you going to tell me what the hell this is all about? I mean, who is she?" Where does she live? You don't just show up with a little girl in the middle of the night without some logical reason."

"You are right, Anita, you don't. Unfortunately, there is no logical explanation. At least not right now. She's been living with some man she calls Uncle Carl. He has been abusing her for I don't know how long. He is not her uncle. Believe me. He is your worst nightmare. Some things happened at her apartment tonight that prevent her from going back. At least tonight. Maybe never, I don't know. You were the only person I could think of. I'm sorry."

"No, by all means, I'm flattered that you thought of me."

"Look, if you can't—"

"I am kidding. Bad joke. Of course, she can stay here as long as she wants. Where are her parents?"

"My mother is dead. I'm not really sure, but I think my father is dead too. I don't think I ever saw him. I live with my Uncle Carl," Melody said as she walked back into the room. "This nice man helped me escape. I don't want to go back there. They are mean men. They always hurt me. They make me do things I don't like. Can I stay here please?" Melody stood there, tears running down her cheeks.

Anita ran over and put her arms around the child.

"Yes, you can stay here. You can stay as long as you like."

PJ just watched. What the hell was going on? How was this all going to play out? He really was getting too old for this kind of stuff. How did he go from a poker game, to killing three men, to becoming the apparent savior of little children.

Anita told her housekeeper to help Melody get ready for bed. She gave the little girl a warm bath, managed somehow to cut down a pair of Anita's pajamas for Melody to sleep in, and then tucked her in bed in one of the two guest rooms. The little girl was asleep before the housekeeper turned off the light.

"Anything else, Mrs. Lippincott?" the housekeeper asked Anita before she went back to her room.

"No, Anna, but do me a favor. Make sure I know as soon as she gets up in the morning."

"Yes, Mrs. Lippincott. Good night. And good night to you, Mr. Gould."

"Good night, Anna."

Anita sat down in the chair opposite PJ, leaned forward and said, "Why don't you stay here tonight? You look exhausted. We can talk about this in the morning."

PJ didn't put up an argument. "Maybe I will," he said.

Anita got up and held out her hand to him to help him get up from the sofa.

"Thanks," he said as he took her hand. There they were. Just standing in the living room, holding each other's hand. He leaned forward and kissed her very gently on the cheek. Her face was warm. He wanted to grab her and hold her and tell her that he never wanted to leave. But she didn't give him time.

"I think we've had enough excitement for one night, Mr. Gould. Why don't you get some sleep? I'll see you in the morning." And once again, another opportunity lost.

CHAPTER FORTY-FIVE

The following morning

When PJ woke up, he could smell the coffee brewing. He slipped into his pants, put on his shirt, and followed the smell of the coffee. Anita was sitting on the patio. He was surprised to see her up and dressed so early. She was wearing a Dior suit she had bought in Paris when she and Walter were there in April. The suit was a rich deep blue that complemented her pale azure eyes, brought out the creamy texture of her skin, and the highlights in her straight light brown hair. In her ears were a pair of diamond earrings. On her lapel was a diamond leopard with sapphire spots and ruby eyes.

"Good morning. Looks like you got up before breakfast," PJ said while pouring himself a cup of coffee. Anna came in and asked him what he wanted for breakfast.

"Nothing, thank you, Anna. Coffee is just fine. Is Melody still sleeping?"

"Yes, I just looked in on her, and she is sleeping like a baby. Poor child. I can't begin to imagine what she has been through."

"I know, Anna, thanks."

He put down his coffee cup and looked at Anita. She was radiant. He thought how lucky Walter was to have been married to her.

"So what's the occasion? All dressed up so early in the morning."

There she was . . . blushing again. "Oh, you mean this old thing?" she said jokingly, pointing to the stunning outfit she was wearing. "I wouldn't call this all dressed up. Well, maybe a little. Anyhow, I'm the chairperson of Children of Our World. It's a charity that funds educational grants to deserving children whose parents can't afford to send them to college. We're having a meeting this morning to approve a couple of scholarships, and I really need to attend. If I wasn't the chairperson, I would have bailed out. But I'm sure I'll be back by lunchtime. What are your plans? Can you stay until I get back? We have to talk about Melody."

"Whew, slow down. I can probably hang around until you get back, but as far as Melody is concerned, I think we need to call the authorities and let them decide what to do about her."

Anita looked surprised. "Authorities! What authorities? The State welfare? Who? We can't do that, PJ. That poor child looks like she has been to hell and back. We have to help her. According to her, she has no parents—for sure, no mother. And this Uncle Carl person, we sure as hell can't send her back to him. I assume he's still there, wherever 'there' is. Was it a house? Tell me . . . exactly where was she living, PJ? She said you saved her from those bad men. What bad men? PJ, if I'm going to help you, I have to know what it is you're doing . . . shit, I'm going to be late," she said, looking at her watch. She got up from the table and stood next to him.

"PJ, promise me one thing. You won't do anything until I get back."

He stood up and put his hands on her shoulders. "I promise."

"Good. I already made a couple of calls to get her some decent clothes. Anna will know what to do when they get here. In the meantime, you can entertain her until I come home . . . When I get back, we'll talk."

"Okay," he said as she turned to leave. Before she walked out the door, he said, "Anita, I appreciate what you're doing, but let's be careful we don't get too involved in Melody's life."

She stopped, looked back at him, and said, "PJ, we already are involved in her life."

Anita was only gone a short time when Anna came in to tell him that Melody was awake. "I'm going to make the child some pancakes Mr. Gould, why don't you have some?"

"Thanks, Anna, that sounds like a good idea."

A few minutes later, PJ and Melody were sitting in the kitchen watching Anna make pancakes. Melody had finished a large glass of orange juice and was now working on a glass of milk and a piece of chocolate cake while waiting for the pancakes. She was a very pretty child with big brown sad eyes. Suddenly, she stopped eating and said to PJ, "Where's your wife?" Anna turned around and let out a chuckle.

"You mean Mrs. Lippincott. She's not my wife. We're just friends."

"Oh, is that her name, Mrs. Lippincott?" she asked.

"Yup, that's her name."

"Should I call her Aunt Anita?" she said, starting to work on the chocolate again.

PJ looked confused. "Why do you ask that?"

"Uncle Carl always told me to call the ladies Aunt."

That dirty son of a bitch, PJ thought to himself. "Sure, you can call her Aunt Anita. I think she would like that."

"What should I call you?" she asked. "I like what Aunt Anita calls you, PJ. I think that's funny."

"Then you call me PJ too. How's that?"

Melody stopped eating her cake again and looked at him. "Am I going to live here now?" she asked.

Anna saved the day. "Pancakes are ready," she said and winked at PJ who gave her a thumbs-up.

While they were having breakfast, a messenger arrived with the clothes that Anita ordered for Melody. She knew the store manager at Bloomingdale's and called him at home. She told him what she needed and had no doubt in her mind he would take care of it. As soon as they finished eating, Anna suggested to Melody they go unpack her new clothes and decide what she was going to wear today. Melody was thrilled. PJ watched her and thought to himself, *She is acting just like any normal ten-year-old.* However, he knew she wasn't like any other ten-year-old. Not by a long shot.

Melody couldn't wait to run back into the living room to show PJ her new outfit. "PJ, look at these jeans! Aren't they cool?"

"They sure are," he said, wishing that Anita would hurry up and come home. He was not used to entertaining a ten-year-old. Besides which, he had a lot of other things on his mind this day. He had to find Tozzi.

Anna and Melody were in the den watching TV. He looked in at the mahogany child and wondered what was going to happen to her. How strange is life? One day, this child was living in hell; and the next day, she is watching television in a luxury apartment on Seventy-ninth Street and Park Avenue. Funny how quickly the cards change.

Melody saw him standing at the doorway, watching them. "Do you want to watch TV with us?" she asked matter-of-factly.

He smiled. "No thanks. But tell you what, when your show is over, how would you like to tell me a little bit about yourself? You know, like where you go to school, what you like to do, stuff like that. How does that sound?"

"I don't go to school," she said without looking away from the TV.

"Really?" PJ said. "Well, what do you do all day?" he asked, almost afraid to hear her answer.

"Mostly just watch TV. Sometime Uncle Carl takes me to the movies, but I don't like that . . . he would . . . oh, look at that," she said, pointing to something happening on TV and evidently not wanting to tell what Uncle Carl did to her in the dark movie theater.

PJ could feel the anger build up in his whole body. *That dirty rotten son of a bitch*, he thought to himself.

When the television program ended, Anna told Melody she had some chores to do and suggested she sit and talk to PJ. "Can I please have some of those chocolate chip cookies first?" she asked, following PJ into the living room.

"So here we are," he said, not really sure how to begin. He didn't want to make her feel uncomfortable asking questions, probably most of which she would rather not answer.

"You know something, Melody, I don't even know your last name."

She laughed like that was supposed to be funny. "It's Walker."

"That's a very nice name. Melody Walker. So, Melody Walker, what should we talk about? I know, let's talk about your friends. Do you have any friends?"

She put her feet up under her as she settled in at the corner of the couch. "I have a social worker. Does that count?"

"It sure does," PJ answered. "Why don't you tell me about her?" *Out of the mouth of babes*, he thought.

"She's okay, I guess. Her name is Ms. Whitman. I think she's kinda sweet on Uncle Carl. Sometime when she comes to the apartment, they go into his bedroom to talk. She told me it's grown-up talk. That's why they have to close the door. One time, she came out crying. She told me never to tell anyone.

"She said I should go to school, but Uncle Carl never took me. Once she left me some books to read. They were really neat." And she wasn't even out of breath.

PJ was surprised she could read. *How did she learn?* he wondered.

"How often does Ms. Whitman come to see you?" he asked.

She put her finger to her head, thinking. "Hmmm, I can't remember. Can I tell you a secret, PJ?"

"Sure you can, sweetheart."

"Well . . . they told me never to tell anybody, and if I did, I would go straight to hell. But I don't think that counts if I tell you, right?"

"Right," he said, afraid to hear what she was about to tell him.

"Okay, one day, when she came to see us, Uncle Carl was sleeping. I think he had too much to drink."

PJ smiled and said, "You were probably right."

She continued, "Here's the part I'm not supposed to tell. Ms. Whitman said we should get undressed and get in bed with him and surprise him."

PJ had difficulty containing his anger. "And did you get in bed with him?" he asked.

"No, I told Ms. Whitman I didn't want to do that. I told her he sometimes comes in my room at night and makes me take off my jammies and then he . . . you know, touches me all over."

"What did she say to that?"

"She said I must have been dreaming. I wasn't dreaming, PJ."

"I know, honey. But that's all in the past. Tell me, how long have you lived with"—the words stuck in his throat—"your Uncle Carl?"

"A long time. My mother used to live there too. She died though. She was always mean to me too. I wanted to run away, but Uncle Carl told me the police would catch me and lock me up in a dark place. I wouldn't like that, would you?"

"No, I wouldn't like that either." He stored the social worker's name in his memory bank. He planned on talking to her at some point. "I'll bet you have a lot of pictures when you were little," he said, hoping he didn't hit a nerve.

"Yup, I keep them in my safe box with my other good stuff. Uncle Carl doesn't know I have it. Can we go back and get it? Then I can show you the pictures." Suddenly, she sat up, put her hands in her lap, and said, "Did you kill Uncle Carl? I don't care if you did. It's okay."

PJ felt the blood rush to his head. "Why would you say such a thing, Melody?"

"Because I saw you had a gun in your hand when you made him and Uncle Sal go upstairs. And you looked angry at them. Really, if you did, I don't care."

Harry Brooks

PJ was at a loss for words. This was not good. He leaned forward and took hold of Melody's hands. "No, sweetheart, I didn't kill anybody. However, I told them they had to go away. I didn't want them to hurt you anymore. They agreed to leave and never come back. You never have to worry about them hurting you ever again."

Melody jumped up from the couch and into PJ's arms. "Oh, thank you, PJ. I love you so much!"

He sat there with his arms around the mahogany child, tears running down his cheeks. That didn't happen very often, if ever.

Anita was back home before noon. She saw Anna and Melody in the kitchen baking something or other. That brought a smile to her face. "Hey, ladies, looks like you're having a good time."

"We're making brownies, Aunt Anita," Melody said without turning around.

Anita stood there, not sure what to say. Anna looked at her and shrugged her shoulders as if to say "I don't know where she got that." She started to walk away from the kitchen, wondering where PJ was. As if reading her mind, Melody called out, "PJ is in his room lying down! Do you want some brownies when they're finished?" She managed all in one breath.

"Sure," she answered, totally confused as to what had happened while she was away.

She went to the guest room. PJ was lying on the bed, his hands behind his head, just staring at the ceiling. "Are you okay?" she asked.

"Define *okay*."

"I guess it's time we talked," she said, sitting down on the side of the bed.

Twenty minutes later, they were sitting in a coffee shop around the corner from her apartment house. PJ had suggested they go someplace where they could talk in private. The waiter delivered coffee and asked them if they wanted to order lunch. "Give us a couple minutes," PJ told him.

The waiter said, "Okay," and left.

"So it seems like you had a very eventful morning," Anita said.

"Guess you can describe it that way," he answered. "I'll tell you one thing—that kid is something else."

"By that you mean what?" she asked.

208

"Oh, not in a bad way. She is very sharp. And considering what she has been through, she's still a little girl, if you know what I mean?"

"Yes, I think I do," she said. "So tell me, what did you two talk about while I was gone?"

PJ proceeded to tell her all the things Melody told him, leaving out her question about him killing Uncle Carl! He told her about Ms. Whitman. He didn't think it would be too difficult to locate that piece-of-shit social worker. Once they did that, they should be able to find out more about the mahogany child. He told her about Melody's safe box and that she wanted to go back and get it. "Did you tell her she could?" Anita asked.

"I told her we would try," he said, but he knew that it was not possible.

The waiter returned, and they ordered the special. Tuna on rye. Not very imaginative. Anita waited until the waiter brought their lunch and then decided it was showdown time. She leaned over the table, getting her face as close to PJ as she could. He could see the fire in her eyes.

"Okay, PJ, no more screwing around. What is it you are doing? And how did you end up with Melody? Tell me the truth, PJ."

He knew he had to tell her something. Something that at least resembled the truth.

"Anita, I'm going to tell you some things that I've never told anyone. They are things about my past. And up until the time that Walter was killed, they stayed in my past.

"However, after what happened to Walter and Cindy, my past is now staring me in the face. Walter was right when he told you I worked with the CIA. I also worked with the Israel government. I was in the Sayeret Matkal, which is Israel's elite commando unit. I was involved in some of Israel's most high-profile security missions. I was trained to be proactive. I was also trained to kill. That is why I can't just sit by and do nothing. I know revenge is not the kind of thing you talk about at cocktail parties, but it is what I did for almost twenty years.

"When I finished college and went to Israel, it was just after the Six-Day War. I can't begin to tell you how impressed I was with the people there. Their total commitment to the things that they believed in. Their strong belief of what was right and what was wrong. I wanted to be part of that. There was a certain excitement about what was going on there."

Anita was too shocked to ask any questions. She just sat there and listened.

"I have been trained to do things the system can't do. It is difficult to explain, but over the years, I have developed a sixth sense about the way the bad guys operate. So when Walter and Cindy were killed, I knew immediately I would somehow be able to find the men that killed them. This is not something I planned to happen. Believe me, Anita, I was perfectly happy with my life before this all began. But now I have to see it through to the end."

Anita had to interrupt. "I don't understand, PJ, see what through to the end? Isn't that what the authorities are paid to do? This entire business doesn't make sense to me."

"I know, Anita, it's not easy to understand."

"Okay, then just tell me how you ended up with Melody. What happened that was so terrible, you had to take the child from her bed in the middle of the night? That should be easy for me to understand. How did you end up with her?"

"Well, first of all, the man she calls Uncle Carl was one of the men who killed Walter."

"Oh my god," Anita said. "Where is he now?"

"He's dead, Anita. That's all you have to know."

He said it with such a finality that she knew there was no point in asking how he died. She wanted to ask "Did you kill him? How did you kill him?" But the words wouldn't come out. She just sat there, one hand over her mouth, the other in her lap.

"Are you okay?" he asked, reaching across the table. She nodded her head yes.

They looked at each other for several minutes without speaking. Finally, she said, "PJ, I don't know if I'm going to be able to handle this."

He gave her that understanding smile that was hard to resist. "I understand. This is not lunch at the Plaza, so to speak. There is no reason for you to be involved in this mess. This is something I have to do. And I don't expect you to sit around and wait for me to finish so that . . ." He wasn't sure what she was supposed to wait for.

"Wait for what, PJ?"

He shook his head. "I don't know what the hell I was expecting you to wait for. Look, Anita, you need to get back to living your life. You have been through enough these past weeks. It isn't fair for me to drag you into my problems. I have to go to Atlantic City soon. After I finish what I have to do there, then if you still want, we can talk about us. I hope you can understand."

"And what happens to Melody in the meantime?" she asked.

"I don't know. To tell you the truth, I hadn't thought about it. I was more concerned about you."

"Well, I have thought about it. I want to become her legal guardian."

"You what? Do you have any idea what you're letting yourself in for? You can't be serious, Anita."

"Oh yes, I am. And I'm going to need your help. So I'm asking you to hold off going to Atlantic City for a couple of weeks so that you can help me. And one more thing. I am not as fragile as you think. I don't want you to put me in the same category as those Park Avenue women whose only interest is . . . lunch at the Plaza."

"Anita, I am sorry. That is not what I meant . . ."

The tables had turned. She was now holding the best cards, and she was making a big bet. Could PJ call her bet?

"When I said I didn't think I could handle it . . . I didn't say that I wouldn't handle it. There is a big difference there."

He held up his coffee cup. "Point to the lady from New York. Okay, what is it you want me to do?"

"Good, I appreciate that. Now one last question about this Uncle Carl. Can I assume he is out of the picture? You said he is dead. Can anything happen to affect Melody because of that? And I assume you took Melody because there was no one else there to take care of her."

PJ reluctantly agreed, hoping he was correct that Melody would not be tied into Wilson's death.

"Good. Now here is my plan."

The following day, Anita contacted her attorney and told him it was important she meet with him as soon as possible. When they met, she told him there was a little girl who had no parents or "living legal guardian" to take care of her, and she wanted to be named her legal guardian. Her attorney was more than curious and asked who the girl was and how did this all come about. After all, Anita was just recently widowed, and he didn't want to see her make a decision like this out of loneliness. She assured him that was not the reason. She then proceeded to tell him the story she and PJ concocted. It went something like this:

Several months ago, I met a social worker by the name of Francis Whitman. She was at an award ceremony being given by Children of Our World. I am sure you remember, I'm chairman of the New York chapter. Anyhow, she was telling me about this little girl, whose mother died from a drug overdose about a year ago, and now she lives with her mother's boyfriend. She is the case worker and is trying to place the little girl in a foster home. She said the little girl is very bright and given the opportunity, can really make something of her life. She asked me if Children of Our World had any kind of a program that would apply to a child like this. I told her that we have made special grants in the past for many different situations. I agreed to meet the child before I made any recommendations to our board of directors. After meeting the child, I knew in my heart she deserved more than being just another name in the welfare system. To make a long story short, Children of Our World is going to sponsor Melody, that's her name, to attend a boarding school for girls in Maine. And since we haven't been able to locate any other relatives, I decided that I wanted to become her legal guardian. So how do we make that happen?

"That's it?" her attorney asked.

"That's it," she said.

Felix Spiro was both a personal friend as well as Walter's attorney. And after Walter died, he was of considerable help to Anita. He looked at her with a smile and said, "So that's your story and you're sticking to it." It didn't require an answer.

After leaving Spiro's office, she immediately called PJ. "The meeting went fine. Now all you have to do is find this Ms. Whitman and have her agree to our story."

PJ said, "No problem. It's as good as done."

"From your mouth to God's ears," she replied.

Chapter Forty-Six

It took PJ only a few days to locate Francis Whitman. A couple of phone calls to some old friends, and he had her office address and job history. She was hired by the New York State Social Services Department right out of college. She graduated from the City College of New York in 1989 with a masters degree in social psychology. Her first year on the job was spent in the office reviewing case reports and making recommendations to one of the department heads. She did such a good job that she was promoted to case worker and has held that job for the last five years.

Now that he had that information, all he needed was some way to identify her. Since he didn't have her picture, he would have to think of another way. He called her office and asked the receptionist when she was scheduled to be there. "Ms. Whitman will be here on Friday." He would have to wait two days.

On Friday morning, PJ arranged for a messenger to deliver a dozen roses to her, with instructions that she sign for them personally. The card simply read, "A secret admirer."

PJ also gave the messenger a $100 to meet him back at the Social Services building at five o'clock. When the employees filed out of the building, the messenger pointed out Francis Whitman to him.

She had only walked about fifty feet from the building when PJ came up from behind and grabbed her by the arm. Before she had a chance to either say anything or possibly scream, he said, "I am not going to hurt you or rob you, so don't try to pull away or call out. I am here to talk to you about Melody Walker."

She felt her knees go weak. He sensed that and tightened his grip on her arm to prevent her from falling down. She was so frightened that she couldn't speak. He eased her over to the building side of the pavement and let her catch her breath.

"Are you okay?" he asked, knowing full well she wasn't.

She nodded. "I need a drink of water," she said, followed by, "You're hurting me. Who are you? What do you want?"

That was good. The shock was wearing off. She should be able to talk to him now.

"There's a restaurant in the next block. We can go in there and talk. Can you make it without falling down or doing something you will be sorry for later?" He scared the shit out her of again. All she could do was nod.

They made it to the restaurant without incident and found an empty table near the back. When they sat down, it was the first time she actually looked at him. She had a pretty face. Her lips were trembling. If it wasn't for the fact that he remembered what Melody told him, he would feel sorry for her. But today, his feelings were anger, not sympathy.

She finally was able to speak, just as the waiter approached. "Can I get you something to drink?" he asked.

"Water please," she said.

"I'll have some coffee," PJ added.

The waiter walked away, thinking, *The last of the big-time spenders.*

They sat in silence until the waiter returned. This was PJ's game, and he knew how to play it. This was intimidation time.

"Water for the lady, and coffee for the gentleman," the waiter said, placing the drinks on the table. "Can I get you nice folks anything else?" he asked sarcastically.

PJ motioned to him with his finger to come closer. When he did, PJ took his hand and held it so tight, the waiter grimaced. At the same time, he put a $20 bill in the waiter's other hand and said, "You go play with the other children until I call you." PJ let go of the waiter's hand and turned his attention back to the social worker.

The waiter looked at the $20 bill in one hand and the red marks on the other hand. Then as politely and courteous as he could, he said, "Yes, sir, thank you, sir," and left.

"Do you think you are calm enough to talk now?" PJ asked her.

"I . . . I think so. But . . . I have to go to the ladies' room . . . can I go?"

PJ looked around to see exactly where it was. It was half-way between where they were sitting and the front door.

He leaned forward and put his hands on the table. "Let me see your hands," he said. Like a robot, she put her hands on his. He smiled as he gently held her hands in his.

"Okay, Francis, you can go to the ladies' room. But please don't get any crazy ideas about leaving the restaurant. I know that when you get up from the table and start to walk to the ladies' room, you will look at the front door and think that you can just walk outside and get lost in the crowd and then this nightmare will be over. That won't happen. Wherever you go, I will find you. Now if you just do as I tell you, this will all be over soon. Do I make myself clear?"

He could feel her hands shaking in his as she nodded yes. He was hoping she hadn't wet her pants by this time.

She was up and back in record time. After she sat back down, he said, "Good girl. Now you want to know who I am and what do I want. My name is Averhim, and I am somebody that you never want to make angry. That's all you need to know for now. Like I told you, I am here to talk about Melody Walker. Francis, you have done a terrible injustice to this poor innocent little girl who never did you any harm."

She managed, "I don't know what you mean."

"You don't know what I mean! You were supposed to protect Melody. Instead, you let her stay in a house with a man who constantly abused her. You knew she was being sexually assaulted, yet you allowed her to stay there! It was your job to get her out of there and into a foster home where she would be taken care of. And to make matters worse, you became sexually involved with the man who was abusing her. How sick is that? And by the way, Francis, Melody told me about the time you were there and suggested to her the two of you get into bed with him."

"No no, I was just kidding with her. I would never do such a thing. You must believe me. I didn't . . . I didn't know . . . he was . . . he was doing anything, I swear . . ."

"Don't swear, Francis, you knew. You had to know. Let me ask you something, when was the last time you visited with her?"

"I'm not sure . . . I . . . I have to look in my book. But I know that I saw her at least once a month . . . I mean I have so many cases . . . I think I saw her last week."

"How about Carl Wilson? Did you see him last week? And, Francis, if you want this to be over, don't lie to me. And stop pretending like you don't remember him. You were sleeping with him for Christ's sake!"

Tears were running down her cheeks. "I . . . I guess I saw him last week also."

"You're lying, Francis. Carl Wilson is dead. He's been dead over a week.

Tell me, where do you think little Melody is now that Carl is dead? Who's taking care of her?"

She couldn't hold back any longer. "I don't know . . . Oh . . . I'm so sorry," she cried. "I should have watched out for her . . . dear God, please forgive me. I am sorry, I am so sorry." She fumbled through her handbag, looking for some Kleenex.

"Exactly what have you done, Francis? What are you sorry for?"

She looked at him, expecting him to tell her. All she got was silence and a look of disapproval. She took a drink of water and wiped some of the tears from her eyes. "Please, Mr. Averhim, tell me what to do. Let me make up for what I did. I am really so sorry. When I first met Carl, I thought he was such a nice man. I thought he was taking care of Melody. And when I told him if he didn't clean up the apartment, I was going to recommend that Melody be placed in a foster home. He promised me he would take care of that. And even when I told him she had to go to school, he said he would do that. He really seemed to care about her. I don't know what happened after that. I never meant to hurt Melody. She is a sweet little girl. Please, Mr. Averhim, tell me, is she all right?"

PJ had a difficult time disliking this poor girl. He didn't know how she became involved with Wilson or why she tried to entice Melody that night. But sitting here today across the table from him, she was a very sad young woman.

"Yes, Francis, Melody is all right. She is staying with a friend of mine."

"You said that Carl . . . was dead. What happened? How did he die?"

"I'm not really sure. According to the newspaper, it had something to do with drugs."

"Oh, how awful," she whimpered.

PJ simply smirked as if to say *"No great loss."*

"Now that he's no longer around, Melody has to have someplace to live. She can't go back to an empty apartment. That's where you come in.

I'm going to give you a chance to make up for what you did. Or I should say, what you didn't do, and that was to look out for Melody. That's what the State was paying you to do."

She started to cry again. "I know . . . I know . . . I'm so sorry . . . Oh god, I want to die." Fortunately, the restaurant wasn't too crowded; however, several customers did turn around to see what was going on. The waiter stood close by in case PJ wanted him. PJ waited for her to calm down and decided it was time to tell her what they needed her to do.

He told her his friend was the head of a charity that was going to send Melody to a boarding school in Maine. She would have the opportunity to grow up in a normal environment and make something of her life. In order to accomplish that, Francis would have to help them. The first thing she had to do was change whatever records she had on Melody to match Anita's story. She would be told what she needed to document. She would also have to confirm Anita's account of how they met. And there was the possibility she might have to make a recommendation to the court in order to help Anita get legal custody. Then he told her, "After the judge grants my friend legal custody, I want her records to disappear."

"I can't do that," she said, "it's illegal."

PJ didn't say anything for several seconds; then he leaned over the table and said to her, "So is what you did, Francis. And not only would you lose your job because of it, but you would also go to jail. Believe me, Francis, if I went to the authorities and told them what I know, your life as you know it now would be over. You have no choice but to help us. And, Francis, after this is all over, I want you to forget you ever knew Melody. I also want you to forget me. Forget our little talk, forget everything about this entire matter." Then he looked at her with a stare that sent chills up her spine and said, "Francis, if one day in the future you feel righteous about all of this and think you need to cleanse your soul by telling the authorities or anybody for that matter about this—don't. Because if you do, I will find you and kill you." The color left her face; her eyes rolled back in her head, and she fainted.

The waiter and several customers all rushed to the table to help him pick her up off the floor. Once she was upright in the chair, he thanked everybody for their help. He told them she was his daughter and the reason she fainted, well, she's pregnant. "Oh, how nice," the customers said, offering their congratulations and then returning to their own table.

The waiter was busy applying wet towels to Francis's head. All things considered, PJ thought the meeting with her went well.

When they left the restaurant, PJ said he would contact her in the next couple of days and tell her what she needed to do. As she turned to walk away, she said, "Mr. Averhim . . . when this is over . . . you're not going to hurt me, are you?"

Now he did feel sorry for her. "No, Francis. As long as you cooperate, I'm not going to hurt you."

She managed a smile and walked away. He definitely was getting too old for this kind of shit.

CHAPTER FORTY-SEVEN

August 22, 1995

During the past six weeks, Anita had meetings with the Department of Social Services, the clerk at the Orphans' Court, the judge who would make the final decision as to whether she would become Melody's legal guardian, and the headmistress at Green Briar School for Girls, the school in Maine. When she took Melody to see the judge, she had to be sure she would give him the right answers, so she told her they were playing a game. "It's like we're pretending," she told her. Melody thought that was fun. On the other hand, Francis wasn't having as much fun. Both PJ and Anita made sure she knew what to say and warned her that if she screwed up, it would be her ass, so to speak. Up to this point, all had gone according to plan.

The Children of Our World board of directors had given their approval for the grant of money to the school in Maine, and Anita was waiting to hear from the school, letting her know Melody had been accepted.

She couldn't understand why they were dragging their feet. She had completed all of the paperwork and took Melody there for an interview and an entrance test, which she passed with flying colors. Finally, the headmistress called and asked if she could come to the school to meet with her. When Anita asked her why that was necessary, she said she would rather not discuss it on the phone. Anita became concerned and asked PJ if he would go with her. Of course, he agreed. They flew up in the Lippincott private jet, went directly to the school, and were now sitting in her office.

When Mrs. Freemont, the headmistress of Green Briar School for Girls walked into the room, she seemed surprised to see someone with Anita.

"Oh, I didn't realize you were bringing your attorney," she said.

Anita looked at her and then at PJ. "What makes you think this is my attorney?" she asked Mrs. Freemont.

"I don't know . . . I just assumed—"

Anita interrupted, "This is my brother-in-law, Mr. Gould."

PJ hadn't heard her refer to him that way before and wasn't sure he liked the sound of it. It sounded too much like a relative.

"How do you do, Mr. Gould? It's nice to meet you."

PJ simply smiled.

"Well, Mrs. Freemont," Anita said, "here we are. So what is it you found so important that we couldn't discuss on the phone?"

"Yes, I appreciate your coming all this way, Mrs. Lippincott," she said, appearing a slight bit uncomfortable. "You must understand, Mrs. Lippincott, things like this can happen sometimes."

"Things like what?"

"Well, it seems that we made a mistake when we told you we had a vacancy for the fall semester."

Anita leaned forward in her chair. "You made a mistake? What kind of mistake?" she asked, raising her voice ever so slightly.

Mrs. Freemont fumbled through a file on her desk and said, "Our enrollment for this fall term is completely full, Mrs. Lippincott." Then very smugly, she took off her glasses and said, "But we would be happy to put Melody on the waiting list for next spring. You never can tell what will happen."

PJ put his hand on Anita's as if to tell her he would take over from here on in. "Mrs. Freemont, as a matter of fact, we can tell you what will happen."

"I beg your pardon," she replied.

"Let me ask you something, Mrs. Freemont. Exactly how many Afro-American girls are enrolled at Green Briar?"

Mrs. Freemont became very flustered. "What do you mean? What are you saying?"

PJ looked at Anita and said, "Do you think that was a difficult question? Did you understand it?"

Anita smiled. "Perfectly," she said.

Mrs. Freemont stood up and folded her arms across her chest as if to protect herself and said, "Now you look here, you two, I don't know what you are trying to insinuate. But Green Briar is a respectable school and has a policy not to discriminate. So if you think we're not accepting Melody because she is black . . . excuse me, Afro-American, well, you are wrong."

"Nicely done, Mrs. Freemont, but no cigar. Now I suggest you sit down so we can figure out some way to make sure Melody is admitted this fall."

Once the headmistress was seated again, PJ got up and walked to the window overlooking the south campus of the school. He turned around and asked, "When do you plan to break ground, Mrs. Freemont?"

"I beg your pardon."

"The new dormitories and library. When do you expect to break ground?" PJ asked, walking back to his seat. Anita didn't know what was going on.

"Not that it has anything to do with what we're talking about, but we are still in the fund-raising mode. Once we reach our goal with donations, the directors will then decide on how to proceed with financing. In answer to your question, I'm not really sure."

"I can understand that, Mrs. Freemont. Getting back to what I asked you before, just how many black students are enrolled here? You see, you can say black instead of Afro-American since it's just us white folks here."

The headmistress jumped up from her seat. "I think it's time you both left . . ."

But before she could finish, PJ stood up, leaned both hands on his side of the desk, and said, "Okay, lady, it's time we stopped playing games. First of all, if it was up to me, I wouldn't send my cat to this school. But the fact of the matter is, Mrs. Lippincott wants Melody to be here, and that's what's going to happen."

The headmistress tried to say something, but PJ held up his hand as if he were stopping traffic and gave her a look that said it all.

"In the history of Green Briar, there have only been five black students," he said. "The last one four years ago, Governor Ingram's daughter. And she was only admitted after the governor pledged $200,000 to the, quote unquote, building fund. I spoke to the governor before we flew up here, and he told me the whole story, how you practically bribed him before you allowed his daughter to attend Green Briar."

She tried to say something, but he didn't let her.

"In case you don't know who my brother was, Mrs. Freemont, let me enlighten you. He was on a first name basis with the president and more senators and other Washington bigwigs than I care to mention. Now, Mrs. Lippincott, is going to make it easy for you. She is prepared to make . . . a sizeable donation to the school's building fund." He turned to Anita and asked, "Isn't that right, Anita?"

She looked at him for a moment and then answered, "Yes yes, of course."

"Now, Mrs. Freemont, if after Mrs. Lippincott fills out her pledge form you still refuse to admit Melody, you leave me no choice. I will go to Washington and speak to some friends of mine who will launch a full-scale investigation of Green Briar. They will investigate the tax-free status you enjoy, the lack of blacks and Jews in your school, and any other skeletons you happen to have in your closet. And believe me, dear lady, you don't want that to happen, do you?"

"No . . . no, of course not. Mr. Gould, I am sure we can work this out."

"I was sure we could. And one last thing, Mrs. Freemont. I plan on holding you personally responsible for Melody's safety while she attends Green Briar. That means no harassment by either teachers, parents, or students. I expect Melody to be treated like all of the other students. No better, and for sure . . . no worse."

Anita had difficulty waiting until they were in the limo on the way back to the airport before she said anything to PJ about what had transpired at the school.

"What the hell was that all about?" she asked, finding it difficult not to burst out laughing. "How did you know all that stuff about Governor Ingram and his daughter?"

"You never played poker, did you?"

"What are you talking about?"

"It's called bluffing."

"I don't understand."

"Okay," PJ said, "it's like this. When you told me Mrs. Freemont called you and said she had to talk to you in person, I became suspicious. So I called a friend of mine and asked him what he knew about the school and their policy about admitting blacks."

"Why would you even think something like that?" she asked him.

"Because that's how my mind works. I was trained to always be proactive. And I thought it might be something like that. It so happens my friend knows Governor Ingram and remembered his daughter attended a private school in Maine. He said he would call him on the chance the school his daughter attended was Green Briar. Bingo. All the governor told him was he made a $200,000 donation to their building fund, and his daughter was admitted to the school. That's all I needed to know. The rest was a bluff."

"My god, you are something else! I don't know what I would have done without you." She bent over and kissed him on the cheek.

He just smiled, then asked her, "Why the hell is it so important she go to that school?"

"Because it's just about the best in the country. And when you graduate from there, you have your pick of colleges. I want Melody to have the best."

"Okay, you got it. She's in."

Anita laughed when she asked PJ if he saw the bitch's face when she gave her the pledge form.

"I don't know how much it was," he said. "But the bitch almost fell off the chair."

"Is that why you told her you wanted the new library to be called the Walter Lippincott Library?"

"Yeah, that okay with you?"

She put her hand on his and said, "Yes, that's fine with me."

CHAPTER FORTY-EIGHT

September 20, 1995

Labor Day came and went, and PJ was still in New York. He had promised Anita he would fly up to Maine with her when she took Melody to school. After they returned to New York, he told her he had to go to Atlantic City to finish what he started. When she asked him to tell her exactly what that meant, he simply told her once again, "You just have to trust me. This will all be over soon."

"Okay," she said, "but before you leave, let's have an old-fashioned New York day. I can't remember the last time I just rode around the city and took it all in." He smiled and agreed. After all, another day or two wouldn't make any difference; besides which, he enjoyed every minute he spent with her.

The following morning, Anita picked him up at his hotel, and they went sightseeing. They went to the Statue of Liberty, Bloomingdale's, the Empire State Building, and the Museum of Modern Art. They drove down Wall Street, the granite heart of capitalism, through SoHo and Chinatown. They stopped in Little Italy for some lunch and then continued their sightseeing in Washington Square and then went uptown to the theater district, the West Side, and Harlem. Anita looked out of the window at the people standing around on the street corners doing absolutely nothing and said to PJ, "It's so seedy, so filthy, yet so alive, don't you agree?"

He just nodded. His mind was somewhere else. Anita could sense that. She knew the sightseeing trip was over. It was time to go home.

CHAPTER FORTY-NINE

Not far from where PJ and Anita were sightseeing, Joey Sconsi was holed up in Maria's apartment building. He had made himself as scarce as he could on the street. He was afraid to go out for fear someone would recognize him and tell Tozzi, not that Tozzi really cared. Maria kept telling him nobody in New York knew who he was, and he was being paranoid. Finally, he became fed up with the dreary life of not going anyplace or seeing other people. He did a complete turnabout. He told Maria he wanted to help her with her modeling career and suggested he go with her to auditions. "I'll be like your agent," he said. "And it won't cost you no 10 percent." She liked Joey and was not adverse to his idea.

Once he decided to leave the apartment, they started going out to dinner and to hangouts Maria used to frequent. After a while, they branched out to other classier places. Places like Sardi's, the renowned Times Square restaurant that was a magnet for the showbiz crowd. Joey told Maria, "You can never tell who you might meet here." And he was right. One night, they met an ad executive for a large advertising firm that was looking for a "new face." With Joey's gift for gab, Maria got an audition and was now doing a layout for *Harper's Magazine*. And Joey was officially her agent.

CHAPTER FIFTY

In 1978, the federal government found a new way to attack the Mafia. It was a statute known as the Racketeering Influenced and Corrupt Organizations Act, called RICO for short. Even though RICO had been passed in 1970, the powerful crime-fighting weapon had mostly gathered dust on the shelf. In part, this was due to the complexity of the statute. Mostly, it was due to prosecutorial shyness. The law had not really created any new crimes. What it did was combine existing criminal behavior into a new offense that carried far stiffer punishment. RICO covered eight state and twenty-four federal crimes. If a prosecutor could prove a person committed any two of the crimes, he'd succeed in showing a pattern of racketeering and the RICO sanctions kicked into action. Federal agents frustrated by meager sentences resulting from gambling and loan-sharking convictions could combine the results and, bingo, nail a wise guy for operating a racket and win some big jail time—at least twenty years. No one ever thought that almost twenty years later, RICO would also end up convicting a U.S. senator of racketeering.

In Washington, there was a bipartisan pledge to clean up their act. Get rid of the bad apples, so to speak. After all, there was an election coming up, and the politicians had to put on their best face. A Senate subcommittee was formed to "look into this." One of the targets of the committee's investigation was Senator Guy Baxter. He had smelled bad for a long time It wasn't long before leaked press reports, made it known that Senator Long was being investigated. As soon as that happened Las Vegas very quickly seperated themselves from the good senator. Las Vegas could make or break you. In this case it was the beginning of the end for Senator Long.

There is a culture of distrust, a general disinclination by the FBI to share information with other investigative agencies. It is organized crime and disorganized law enforcement. Taken to its most deadly and damaging extreme, it is that kind of smug arrogance and righteous posturing that would open the door in 2001 for an American tragedy simply to be referred to as 9/11. However, in September of 1995, on a much smaller scale, the FBI refused to share what they knew about the shooting at PJ's apartment in Las Vegas with either the CIA or, for that matter, the local authorities. As a result, Detective Sandy Keller of the Las Vegas Homicide Division convinced his superior to close the case. "We got one of the bad guys, and the other one is dead. We all know PJ was a victim. The fact he shot and killed one of the bad guys simply helped us. It's a damn shame that his girlfriend got taken out in this mess, but again, I'm sure he had nothing to do with that. And as far as I'm concerned, I suggest we don't waste our money or time trying to find the guy back East who set up the hit. These things seem to have a way of working themselves out."

And so the case was closed. Sandy couldn't wait to call his friend PJ and tell him the good news.

And the CIA and FBI were doing no better in New York trying to solve the murder of PJ's brother, his associate, his chauffer, and the doorman from his apartment. The New York State Police had one theory and the FBI another, which they claimed involved national security, so they could not share. And the CIA was so far out in left field they didn't want to look bad if they were wrong. So the incident became another unsolved murder in the Big Apple. None of the agencies connected the murder of Angie in Chicago and Sal Morreti and Carl Wilson in New York to the Lippincott shooting. The Chicago police chalked Angie's death up to "gang-related revenge." And in New York, the deaths of Carl, Sal, and some black transvestite were drug related. End of story. Initially, Anita kept pressing the FBI and the state police for answers, but PJ convinced her to let it go. He was taking care of it. Trust him. She was scared to death to try and imagine what he was doing, but she did trust him. More important, she worried for his safety.

On September 25, 1995, driving the black Buick rental car, PJ was on his way to Atlantic City to . . . finish what he started. Before he left New York, he called Phil Cantor, Joseph Cantelli's lawyer, in Chicago.

He wanted to make sure Tozzi was still in Atlantic City. The lawyer assured him that he was, and, as a matter of fact, was living with a waitress who worked at the Trump Plaza. He told PJ that it appeared Tozzi was planning on staying in Atlantic City. He was hanging around the casinos, scamming wherever he could. The lawyer had good information. He gave PJ Tozzi's address, a description of his waitress girlfriend, and the lowdown on their next-door neighbor—a prissy old woman who needed money to gamble and was not above doing most anything to earn that money. "Let me know how you make out," the lawyer said before hanging up the phone. PJ assured him he would.

CHAPTER FIFTY-ONE

On September 27, the plans that Tozzi had outlined to test his new car's roadworthiness that afternoon went awry. Instead, he was now driving on Atlantic Avenue on his way home to see what was wrong with his live-in girlfriend. Had he had the presence of mind to phone her from the saloon before he left, he would have learned from her that she was perfectly fine. But he was so uptight when he got the call from his prissy neighbor that all his senses were dulled. "She fainted on the steps," the woman said to Tozzi. "You best come right home. She told me where to reach you. She is real sick, Mr. Tozzi."

But his senses were not so dulled that when he stopped for a red traffic light, he didn't notice the black Buick sedan behind him. The car itself may not have disturbed him so much as its occupant. He saw the man's face in his rearview mirror. It was like the face of death.

It shouldn't be hard to guess what must have actually flashed through his head as the Buick tailed him doggedly after the light changed. He turned the corner on to Morris Avenue so sharply that he almost lost control of the car.

The Buick gained speed and was closing in.

In seconds, the Buick pulled alongside the Lincoln Tozzi was driving. Up ahead, children were playing kick-the-can in the middle of the street in front of a school. Suddenly, the children saw the cars bearing down on them. Screaming, they scattered off the pavement to the safety of the sidewalks on both sides of the street. The cars tore past them.

The children's cries attracted the ladies at Mrs. Kaufman's garden party, who turned to see what was happening. The Lincoln and Buick were now nose to nose; and suddenly, there was a loud, earsplitting blast.

It was the explosion from the muzzle of a sawed-off shotgun sticking out the front window of the Buick. The shots burst into the driver's side of the Lincoln; and the man behind the wheel, Tozzi, lurched forward.

As Tozzi slumped over the steering wheel, blood pouring from a countless number of bullet holes in his head, face, neck, and upper torso, the Lincoln went out of control. It veered all at once to the right and mounted the sidewalk.

By now, the children on the street and the ladies at the garden party were shrieking hysterically. The black Buick never slowed down as it roared toward the corner. There was a piercing squeal of tires; the car made a sharp right turn on Pacific Avenue and disappeared from view. Within minutes, the driver of the black Buick was at the $2 toll plaza, entering the Atlantic City Expressway headed toward the Garden State Parkway to New York. Like the many drivers in the other cars on the road alongside him, he was wearing his seat belt, observing the speed limit, and listening to a local Atlantic City sports station. Looking like just another loser leaving the city on his way home.

Meanwhile, the careening Lincoln skirted past the privets alongside Mrs. Kaufman's garden and rammed into the stone stoops of the house next to the school. The impact spun the car almost completely around and brought it smashing into the brick front wall of the house. The force with which the vehicle hit sprung open the driver's door, and Tozzi's limp, bleeding body was catapulted out of the car. It landed on the sidewalk not far from the feet of the terrified women in Mrs. Kaufman's garden.

On the six o'clock news that evening, the lead story was GANGLAND-STYLE KILLING IN ATLANTIC CITY. The news anchor went on to say, "The killing was a virtuoso performance by organized crime. Few gangland murders matched the high drama and unique horror of this assassination."

CHAPTER FIFTY-TWO

When PJ left Atlantic City, he drove straight to the Avis car rental lot at the Newark Airport. He returned the black Buick he had rented and took the shuttle bus to the airport. Once at the airport, he hired a limo and driver to take him to the Plaza Hotel in New York City where he was already registered. He put a Do Not Disturb sign on his door when he left that morning and told the operator to hold his calls. When he arrived back at the hotel, he went to his room, removed the Do Not Disturb sign, and called room service. Then he called the hotel operator and told her that he was awake and that she could put his calls through. He had one message. Anita called. When he returned her call, he told her he had slept in; that's why he turned off the phone. "And your cell?" she asked. "Was that turned off also?" They both knew what was going on.

"Tell you what," he said, "how about you come to the Plaza, we hire a horse and buggy, and take a ride in the park? I have to talk to you about something." She didn't like the sound of that but had been expecting it nevertheless. He was in the lobby when she arrived.

"Are you all right?" she asked.

"I'm good," he answered. "And before you ask me, I'm finished with what I had to do. It's over."

"Oh, I'm so glad," she said, still not sure what it was he had done. "Does this mean you can move to New York now?" They had discussed that several times, and he always avoided making a commitment.

He took her hand as they walked out of the hotel lobby and asked the doorman to get them a horse and buggy. Once they were seated in the buggy and the driver headed into Central Park, PJ turned toward her and gently kissed her on the cheek. Before she could respond, he said, "I think you know how I feel about you."

She simply nodded, afraid to speak for fear that she would say the wrong thing, like "I love you, PJ, and I don't ever want you to leave me again."

He could tell by the look on her face what she was thinking. "But it's too soon, Anita. We need to give this time. These last couple months have been like a whirlwind. Both of us have been going a hundred miles an hour. You need to finish up with Walter's estate, and I need to wind up my affairs in Vegas before I can even think about moving to New York. And just so you know, the only reason I would even consider moving here is so that I could be with you." He saw the tears running down her cheeks. He wiped them away with the back of his hand and put his arm around her. Then he quietly whispered those famous words, "Trust me, Anita. This will all work out."

CHAPTER FIFTY-THREE

About a year later (the fall of 1996)

The hairdresser had arranged her hair in a loose upsweep of curls, but Anita decided that with the cream-colored silk Vicky Tiel pajama suit she was wearing, she preferred it down. She was combing it out when her cell phone rang. It was on the nightstand on the other side of the room. She leaped up from her dressing table to answer it. She heard a voice say her name, but the connection was not clear, and the voice did not sound familiar.

"Who is it?" she answered cautiously.

"What's the matter, you don't recognize my voice?" PJ asked with a slight chuckle.

"PJ! Oh, I'm sorry. I'm so glad you called."

"Didn't you think I would? It hasn't been that long."

"Of course, of course. You know what I mean. It's just that I wasn't expecting your call tonight. Oh, damn it, why do I always end up sounding like a teenager around you? What I really meant was, I was hoping you would, but I wasn't sure when. There, how's that?"

"That's just fine. Is it too late, or can I stop by for a nightcap?"

She was totally surprised that he was in New York. "Where are you? Are you here? I mean, here in New York?"

"Yup, got in about an hour ago. I just picked up a rental car, and I'm headed out of the airport."

"Why didn't you let me know you were coming? I would have sent the car for you."

He laughed. "That's why I didn't let you know."

"Ha-ha," she replied. "How long do you plan on staying this time?"

"Oh, that was a low blow," he said.

"You think so? The last time you were here, you stayed less than a week and then had to fly back to Vegas. When are you going to wind up your affairs out there and move to New York? I miss you when you're not here, PJ. You're my best friend, you know." Without being able to see his face, to watch his expressions, it was difficult for her to guess what he was thinking or feeling. But that didn't matter. She was glad he was back in New York. She wanted to see him again, soon. "How soon will you be here?" she asked, trying not to sound like she was sixteen years old, waiting for her prom date.

"It shouldn't take me too long. There doesn't seem to be too much traffic. By the way . . . I miss you too."

She glanced at the clock and returned hurriedly to the dressing table, reached for the gold-plated Canovas makeup case, and powdered her face, repairing the damage a few tears had caused. She drew a comb through her hair and waited. When the doorman finally called her to tell her that he was on his way up to her apartment, she thought her heart would jump out of her chest. As soon as he came into the apartment, she raced across the room to greet him. "Oh, I am so glad you are here," she said, flinging her arms around his neck as eager as a schoolgirl for that first kiss. How lucky she was to be able to feel this again, the rush of excitement, the surge of pure joy, just seeing the face of the man she loved. And when he touched her! Then her whole body began to vibrate as if in the grip of a small but pleasant earthquake.

During the past year, he visited her in New York five times. Each time he was there, she hoped he would tell her he was moving to New York to be with her, but that didn't happen. Although she wanted him to stay at the apartment, he chose to stay at the Plaza. The visits usually lasted less than a week, and when he left to return to Las Vegas, she was very sad. She had fallen in love with him but was not totally sure he felt the same way. Neither of them said the words "I love you." There was "I will miss you when you leave" and "You know how I feel about you," but never "I love you."

The last time he was in New York, he told her he put his condo up for sale. "And what happens then?" she asked.

"We'll see," he said. They never spoke about Walter's "assassination" or his girlfriend Cindy's murder.

The lawyers were finished working out the details of Walter's will, and she told him she was invited to join the board of Walter's company as a director.

Since she was now the major stockholder, it was in their best interests to have her "close by." PJ thought it was a good idea, and so she accepted.

Melody was doing well at school. And during the summer break, she came to New York and stayed with Anita for three weeks. She spent the balance of the summer at her roommate's home in New Hampton. A big change from where she grew up.

"So you never answered my question," Anita said after taking her arms from around PJ's neck.

"What question was that?" he asked, taking her hand in his and walking with her to the sofa.

"You know damn well what question. How long do you plan to stay in New York?" And then without thinking, she said, "I need a man, PJ. And if I don't get one soon, I'm going to bust!" They looked at each other, and the both of them fell back on the sofa, laughing. "I'm embarrassed," she said, holding her hands over her face. He reached over and took her hands away from her face and kissed each one very gently.

"Don't be, Anita, that's the nicest thing anybody ever said to me."

They sat looking at each other for several seconds, and then when he finally put his arms around her, she realized she had been holding her breath. His mouth covered hers; and soon, she felt his tongue flicking here, there, eliciting small explosions of feeling. He touched her ever so gently, his hands finding their way under her thin layer of clothing, caressing her skin. She wrapped her arms around him and ground herself into him, wanting to be closer, as close as it was possible to be.

She finally had to come up for air. "Wow," she said, moving away just far enough to breathe. "You are one hell of a kisser," she managed, holding his face in her hands.

"You're not too bad yourself, young lady. By the way, I'm planning on moving to New York. Do you know if there are any apartments for sale in this building?"

"Oh my god," she said, "oh my god. That's wonderful! When? Oh, PJ, I am so happy." Then she said it, "I love you. I love you."

He smiled and said, "And I love you back."

They got up from the couch without saying a word and went into her bedroom. She walked toward the bed at the same time, taking off her pajama top and then unloosening the string on the pants, allowing them to fall to the floor.

"Turn around," he said when she was naked. "Completely around. I want to see you." It was as if she had no will of her own, only his. She turned slowly, without embarrassment. "You're so beautiful," he said. "Your body is perfect." She felt like it took him forever to close the distance between them, and when he finally did, he wrapped his arms around her and moved with her to the bed. He caressed her breasts first with his fingers, then with his mouth. Taking her hands, he put them on his belt. "Help me," he whispered, his breath against her ear. She unbuckled his belt and unzipped the fly of his trousers while he stood with his arms loosely around her, caressing her buttocks. When they reached the bed, he stripped off his clothes and pressed his naked body against hers. Then he gently lifted her up and laid her on the bed. She stretched out her arms, and he slowly put himself on top of her. He could feel the heat of her body all over his.

"You don't know how much I want you," he said. "I told myself, take it slow, there's no hurry. But goddamn it, I'm no good at taking things slow. Not anymore. Life is so short, Anita. Too short. I don't want to waste it playing games. I want you. I want to make love to you."

He kissed her, and she responded eagerly. He reawakened in her a desire for love, for sex, which her healthy young body had gone without for over a year. And when she felt his tongue slip gently into her mouth, his hand settle tentatively on her breast, she felt a spark flare and catch and blaze into the need to make love. It was a feeling different from anything she had ever felt before. It was desire tinged with the tenderness of love. And then she felt him inside of her. She wanted to scream in delight. She wanted the feeling to last forever. Their bodies moved together. First, very slowly, then more rapidly as they both could feel the joy of making love. And when he pulled back for a moment and looked at her, she said nothing but just lowered her mouth again to his. Lying naked with her in her large double bed, he thought to himself, *Is this where she made love to Walter?* No matter. Now she was his. They were in love. It felt so completely familiar and natural and good to be together because they were, just then, the most important people in each other's world.

This game is over. There will be other games, but not necessarily with all of the same players.

What happened to the players after the game ended?

After Francis Whitman, the social service employee, knew that Melody was admitted to the school in Maine, she took a six-month leave of absence to "get her head back on straight." When she returned to work, she was committed to be an advocate for children like Melody. She vowed that she would never allow another child to be treated the way Melody was. She eventually became the administrator of the department and never gave up the fight to help children like Melody. She really was a good person.

In June of 1996, Sid Mastro, the small-time bookie and bar owner, decided to leave Chicago. His wife had left him, and the Cantelli family refused to do business with him. Besides which, he kept looking over his shoulder, waiting for the police to question him about his friend Angie. He assumed either the Cantelli family or PJ killed him. Either way, he didn't want to be around to answer questions. He had enough of Chicago's bad weather, the wise guys, and his parole officer. He wanted to live out the rest of his life in peace. So he sold the bar and moved to Key West, Florida. It was perfect. He found a nice little apartment only two blocks from the beach and got a job tending bar at a joint on the main drag. Life was good. Unfortunately, Sid didn't know the bar was owned by the Frantalio crime family in Tampa. Poor Sid, who knows what will happen to him now.

After the election in 1996, the new Republican president signed into law the right to have legalized gambling in all fifty states. Of course, it was up to each state to decide whether they wanted gambling. But everyone knew "there was a new game in town." And although it was still business as usual in Las Vegas, the men in the fedoras who built the city are long gone. The gamblers with no last names and suitcases filled with cash are reluctant to show up in the new Las Vegas for fear of being turned in to the IRS by a twenty-five-year-old hotel school graduate working casino credit on weekends. The backroom cash poker games played on old round wooden tables with sawdust on the floor have been replaced by high-stakes games, with a TV audience of millions watching. Where the winner can go home with five to ten million dollars if he (or she) has the guts to go . . . all in. Las Vegas has become an adult theme park, a place where parents can take their kids and have a little fun themselves. While the kids play cardboard pirate at the Treasure Island Casino, Daddy can lose the mortgage money or Junior's college tuition.

In December of 1996, PJ's friend, homicide detective Sandy Keller, resigned from the Las Vegas Police Department and went to work for Sonny Cantelli at the Casino Royal. He was hired as chief of security. His salary was more than double what he was making as a detective, and the job allowed him to rub elbows with the rich and famous.

His partner, Josh Hayward, graduated law school, left the Las Vegas Police Department, and joined the FBI. As a reward for getting them involved in the shooting at PJ's apartment, which was a real pain in the ass to them, he was assigned to a desk job in a small town in Arkansas, never to be heard from again.

Also during 1996, Senator Guy Baxter was forced to withdraw his name from the Republican primary race for president due to the ongoing senatorial investigation. Then shortly after the new Republican president took office in 1997, he was officially charged and indicted on sixteen different counts of obstruction of justice, conspiracy to obstruct justice, racketeering, money laundering, bribery, and, so Wall Street wasn't left out, insider trading. Only a few at the justice and in law enforcement around the nation saw something even deeper behind Baxter's "elbowing" the administration. His fellow politicians didn't want to believe what a really bad guy this dude was. In a plea bargaining agreement, he gave the justice department the names of some "dirty" people in Washington and Las Vegas. If necessary, he agreed to testify against them. He was a real sleaze. He ended up paying over two million dollars in fines and was sentenced to three to five years in a white-collar federal prison. No good deed goes undone.

In March of 1997, Nick Paraphas, the man arrested in Las Vegas for taking part in the shooting at PJ's house, was serving time at a federal prison in Seattle, Washington. One morning, while taking a shower, he slipped on the soap, hit his head on the tile floor, and bled to death. He was the last of the hired killers who took part in the murders of PJ's girlfriend and brother. The only one left unpunished (at this time) was Joey Sconsi.

In August of 2000, Joey Sconsi and his girlfriend, Maria Falcone, were having dinner at Umberto's Restaurant in Little Italy. The night started out like any other night. Maria came home from work; they had a couple of drinks and would either eat at home or go out to dinner. On this particular night, they went out. Seated behind them in the restaurant was a man by the name of Albert the Greek and two of his bodyguards. Albert the Greek was at odds with the Colombo crime family. He was muscling his way into their numbers and loan-sharking business. So the Colombo family decide to "eliminate" him. Unfortunately for Joey and his girlfriend, they happened to be in the wrong place at the wrong time. Neither Joey, Albert the Greek, or his two bodyguards saw the four men with drawn pistols enter the restaurant through a side entrance and make their way toward the Greek's table. As they got closer, the Greek caught sight of them. "You sons of bitches!" he screamed as all four gunmen, as well as one of the Greek's bodyguards, began firing. In the end, Albert the Greek, one of his bodyguards, two of the intruders, and Joey all lay dead on the restaurant floor. Maria was not injured but was in total shock. After being questioned by the police, she went home, packed whatever belongings she could take with her, and told her landlady to sell the rest, keep whatever money she owed her, and send her the rest. She then went to the bus station and took the first bus to Chicago. Two years later, she married someone from the neighborhood, had two kids, got fat, and stayed at home most of the time watching TV.

In September of 2000, Clarence Efont, PJ's friend who worked for the CIA in New York, retrieved some coded dialog from a cell phone belonging to an Afghanistan with a forged passport. He told his superiors from what he could determine, it sounded like the message had something to do with a terrorist attack in New York within the next year. He suggested they cross-check the message with any intelligence they now have. His superior never followed through. This was about a year before 9-11!

Melody, the years 2000-2007

By the time she was fifteen years old, Melody was on the verge of womanhood. All her baby fat had gone. She was tall, already five feet seven, and slender, with just a hint of roundness to her shape. Her long dark braids had been sacrificed for a more fashionable short haircut, framing her face, emphasizing her mahogany complexion, her green eyes with their thick fringe of dark lashes and heavy arched brows, her high cheekbones, and full mouth. But still, there was something adolescently awkward about her as if all the pieces didn't quite fit right.

Even at fifteen, disapproval was not a value judgment she arrived at after serious thought; dissatisfaction was not an emotion resulting from genuine disappointment. Both were simply techniques her unconscious had learned to use to her advantage at a very early age. Had she been a less adorable child, a less beautiful and engaging woman, she never would have got away with it. Her refusal to be satisfied, she had discovered somewhere along the way, encouraged people to try harder to please her. Especially boys, and then as she got older, men. Her perpetual air of discontent made her more desirable. She was both lovely and clever, had an ample supply of wit and charm, and men flocked to her like a bee to honey. As Anita and PJ watched her grow from a child to a young woman, it was difficult for them to believe this was the same little girl they rescued from a tenement in New York. She grew lovelier every day, they thought. The young pretty child had turned into a remarkably beautiful young woman. She was like a magnet that drew all eyes.

She graduated from Green Briar second in her class. PJ and Anita were delighted. Melody was not. She did not like finishing second. She received an invitation from Harvard for a full scholarship but told Anita and PJ she was offered a job modeling. "From who?" Anita asked, totally surprised that Melody was not considering college.

"From a man I met in New Hampton when I was there last summer."

"From a man? What man?" Anita asked.

Melody didn't like being questioned, and Anita could tell she was becoming agitated. "From an agent, Aunt Anita. He has a modeling agency in New York, and he told me I was a natural."

"But you are only eighteen years old," Anita insisted. "That is much too young to jump into the world of modeling. That is a dog-eat-dog business. First, get a college education. Then you can decide if you want to do modeling." But no matter what Anita said, she couldn't convince her to change her mind. She was as independent as she was beautiful. As far as Melody was concerned, she was finished answering questions.

"And just think, the job is in New York," she said. "We'll be able to see each other all the time."

"Where will you live?" Anita asked her.

She laughed and said, "With you guys, of course!"

Once she moved in, Anita generously encouraged her to stay as long as she liked. However, as soon as she had saved a little money, she started looking for an apartment of her own. She refused to take the money Anita offered her. "You can pay me back when you get rich," Anita told her jokingly, but Melody insisted she wanted to "do it on her own." She soon found an apartment in the Village, not far from the modeling agency, inexpensive enough for her to afford on what she made modeling and working part-time at Saks as a makeup consultant. It was a tiny one-bedroom apartment, but it was all hers.

It was not too long before she started to get more modeling jobs, and as her modeling career became more successful, juggling the two jobs became difficult. So fifteen months after her arrival in New York, she left Saks. She was already earning $500 a day as a house model and $200 an hour for runway shows. And then the big break. She was asked to audition for the job as cover girl for a large cosmetic company. It was on her twentieth birthday that she got the job. She never knew that Anita called the president of the company, who had large loans at her bank, and "convinced" him Melody should get the job.

Soon, her schedule became more hectic than she could have ever dreamed. Life as a model was demanding. First, there were the designer studios, followed quickly by catwalk shows, then more and more print work. To meet magazine deadlines, she sweltered modeling furs in summer and froze in bathing suits in midwinter. For runway shows, she was up at six for fittings, rehearsals, and makeup. The clothes would be hung on one peg, hat and underwear on top, shoes and stockings underneath. With the aid of a dresser, she would put on outfit after outfit, changing from top to bottom, inside out, scarf over her head to keep her hair in place. When she was ready, she danced out onto the runway to as many as sixteen choreographed routines learned on short notice. Even more exhausting was the showroom work when she would model samples chosen from endless racks of clothing by buyers from the most expensive stores in this country and Europe.

During this period, she met Katrina, a Swedish model who became her best friend. As the months passed, they became so close that both of them wondered from time to time why they were not lovers but decided that the "chemistry" was not there. Katrina introduced Melody to a lot of very rich and generous men. Some single, many married. And although Melody lost her virginity when she was still a teenager, she was very particular about who she took to the bedroom. She soon learned that men would pay any price just to be with her. She had no problem accepting both gifts and cash from her admirers. Her experience with Uncle Carl had left a bad taste in her mouth for men. If she could use them to her advantage, that is what she would do.

One night, after a hectic day of modeling in Paris, she was sprawled out on a king-size bed in a suite at the Ritz Hotel while Katrina curled up in a ball at the foot of the bed. Both of them totally exhausted. Out of the clear blue sky, Melody said, "I can't believe how many girls are 'giving it away for free' when men are willing to pay for it."

Katrina sat up and looked at her friend, not sure what to say.

"We bust our ass day and night when we could make the same money by lying on our ass instead," Melody said.

"What are you talking about?" Katrina asked.

"What if we started an escort service? We know enough models who would love to make some extra money," Melody said.

"Are you freakin' crazy? You can't do that," Katrina said, now sitting on her knees and holding her head in her hands.

"Look, Katrina, Alex Kowinsky, the guy who owns Astor Fur Company, gave me a mink jacket and $1,000 last month after I spent a day with him at the racetrack. And in case you're wondering . . . he didn't get any!"

"You're serious, aren't you?" Katrina asked.

"You're damn straight I'm serious! I've been thinking about this for some time. Do you want in?"

Katrina just sat there, looking at her friend for several seconds, then laughingly said, "You're damn straight I'm in."

The following morning, Melody called several models she knew and asked them if they would like to have dinner with a very nice, very rich man and get paid for it. Three out of the four girls she called said yes. Only one asked, "And what else do I have to do?"

"That's completely up to you," Melody answered.

A year later, she had over fifty girls working for her. Some full-time, others only part-time while they were saving money to get married or needed money to pay their college tuition. Melody continued working as a model for the first three months after she started the escort service, then left the modeling business to devote full-time to her new venture. Katrina was in charge of hiring the girls, making sure they had no criminal background or sexually transmittable diseases. She also did most of the scheduling.

By the time she was only twenty-two years old, Melody was operating the largest escort service in New York, supplying girls to politicians, corporate executives, big-name athletes, and some of the most famous entertainers in the country. She very rarely booked herself with a client. If she did, it was usually someone she knew from her modeling days who had been more than generous in the past or a "new foreign dignitary" she thought she could cultivate into a top client. She had computer profiles on each and every client, which indicated their likes and dislikes, their quirks, their favorite girls, were they married or single, and, most important, their gifts—plus how much cash they paid over and above the escort service charge. She lived in a very expensive condo on Park Avenue, had a chauffer-driven Rolls-Royce, and more money than she dreamed was possible. She had gone all in . . . and won. Her relationship with Anita and PJ had deteriorated, and they very seldom spoke to one another. Once again, no good deed goes unpunished.

PJ and Anita, the years 1995 forward.

As promised, PJ bought a condo in New York in a building only two blocks from where Anita lived. She tried her best to convince him to move in with her, but that was not to be. At least not yet. However, she either spent the nights at his apartment, or he at hers. They were like two kids in love. PJ took her to Vegas, to the racetrack, and to sporting events. She took him to the opera, museums, and art show openings in New York. She had a busy social calendar, and PJ had no problem fitting right in.

To his surprise, when Walter's will was finally probated, the lawyers informed him Walter left him ten million dollars. He was flabbergasted. He knew Walter was rich but had no idea how rich.

"There's no way I can accept that kind of money," he told Anita.

"Don't tell me," she said. "Tell it to the lawyers."

"Very funny," he said. "I am serious. That money belongs to you," he said.

"PJ, do you have any idea how much I am worth?"

"No, but I bet you're going to tell me."

"No, I'm not. Look, Walter wanted you to have that money. He often said it was just the luck of the draw the doctor picked him to become a Lippincott instead of you. And besides which, now people won't say you're marrying me for my money."

"Ha, that's what they might say, but they're wrong. Why else would I want to marry you? And who said I'm going to marry you anyhow?"

She put her arms around him and said, "I did!"

Finally, after several meetings with the lawyers and a lot of soul-searching, PJ agreed to accept the money. "Great," she said, "now where can we go to celebrate your new fortune?"

"Let's take an extended trip to Israel and then to London. I want to show you some of the places I lived and maybe even meet some of the people I knew back then. It might better help you understand why I did the things I did."

"You don't have to justify to me anything you have done in the past, PJ. I know who you are. You are a good person. A brave person. Someone who fights for what he believes in. That's all I need to know. That notwithstanding, I love the idea. Let's go."

And so in April of 1996, they left New York for Israel. After they arrived and were checked in at the King David Hotel, he took her to the country house owned by Ronit's parents in Tel Aviv. Ronit was the girl he lived with before joining the Sayeret Matkal. He told Anita some of the many fascinating stories that happened when he was there, but as Thomas Wolfe said, "You can't go home again." He was sad to learn that Ronit, her father, and her brother, Shomal, were all killed in terrorists attacks in Tel Aviv; and Ronit's mother really didn't remember PJ although she offered them to stay the night with her. "Hardly anyone comes to visit anymore," she said

They left Ronit's house and took a tour through Israel and the surrounding area. Anita had accompanied Walter on a business trip here in 1990; however, they were there for only two days, and she didn't see very much of the country. PJ tried to think back and wasn't sure if he was there at that time. It was possible he was off somewhere killing the bad guys!

Before leaving the States, PJ arranged a meeting with Colonel Shamonam, an officer in the Sayeret Matkal, at the prime minister's office. This was not an easy task; however, the prime minister agreed to a short meeting. The agreement was no questions about what the Matkal does or who supports it. Just general "make you feel proud you're a Jew" stories.

The colonel was almost two hours late for the meeting and never apologized. Neither the prime minister or anyone else for that matter expected an apology. That is, no one except Anita, but she didn't show it. As it turned out, the colonel was a charming man; and although he avoided naming names and actual places, the stories he told were fascinating. He made sure to include stories about PJ. PJ knew he was embellishing them for Anita's sake. Half the time, Anita just sat with her mouth half open, looking back and forth between the colonel and PJ. *What a life he must have had*, she thought. *How am I going to keep him down on the farm?*

PJ could sense what she was thinking. He reached over and took her hand in his and whispered, "That was all in the past before I had you. Now you're all the excitement I can handle."

The prime minister could hear him, winked at him, and gave an approving smile.

It turned out to be an enjoyable afternoon. After all of the thank-yous and obligatory hugs, PJ and Anita politely declined an offer to have dinner there and left to go back to their hotel. When they got into the chauffeured BMW they had hired for the trip, Anita snuggled up against PJ and said, "Promise me you won't go around killing people anymore. Promise?"

He gave her a hug and laughingly said, "Well, if that's what you want. But maybe just one more for old times' sake."

She punched him in his side and moved as close to him as she could. He hugged her even tighter as they both said at the same time. "I love you."

After three weeks in Israel, they decided it was time leave. PJ had enough of the past; now it was time for the future. "How long are we going to stay in London?" Anita asked.

"Until the money runs out," PJ said jokingly.

"Oh my god," she said, "we'll be there forever."

It had snowed the week before they arrived in London; and amazingly, the drifts had accumulated to heights of twelve inches and more in some places, a phenomenon no one could recall happening in living memory. At the suggestion of a friend, they were staying at a small hotel called the Royal on a small street off St. James, not far from Piccadilly, an excellent location near all the smart men's clubs. It was the former town house of an English duke. Its paneled walls, Grinling Gibbons carving, painted ceilings, and Robert Adam library had survived its conversion to a hotel after it was sold for taxes. Anita fell in love with the hotel. "Let's buy it," she said to PJ after the second day they were there.

"And then what?" he asked.

"We will have it all to ourselves when we visit London."

"And how often will that be?" he asked.

"What difference. I love it. Let's buy it. You and me. We'll be partners. After all, you just got ten million dollars. What do you say?"

"I say you're nuts, that's what I say. But if you want to buy it, let's go . . . I'm all in."

She laughed and put her arms around him. "Just testing you, big guy. You passed."

He threw her on the bed and gently lay down on top of her. He kissed her on the neck and then slowly undressed her. "What about dinner?" she asked.

"This is it," he whispered.

The next day, they drove to Newbury, heart of England's racing country, in the Jaguar he ordered before they left Israel. After all, he just inherited ten million dollars. The snow that remained in the countryside was all white as compared with the small gray piles of grit-covered ice patches in the city. The verges of the road were lined with mounds of snow resembling a line of cumulus clouds stretched along the horizon.

They stopped in a pub with a thatched roof and ate a traditional ploughman's lunch of cheese and bread. "How about we go to the races?" PJ asked while they were eating lunch.

"In this weather?" she asked.

"They race all year round. I'll call and have them reserve a box."

When they finished lunch, PJ asked the waitress to bring them a bottle of their best wine. "We only have two different kinds," she told him politely.

PJ smiled and said, "Fine, bring me the most inexpensive."

"Yes, sir," she said, completely missing the humor.

After the waitress opened the wine and let PJ taste it, she poured them each a glass and left.

"What's the occasion?" Anita asked, holding out her glass, waiting for PJ to make a toast.

PJ smiled his magic smile and said, "Will you marry me?"

On January 15, 1998, Anita and PJ were married by the Supreme Court justice of New York. The ceremony was held at the Plaza Hotel in New York. There were approximately fifty guests made up of close personal friends and several obligatory invites from Lippincott Industries. Anita sent the company jet to Maine so that Melody could attend. Anita also offered to send the jet to California to pick up PJ's father; however, when PJ called him, he said he wasn't able to make it.

"Why not?" PJ asked.

"Well, first of all, I have a men's club meeting that day. And the following day, the dining committee, of which I'm a member, is meeting to decide on a mew menu for the spring. You'll send me some pictures."

PJ simply smiled and wished his father well.

On June 1, 1998, the board of directors for Lippincott Industries sent a proxy notice to its shareholders, notifying them that Anita Lippincott Gould was resigning her position as a director. Since PJ and Anita were the major shareholders, the proxy recommended PJ be appointed in her place. On September 1, PJ became a director.

Six months after becoming a director, Eli Cunningham, the CEO of Lippincott Industries, asked PJ if he would do him a favor. They were having security problems at some of their bank locations and were in the process of implementing new security procedures company-wide. He asked PJ if he would oversee the project for him. Of course, PJ agreed. By the time PJ completed the project, he and Eli had become close friends. It was an odd situation. PJ and Anita the major shareholders of the company, and Eli the CEO. However, PJ enjoyed working with him and continued to handle some special projects for him whenever asked. Anita teased PJ about his new job, "You'll love it," she said, "telling all those suits how to get things done."

PJ thought to himself, *Not too bad for a former assassin.*

March 2000

Over the next two years, PJ found himself becoming more and more involved in Lippincott Industries. Part of the reason was his friendship with Eli Cunningham. He enjoyed working with him. On March 20, 2000, he and Eli were having lunch at the Bankers Club in New York. During lunch, Eli told him he was resigning as the CEO to become chairman of the board on January 1, and he would be honored if PJ would accept the job as CEO.

"You must be kidding," PJ said. "First of all, I'm not looking for a nine-to-five job, and secondly ... secondly, I don't want the job. I'm having fun doing what I'm doing, which is really not a hell of a lot. And besides which, I'm not a business guy, you know that. And by the way," he said laughing, "I'm too goddamn rich to work."

"Ah, but that's what makes you perfect," Cunningham said. "And you have the ability to analyze a situation very quickly and then make a decision. You understand people. You know how to motivate them. You have been trained how to negotiate from both strength and weakness, which is something not many people know how to do. And most importantly, you command respect. Do it for just a little while. Believe me, when I tell you, if Walter were alive, he would approve." PJ was very flattered.

When he entered the apartment, Anita was sitting on the couch, reading a magazine. She was wearing a transparent embroidered dressing gown over a satin underslip. Her hair was down over her shoulders, so you could barely see the diamond earrings that PJ had given her as a wedding gift. He whistled softly in appreciation when he saw her.

"Lady, you sure know how to dress, or should I say . . . not dress."

She thanked him and returned the compliment, and he smiled a little sheepishly. He was wearing a dark Armani suit, with a pale blue button-down collar shirt and a flowered tie. His style of dressing was casual and unaffected as he did not care much about what he put on; yet everything he wore was expensive, stylish, and in the best of taste.

He bent over her and kissed the top of her head. "Hmm, you smell good," he said.

She pulled him down beside her. "You know, I really love you," she said while stroking his face.

"Hey, have I got something to tell you," he suddenly said.

"Me too," she said. "But you go first."

"Okay," he said. "I had lunch with Eli today. He is going to accept the position as board chairman the first of the year, and he wants me to be the CEO. Is that a joke or what?"

"Really?" she said. "That sounds like fun! So tell me, what did you say?"

"You're looking at the new CEO, baby!"

"Get out of here!" she screamed. "Are you serious?"

"Does a bear shit in the woods?" he said laughingly.

"Oh, that's wonderful, PJ, I am so proud," she said, hugging him.

"It's really funny," he said. "All the years doing the things I did and to end up a New York businessman. Who would have thunk it?"

They both just smiled at each other. She thought to herself, *Life is good.*

"You hungry?" he asked.

"Not really, we can eat later."

"That's good," he said as his hand slid under her dressing gown and inside the thin strip of her bikini panties. In an instant, her body turned toward him; and her hands fumbled with his belt, rushing him to undress so that they could make love. And then when they were both naked, he kissed her all over and gently placed his body on top of hers and then was inside her. Each time, they made love, it was like the first time all over.

Later, she lay with him, cradled in her arms, his head resting on her breast. "You know, they are bigger," he said sleepily. "I'd swear it." His hand followed the line of her hip for a moment and came to rest on her belly. "You've gained weight. I never would have believed it. I'm not complaining if you're wondering. I like it."

"For real?" she asked like a schoolgirl.

"Yeah, for real. I like it."

"Well, that's good . . . because I'm pregnant."

He sat up and stared at her. "You are what?"

"I'm pregnant. You know, like in we're going to have a baby."

"Is that any way to break news like that? I could have had a heart attack."

"I did practice how to tell you. I was going to lead up to it gently at dinner. But then you wouldn't eat."

"Not dinner anyway," he said, forcing a smile. He was on automatic pilot, responding instinctively while his mind tried to take in what she had just told him. "You're sure?"

She nodded.

"How far along are you?"

"Three months."

"Three months! And you just got around to telling me now?"

"I did see the doctor only this morning."

"Oh, honey," he said, leaning down to kiss her. And then it dawned on him. She wasn't able to have children. She told him that she and Walter tried, but the doctors told them she was unable to conceive. He sat up and looked at her with a blank stare. "But how can you be? You said the doctor told you that you couldn't have children. How did this happen? I mean, I know how it happened. What I mean is . . . how did you get pregnant? Oh shit, you know what I mean!"

She started to laugh. "Calm down. I know what you mean." She put his head back on her chest.

"When the doctor told me and Walter that we couldn't have children, I assumed he knew what he was talking about. Like I told you, we had very little sex after that even though I told Walter we should keep trying. But of course, nothing ever happened. For so many years, I tried to get pregnant and didn't. I just stopped thinking about it. And so I didn't even think I was pregnant now. Then when I went to the doctor this morning and he told me I was three months pregnant, I couldn't believe it. I asked him the same thing. How come after all this time, I suddenly was able to conceive?"

"And what did the witch doctor say?" he asked, his weight still resting on her, his head buried in her neck.

She touched his hair, the pale luster of corn silk and silver mixed. "He said . . . these things just happen. Are you happy?"

"Happy?" he murmured without looking at her. "Terrified is more like it."

"I do want this baby so much," she said.

He lifted himself on his hands and looked down at her again. "And so do I. But can you? I mean, I thought after a certain age, it was too dangerous."

"I'm only fifty-one. Many women my age have children."

"Yeah, of course, I know that. I mean, you'll be okay, right?"

She continued to stroke his hair. "I'll be fine. It's you I'm worried about, old man."

"Old man, I'll give you old man," he said positioning her so that he could make love to her again. "Forgetaboutit, Charlie, I'm hungry."

She pushed gently against him and, when he moved aside, got out of the bed. As he watched her, she turned back to look at him with a smile on her face, then went into the bathroom. She returned a few minutes later wearing a silk robe. Sitting on the side of the bed beside him, she smiled and said, "I know this is a shock to you. We had our life all planned out. And now at age fifty-eight, all of a sudden, you're going to be a father. Are you sure you're okay with this?"

He leaned over and gave her a kiss. "I couldn't be more okay if I wanted to. I love you, and I'm going to love our baby. I am the luckiest guy in the world," he said, tears running down his face.

She put her hands on his face, kissed him on the lips, and said, "Tell me the truth, did you really travel around the world looking for people to kill? I don't think so."

And so there you have it. On September 11, 2000, Anita gave birth to twin boys. Both she and PJ could not have been happier. They were about to start a new life. PJ was the perfect husband and father. He was running Lippincott Industries and enjoyed every minute of it. However, he often thought of the irony of the whole situation. Here he was running Walter's business, married to his widow, and with children that Walter never had. God sure had a funny way of doin things sometimes.

On the morning of September 11, 2001, Anita and PJ were having breakfast with the twins; it was their first birthday. Reaching out and taking hold of PJ's hand, Anita looked around the table at the smiling faces of her husband and two sons and thought of the joy this past year had brought. She wondered for an instant what changes the next few years would bring, what pain, and what happiness, then pushed the thought away. This was not the time to worry about that. Here now surrounded by the people she loved most in the world, for this moment, however brief, however long, she had it all.

Suddenly, the housekeeper came running into the dining room, hollering, "Mrs. Gould, Mr. PJ, quick! Turn on the TV! Something terrible has happened! Oh my god, what has happened? Oh my god! Oh my god!"

A new and terrible game was about to start.

The end. (For now.)